Als
Gavin May

ISBN9781800944176

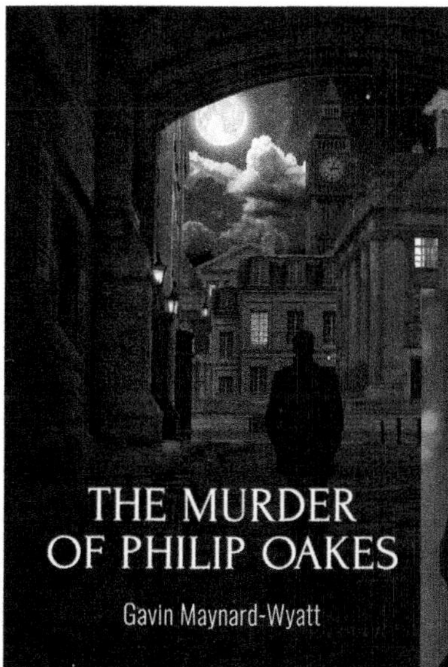

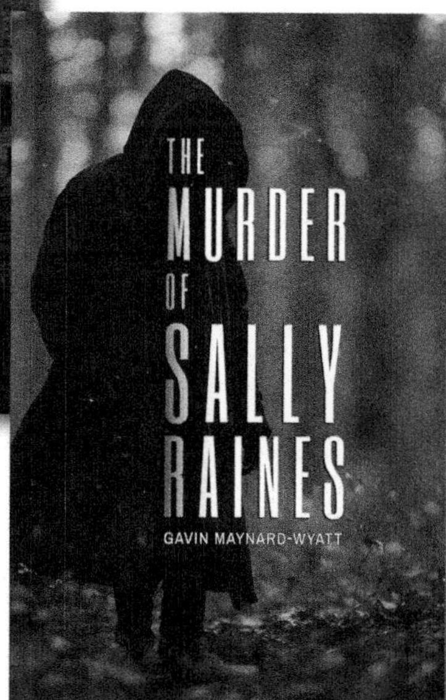

ISBN 9781800946460

GAVIN MAYNARD-WYATT

THE MURDER OF RAVI PATEL

This edition first published in paperback by
Michael Terence Publishing in 2024
www.mtp.agency

ISBN 9781800948709

Michael Terence
Publishing

Dedicated to Liz Hudson

Liz has been by my side for each of my three books. She has read them, helped me with spelling and grammar, and made suggestions to help the sentences read better. I dedicate this book to her, as a thank you for all the hours she has spent helping me create the perfect murders!

Acknowledgements

Glenn Chaplin

With Thanks

Bilam Datta

Characters

Victim:

Ravi Patel

Suspects:

Rakesh Kumar: Ravi's husband

Dipen Patel: Ravi's cousin

Parveena Johal: Ravi's colleague (vet)

Norton Greene: Ravi's friend (psychologist)

Agatha Hawksworth: Ravi's friend

Detectives:

Isaac Davidson: Detective Chief Inspector (Brother: Alan)

Jian Wong: Detective Sergeant

Anne Michaels: Detective Constable

Hamish Potter: Detective Constable

Faisal Asher: Detective Constable

Lily Tovey: Detective Constable

Alex Poole: Forensic Lead

1

29th October 2019

The Body!

08:30 a.m.

The bright blue sky without a single cloud helped make this autumnal morning glorious. The large oak tree near the river was still shedding its leaves and in the distance, there was the unsettling scream of a female fox. Joggers were running along the pathway and a few people were walking their dogs. This was a quiet part of the Thames towpath and today was no exception.

Two older women casually walked along. They were chatting about their medications, family, and the new librarian they believed was too inexperienced. His mauve hair, neck tattoo, and nose ring were also mentioned. Plus, the fact he was meticulous with the "no-talking" policy was another reason they frowned upon him.

Both women wore brightly coloured raincoats and headscarves despite it being mild for the time of year. They were heading toward their favourite coffee shop that had beautiful views across the river. This walk had become a weekly event that they both looked forward to. In truth, they were two lonely women who were mostly ignored by their families. It was the only time they each got a bit of company. The content of their conversations was irrelevant. Just the fact they were talking was what mattered to them.

'What blood pressure tablets did Dr Raj put you on?' Molly Ferres asked her friend, Mrs Latimer.

'Felodipine.'

'I haven't heard of that one,' Molly said.

'You?' Joyce enquired.

'He put me on Ramipril. I wonder how they decide which one to start us on?'

'I miss Dr Aherne,' Mrs Latimer said, ignoring Molly's question. 'I used to enjoy seeing him and discussing all of my health issues that seem to increase each year. Such a shame he committed suicide following that murder.'

'I know,' Molly gestured. 'Wasn't it something to do with one of the receptionists? Anyhow, that's what I heard.'

'Yes, that's right.'

'I was there when they found her body you know,' Molly smiled and gloated with a sense of pride.

Mrs Latimer was used to her neighbour boasting. She wouldn't go as far as calling her a friend, but she gained something from her company, even if it was just for all the local gossip that Molly Ferres was so good at getting hold of.

'I thought a man with his dogs found the body?' she said with a touch of venom in her tone and a smirk on her face.

Molly glared at her. She hated the fact that, technically; she was correct. Molly had been among the gathering of people in the park but had felt frustrated being kept behind the crime scene tape. It would have made her day to have been the person who had stumbled upon the wretched girl.

'I don't know why you must be like this, Joyce!' Molly wasn't pleased. 'It's typical of you to rain on my parade.'

Joyce Latimer inwardly laughed, knowing the film Funny Girl had been on the night before, hence Molly's reference to the famous song.

'All I was saying,' Molly continued to articulate with much irritation, 'was I was there. I'd already helped in the *"Philip Oakes"* murder that happened in the house next to mine, and I was there for this murder.'

Joyce took a deep breath. She was sick of hearing about the murder Molly helped the police with.

'Do you know what? I think I'm drawn to dead people. It wouldn't surprise me if they started talking through me somehow. I could be one of them physics on a stage, regaling the lives of those who have gone beyond, channelling their spirits through me. I remarked so to Mr Chang who lives three doors down from the funeral directors just off Tennyson Avenue, on the corner of Vine Crescent. He was so impressed.'

'I think you mean psychic,' Mrs Latimer interrupted.

'What?' was Molly's sharp reply.

'You said "physics" but you should have said "psychic" I believe.'

'There you go again, always ready to make me feel small. Well, Joyce Latimer, that's the last time I'll bring you a lemon drizzle cake for afternoon tea!'

After about half an hour, the coffee shop came into view. Nestled between three impressive trees, it resided on the river's edge. Usually, a handful of ducks swam up and hoped some kind person would throw a few crumbs their way. When inside, the ladies always had the same each visit. Two cappuccinos and whichever cake was the freshest. Once they had a flat white coffee but didn't understand what it was, so they returned to the comfort of what they knew.

The wind had now picked up and both women pulled their coats tighter around their bodies. The clouds were now darker and the birds had stopped their calls. However, the fox's cry was still distinct.

'The weather is turning, Molly,' Mrs Latimer proclaimed.

'I can see!' Molly curtly responded. 'That's you all over, always pointing out the obvious.'

Mrs Latimer rolled her eyes. She was used to her so-called friend going "off on one" occasionally.

As the bickering women headed for refreshments, they missed the slow-moving body of a man who was face down in the river, floating past them. He had a piece of material tied tightly around his neck.

Six Weeks Earlier…

2

Ravi

16th September 2019

08:00 a.m.

Ravi stretched his whole body until he heard the bones cracking in his shoulders. This sound always made him feel a little queasy. Why? He had no clue. Exhausted from his broken four-hour sleep, he lay on his bed staring at a large, scary-looking spider creeping along the ceiling. There was also a dull ache in his head. The night before, they had had friends round for dinner to celebrate his birthday. He had turned thirty-eight.

Ravi hadn't fancied an expensive night going out to an over-rated fine dining restaurant like Rakesh, his husband had craved. His only wish was for a quiet night with his friends: Rakesh, Dipen, his cousin, Parveena, his school friend and partner in their veterinary business, Norton and Agatha, his friends from university.

Their night had started as a subdued occasion and it only got worse. Familiar arguments began around 9 p.m. Ending abruptly at 11 p.m. Ravi, having had enough, stupidly lost his temper and shared too many secrets which belonged to the people around the table.

Ravi can only really be described as beautiful. Handsome doesn't establish the correct imagery. His jawline is prominent, cheekbones high, and his eyes are deep-set with a curious dark brown hue. His abundant black hair is slightly wavy, and his eyebrows are just the right thickness to help frame his face. He has a well-groomed, thick beard, and a diamond stud in his left ear. With his pearly white teeth, Ravi's smile lights up any room he enters and instantly draws people to him. Despite never going to the gym, he has muscular arms and a slim build, even with his love for chocolate and a ferocious appetite.

Ravi wasn't interested in designer clothes despite Rakesh constantly trying to mould him into this type of person. Simpler things in life were his preference. He loved his job, but after working all day he just wanted to come home and throw on a t-shirt that often depicted a scene from a film involving dinosaurs and a pair of jogging bottoms. He would then chill for the rest of the evening.

Ravi was the only child of parents who had both died tragically one year ago in a road traffic accident. His mother had no family left on her side, but his father had a brother with two children: Dipen and Beena.

Fragmented thoughts of the night before were ravaging his mind.

'Why does it always have to end up in fights?' he thought as he turned to sit on the edge of the bed and placed his feet on the floor. This movement caused a brief dizziness. 'What did I say to them all?' He ruffled his hair with his hands, stood and stretched again, which caused more of his bones to crack.

Picking up his phone, Ravi typed out a WhatsApp message to their friend group chat.

"Not completely sure what I said last night because my memory of events is vague. Sorry if I revealed too much."

Rakesh was in the kitchen loading things from last night into the dishwasher. He was only wearing his white designer underwear, which stood out against the colour of his skin. He was slim and tall, and his hair was receding at an alarming rate. This had bothered him for more years than he cared to remember. His confidence had plummeted and his self-esteem left him feeling unworthy.

Ravi entered the kitchen at a slow pace. He wasn't sure what the atmosphere between the two of them would be like. Rakesh had been the main instigator of the issues the previous night, yet he had been unprepared for Ravi's unexpected revelations.

Seeing his husband standing at the sink in just his underwear was a pleasant sight. The morning light streaming in from the window gave Rakesh an almost angelic glow. Ravi walked over, stood directly behind him, put his arms tightly around his waist and pulled his husband into him. The warmth coming from his body was welcoming.

They met at a mutual friend's wedding in 2011. They got married in 2017 at an expensive ceremony, obliterating their savings. Ravi had wanted to go away for a tranquil time but Rakesh set his heart on a full-on event with a marquee, caterers, fireworks, and the whole shebang! Rakesh won. They kept their birth surnames because of Ravi's business but their marriage certificate listed them as Patel-Kumar.

Ravi held on to Rakesh and kissed the back of his neck. It felt good until a sharp shudder dislodged his grip, and before he knew it, he was standing alone at the sink in the kitchen. Ravi closed his eyes and slowly shook his head. The situation between him and his husband had been deteriorating. Rakesh had a penchant for living dangerously, taking risks, wasting money, and frequently arriving home late or not at all! Ravi was growing tired of this, but he was quickly hushed each time he tried to raise the issue. Rakesh had told Ravi frequently he was sucking the life out of him.

The two men got themselves ready for the day in near silence. The atmosphere was thick and uncomfortable.

'I don't understand why you're in such a bad mood and not talking to me,' Ravi said. No answer came back. 'You're the one who started dragging up the past again, which got everyone arguing. You! Not me. Why aren't you talking to me?'

'Shut up, Ravi.'

'Are you still coming to Paris with me next week?'

'You've changed over the last six months,' Rakesh said in an unpleasant tone. 'I don't even know who you are most of the time.'

'Have I? In what way?'

'I'm off to work.' Rakesh left without further interaction.

'Please, talk to me. I don't know what I have done wrong. PLEASE!' he screamed.

Ravi sat on the bed and hurled himself backwards. As his head hit the pillows, he burst into tears.

3

Through the Eyes of a Murderer!

(Part One)

16th September 2019

10:30 a.m.

The number of people milling around was less than usual, and this wasn't helping the situation. Crowds were required. Through the scatterings of people, the lone person gazed directly at an unaware man who was casually shopping before heading off to work for his afternoon shift at his veterinary practice.

On a Monday, their late opening day, Ravi and Parveena took turns doing the later shift. It made good business sense and brought in much-needed funds for the practice, which was falling on hard times. However, they both agreed to take this morning off following the party the night before.

'I can see you, Ravi Patel! I assume you're looking through the clothes shops for items to take to Paris next week. Oh, I'll also be there, keeping my eyes firmly focused on you. Please don't pick the green jumper, it isn't your colour. You'd be better in a pale blue. It will blend beautifully with your skin tone. I bought you a cashmere scarf for your birthday a few years ago. Do you remember? It was a pastel blue shade, or sky blue to be more exact, with delicate white and grey highlights. It was such a beautiful piece of material and to my knowledge, you have never worn it. So ungrateful of you.'

Ravi continued to shop.

'I have decided that 27th October is the day you die. It's a Sunday. We are all together for a concert, so you won't see it coming. I'll choose the scarf that I will use to kill you with when I get to Paris next week. Yes, strangulation I think is best. I'll come from behind so you won't be able to see me. It'll come as a complete surprise, and just before you take your final breath, I'll whisper my name into your ear. Why am I going to kill you? It's simple. After what you revealed to everyone last night, plus my rage, which has been building up for what feels like ages, Ravi Patel, I hate you!'

Ravi continued shopping, oblivious to the revengeful eyes burning a hole in his back.

4

Parveena

16th September 2019

12:30 p.m.

Parveena Johal sat in a bar almost hidden down a side street off the principal thoroughfare. She was holding her second glass of whisky since arriving at the venue at midday. It was, however, her fourth since waking.

Parv, known as such by some of her friends, of whom there were few, had a slender physique. When her hair wasn't tied back, it reached just below her bottom and was raven black and glossy. She had an awkward-looking face because her eyes were slightly asymmetrical. She also had a sizeable nose with two smallish rings on the side of one nostril. This feature was from her father's side of the family. Parveena hated her appearance. She only felt remotely feminine when she wore a sari on traditional occasions. Her favourite was a green and white one her much-missed grandfather had given to her. Her arms were fairly muscly due to lifting heavy animals at work, and despite being slight in appearance, she had an immense strength about her which could match most men.

Parveena sat nursing a third drink she had ordered using the app on her phone, even though the bar was empty. It made her feel less conspicuous getting her drink delivered than standing at the bar ordering it herself. Ravi frequently warned her about her excessive drinking, which was negatively affecting the business. This was never truer than over the past few months. Terrible things had happened that she could never forgive herself for. Only Ravi and one other had known what had occurred; until last night, that is.

Her drinking had started at an early age. There was never any alcohol at home as her parents didn't like it, so she relied on the guy she was seeing behind her parent's backs. By the age of fifteen, she had been drunk many times and had used the morning-after pill on three occasions. Her behaviour disgusted her older brothers who kept the truth from their parents, knowing it would break their hearts.

Parveena had been a bright student at school, and despite the drinking had maintained top grades, which enabled her to get into the university of her choice. She and Ravi had been school friends. They had spent most of their time together and at age ten, both decided they would become vets and open a practice together. They were so close that both parents believed they would eventually get married. This was a partnership they all relished.

When they arrived at the university, Parveena and Ravi shared a house with Agatha Hawksworth and Norton Greene. Agatha was studying economics and Norton was taking psychology. Parveena never understood Ravi's friendship with them. She tolerated them and still did, but Ravi wasted too much time with them, especially Agatha in the first year.

Parveena looked at the time on her new smartphone. It was now 2 p.m. and she was late for work. She didn't care. After what Ravi told the group last night, he can rot in hell. Using the app, she ordered another whisky, then her thoughts shifted to the conference in Paris next week. Ravi had booked them both onto it as he thought they should get their names "out there" and become better at sharing their professional achievements; even though they had very few. However, he wasn't presenting but Parveena was: *Dealing with respiratory complications in rabbits and other small domestic animals.* Ravi had told her several times that the subject was boring and that she didn't have enough evidence. In addition, there was a strong possibility she would make their practice a laughingstock throughout Europe. This was a reputation they could do without, especially as Ravi was hoping for the exact opposite.

'Screw you, Ravi fucking Patel,' she said into her whisky glass. 'I'll prove to you exactly what I'm capable of. I'm sick to death of you putting me down, making me feel small, inferior and useless at my job. You're always watching me, evaluating me, and wishing I was no longer your partner. Believe me when I say your comeuppance is coming. My feelings for you have changed. I detested you long before your rotten party. Please don't underestimate me. I'll prove what I am capable of. You'll be sorry you ever crossed me!'

Parveena downed the liquid in her glass and contemplated ordering another, but left instead. She had no thoughts about her destination, but it wouldn't involve work.

5

Norton

16th September 2019

2:30 p.m.

Norton stood by the substantial window in his office, which overlooked Trafalgar Square. There were crowds of people milling about and making use of the space. Some were sitting on the lions at the base of Nelson's column, and a few were messing with the water features. There were hordes of tourists going in and out of the national gallery. Their guides periodically waving small flags from different countries, made it clear they were from overseas.

The gallery was a major London attraction and Norton liked to visit it frequently. He would often peruse in between his clients. His preferences were the Van Gogh pictures, as he was his favourite artist of all time. He found the paintings truly mesmerising. The colours, with the textures employed, were beautiful and thought-provoking. Norton believed he could see the tortured soul in every one of his paintings. In July, he was on a business trip to Lille in France and visited an art museum. When his friend Sue pointed out "The Cows" painting by Van Gogh, he was thrilled. Norton had been unaware that it was on display at this venue. It was a wonderful find. He was looking forward immensely to visiting the Musée d'Orsay in Paris next week. He had been countless times, but never tired of the beautiful artwork on display.

Doctor Norton Greene was thirty-eight, left-handed, and hated that he shared his name with a hamlet on the Isle of Wight. While infrequent, there were a few instances where he was asked if his name was based on the location of his conception. He despised his parents and hadn't seen them for nearly fifteen years; therefore detested questions that made him think of them. He was an impressive-looking man with an intellectual air about him. His hair was a standard dreary-looking brown with a large streak of grey on the left side above his ear. He usually had a few days of stubble on his face with random flecks of grey and ginger. His glasses were square and had clear frames that frequently slipped to the end of his nose. This meant he was constantly using his middle finger on his right hand to push them back into place. In certain instances, he would subtly make this gesture to show his displeasure towards someone who had irritated him. The only other prominent feature about him was his large teeth. It gave the impression that he had too many in his mouth. He hated this aspect of his appearance so rarely smiled.

While the daily activities of others fascinated Norton, he had a sudden realisation that someone was speaking behind him.

'Are you listening to me, Dr Greene?' A disgruntled voice spoke. 'I've been talking to you about a significant and traumatic episode in my past, but you've been staring out of the window!'

It took a few moments for the psychologist to ground himself and become present again.

'I'm sorry, Edward. I will admit I lapsed in concentration, but I promise you it was only a brief instant.'

'I'm not paying you £125 per hour for you to have "lapses." I've also come to you on my lunch break.'

'I've said I'm sorry,' Norton snapped. 'Why don't you make another appointment with my secretary in the other room for next week?'

The angry man was gobsmacked. He stood abruptly, grabbed his coat and headed for the door.

'You can forget about another appointment. I've heard things about you but thought I'd not listen to gossip and give you a chance. However, after today, I can assure you that I won't be coming back!'

The door slammed just as the psychologist called out; 'What gossip?'

Norton slumped onto his sofa, put his hands on his head and exhaled. He knew he wouldn't be getting the £125 as payment.

'Damn you, Ravi,' he murmured to himself, his voice a soft echo as the memories of the previous night's events engulfed his mind. 'You didn't appear drunk, yet secrets tumbled from your lips. Damaging ones. Why did you choose to shame us all? Rakesh instigated the gloomy atmosphere, but that wasn't new, so what triggered you? Sorel,' he called out to his secretary.

The young woman with a heavily made-up face and a haircut which gave others the impression she'd done it herself popped her head around the door.

'Yes, Dr Greene?'

'Did that man pay for his session?'

'No, he didn't.'

'Damn!'

'He told me if you tried to get the money, he'd make serious trouble for you!'

'This is beyond a joke,' Norton griped.

'What happened?' she asked, but knew he wouldn't tell her.

'That is none of your business. Bring me a black coffee; I don't want to be disturbed for the rest of the afternoon.'

'But you have two more clients booked in. Miss Conway has already arrived.' Sorel was confused.

'Tell her I've had a family emergency and can't see her. Just do it!' he yelled.

His secretary backed out of the office with tears in her eyes. The psychologist noticed this as she went and felt a pang of remorse.

'Ravi Patel, this is on you! My head is full of what you regurgitated last night. How dare you say what you did! How fucking dare you! I thought I couldn't despise you more than I already did, but it seems each day my hatred increases!'

6

Agatha

16th September 2019

3:30 p.m.

At thirty-nine, Agatha was the oldest of the six at the party last night and felt like the least successful in life. She didn't mind her name, although she thought it old-fashioned. Over the years her friends had tried to shorten it to Ags or Aggie, but she always corrected them. Her name was Agatha; therefore, it wasn't to be anything else.

When she started university, she was full of dreams and ambitions. Back then she had been a size eight. Now, at a size eighteen, she tried to embrace her appearance. Being a larger woman had concerned her, but certain aspects she liked. She was OK with how her curves had developed as the weight went on. Or at least that is what she led people to believe. Social media meant she needed a thick skin because the trolls made their presence known. She could almost guarantee a barrage of abuse for every "like" she received for a selfie she posted on Instagram. These comments caused low moods, which sometimes led to suicidal thoughts.

Agatha adored wearing brightly coloured glasses that were twice the size they needed to be. She had a mop of frizzy ginger hair, a heavily freckled face, and lips so red she'd never had to buy lipstick. She spent hundreds of pounds in her local nail bar, always presenting herself with themed nails. They mostly followed events of the year:

birthdays, Easter, Christmas, and summer holidays. Currently, they had palm trees because she had recently been to Jamaica.

Agatha lived by herself in a studio flat on the ground floor. She had made it feel homely, but it wasn't what she had envisaged for herself as she approached forty. By this time, she assumed she'd have been married with three or four children, living in a huge detached house in the countryside or by the sea. None of these things had happened. Relationships had always been short-lived. There had been about six guys she had dated since leaving university. Each one was more useless than the last. The longest she had managed to sustain was nine months because he worked away during the week. This meant he was at home with his wife and kids. Her one true love had been at university. They only dated for six months, but it was the happiest time of her life. He had made her feel special, safe, beautiful, and wanted. Agatha's heart shattered and her world crumbled when he told her it was over. He had found someone new. This betrayal triggered her initial stint of depression and her first suicide attempt. There would be many more of each to follow.

The consequence of being unemployed was having to endure long days. Agatha consistently overslept, which effectively squandered her day. Jamaica had been a treat her parents had paid for, trying to lift her spirits. The trip had been for one, which meant she was as lonely, but lonely in a different country. It had never occurred to her parents to buy two plane tickets. Sunbathing had taken up most hours of her day, but she could only protect her front side from the sun because of the absence of someone to apply sunscreen on her back. She also had to be careful as she had burnt herself badly in the past because of her hair colouring and pale skin. In the evenings she drank cocktails, ate huge amounts of food at the all-inclusive restaurant, then hooked up with a few locals who enjoyed the "fuller" figured woman.

Agatha had learnt to be the life and soul of the party. If someone told a joke, Agatha laughed hardest. If Karaoke was happening, Agatha sang the most. Because of her inability to sing in tune, she became the hilarious focus of the night. Everybody loved being around her. She made their evenings, and she often heard: "You've made our holiday" or "I can't believe you haven't got a fella, you're dead funny." In truth, Agatha was the loneliest person in the crowd. Being dumped at university by the only person she had loved had caused her self-esteem to decline at a fast rate. She felt worthless, and it was only because of the anti-depressants that there hadn't been even more attempts to end her life.

As she wallowed in her bed eating her way through a packet of chocolate biscuits, there was the sound of a key in the front door. Agatha instantly felt annoyed and silently screamed inside her head. A woman in her sixties, wearing a trench coat and carrying a shopping bag, entered.

'Afternoon,' she hollered.

'Mum, I've told you countless times, let me know if you are coming over, or knock first.'

'I have no interest in dealing with any of that. What have you got to hide from your mother?'

'Why are you here?' Agatha snorted.

'I wanted to see how you are. You have seemed a little, well, fragile lately. I'm scared you're going to hurt yourself again. I couldn't face finding you in the bath again when you slit your, well, you know what you did.'

'Yes, I do. I don't need you constantly reminding me. It doesn't help.'

Agatha climbed out of her bed, adjusted her sleepwear, and then put the kettle on. Biscuit crumbs were dropping to the floor.

'Just look at the state of you. It's mid-afternoon and you're only just getting up. It just isn't good enough, Agatha.'

'Do you want tea?' Agatha asked, ignoring what her mother had uttered.

This type of conversation was normal practice so washed over her head.

'I also came over last night, but you weren't in. Where were you?'

'I was out with my friends at a dinner party, if you must know!'

'I assume with the usual five?'

'Yes,' Agatha replied with an exasperated tone.

'I can't comprehend why you still see them, particularly him.'

'Please, let's not have this conversation for the umpteenth time.'

'Agatha Hawksworth, that man, Ravi, caused you to take your first overdose! He dumped you when you were at university, which broke your heart. You have never recovered from it. Ravi Patel destroyed your life!'

'I KNOW!' screamed Agatha as she threw a mug against the wall and stormed back to bed.

7

Dipen

16th September 2019

4:30 p.m.

Dipen was twenty-nine and Ravi's cousin on his dad's side of the family. Although roughly ten years younger than the rest of the people at the party last night, he had entrenched himself in their friendship circle five years ago. His relationship with Ravi had always been a good one, and during the past year since the death of his cousin's parents, he ensured he stayed in constant touch. Rakesh, who was convinced that Dipen had an ulterior motive, had grown increasingly angered by this intensity of frequent visits, which he felt also affected Ravi.

Dipen's youthful features were still apparent, especially when he flashed his mischievous smile. His hair was jet black with a small quiff at the front and cut extremely close to the sides of his head. This resulted in a slimming effect on his face. His eyes were a caramel brown and a fraction too close together. This was the only thing that stopped him from being beautiful like Ravi. His perfectly proportioned nose bent slightly to the right, but it didn't detract from his overall attractiveness.

Dipen was a man-about-town. Everybody knew him whichever shops or establishments he entered. Many locals were fond of him because he had a great sense of humour and was someone they could joke around with. However, these same individuals had become cautious about spending time with him. News travels fast and his increasing financial problems weren't going unnoticed.

He proceeded down the high street with a clear destination in mind. Dipen was torn between greeting passersby with friendly waves and hurrying to the betting shop, where he hoped to overturn his recent streak of misfortune.

The sizeable television on the wall showed the line-up for Doncaster's next horse race. Men primarily occupied the shop, with a few women dotted about, each keeping to themselves. Someone occasionally asks for advice or opinions from another customer before placing a bet. Dipen was analysing the horse's form in the newspaper to determine the best one to back. This form of gambling wasn't his forte, but he was desperate. Poker was his genuine passion, but there wasn't another game for a few days, so horse racing would have to suffice.

After scrutinising the newspaper for a couple more minutes, he was ready to place the bet. Behind the counter was Sonia, a hard-faced woman who had a heavily wrinkled face and looked older than she was. Her poorly executed tattoos on her body were visible, especially on her arms, which were bare in the vest top.

'Oh, it's you,' she grunted in a hard tone as Dipen approached her.

'Delighted as always, Sonia,' he sarcastically responded.

Her malignant expression told him all that he needed to know.

'What do you want?' she replied.

Dipen scanned the shop, then over at the television, at the betting slips he was holding, and gave her a disgruntled smirk.

'I'd like to ask you for a recipe for a Rogan Josh curry, please! Oh, wait, I've been making them for 10 years, seeing that I work in an Indian restaurant.'

Sonia glared back but chose not to speak.

'I'm stuck between two horses. Lemon Bramble and Lord Slocombe. Any advice?'

'I'm not here to give out tips. Do you want to place a bet, or don't you?'

'£300 on Lemon Bramble to win, please.'

Sonia placed the bet for Dipen, who went over to the vending machines to grab a coffee and a packet of crisps, unaware of the conversation happening behind him between Sonia and her boss.

'I said we're refusing to take any further bets from him. He's not someone you want to associate with, and there's talk that he's deeply in debt and for a substantial amount. I don't want this establishment to be part of it. Give him his money back and cancel the bet,' Sonia's boss ordered with an angry edge to her voice.

'OK. I forgot.'

The boss went back into her office, slamming the door, causing some papers pinned to a noticeboard to fall onto the floor.

Ignoring what she had been told, Sonia kept the money and silently prayed for his horse to fail. It had done so on its last two races, something Dipen hadn't picked up on when reading the newspaper.

The race started, and Sonia viewed the television surreptitiously with a wide smirk. Dipen was also watching. His fingers gripped his betting slip, making a fist that he pumped into the air.

'Come on!' he shouted.

Sonia's smile grew as she realised that his horse wasn't even in the top five. As the race neared its end, Lord Slocombe maintained a significant lead.

Dipen clenched both fists like he was riding the horse and was vocally getting louder.

As the race ended, the deflated man, still holding the betting slip, screwed it up into a tight ball and threw it to the floor and stormed out of the shop. Sonia was now laughing to herself and planning on how to spend her £300.

The weather had turned and rain was slamming down. Dipen, who hadn't planned for such conditions was only wearing a light jumper and no coat. Despite being uncomfortable, his sole focus was to get home. However, thoughts from the party last night entered his mind as he dashed through the streets.

'Why did you tell them, Ravi?' he mumbled. 'It was something between you and me! They had no right to that information. No right at all and I'm disgusted with you.'

8

Rakesh

16th September 2019

7:30 p.m.

The streets were busier than usual because the torrential rain and high winds were causing havoc. They were littered with people hurrying to get to their destinations. Some were fighting with their umbrellas and others had hoisted their coats over their heads for some protection. Uber cars and black cabs were all touting for business and doing well in the inclement conditions. According to reports on social media and station platform announcements, trains were experiencing delays or cancellations. This was a regular occurrence, as it didn't matter what the weather was doing.

Rakesh rushed along the busy thoroughfare with his head down and his expensive Canada Goose jacket keeping him suitably warm.

'How much did that cost?' Ravi had asked him when he arrived home with it a few weeks ago.

'Shut up! I paid for it using my money so it doesn't concern you,' had been Rakesh's angry reply.

'Where did you get the money from?'

'Just leave me alone, Ravi! You're strange lately and you're doing my head in!'

'Money doesn't grow on trees, husband of mine!' Ravi had groaned with some tension in his body language.

'What about your inheritance? You never fully explained what happened there. I have a right to know as your next of kin.'

'As I mentioned before, I used the money from selling their house to settle their debts and cover the funeral expenses, leaving only a small amount remaining. Regrettably, my parents made several unwise investments throughout the years, leaving me to resolve the issues they created.'

That conversation had made Rakesh furious when it happened, and following last night's revelation at the party, even more so now.

After another few minutes of dashing through the streets, he arrived at the designated hotel. The building was incredibly beautiful, both inside and out. Rakesh took his time to absorb all that he was seeing. He went over to adjust himself in the grandiose mirror in the foyer.

'Looking good, Mr Patel-Kumar,' he said to himself and winked.

Rakesh blushed when a young couple passed by as he said these words.

'Twat!' he heard one of them say.

Parched, he took the lift to the revolving bar on the 52nd floor, secured a comfortable window seat, and ordered the priciest cocktail on the menu. Another shortly followed this. Experiencing this extravagant environment was the life he so desperately craved. Even the bar snacks presented with his drinks probably cost more than a full round for six at their local pub; a place he despised with every bone in his body. Rakesh, therefore savoured every morsel that he placed into his mouth. Even the plush feel of the elegant chairs excited him.

The views of London from this high level were stunning, and he relished eyeballing all the people wearing their best. Observing them stirred a memory of when he took Ravi to the Savoy grill pre-theatre for his birthday a few years ago. It had ended in disaster. Rakesh had been wearing his finest clothes that had cost him a substantial amount of money on his credit card. Ravi, on the other hand, removed his coat and was wearing jeans and a T-shirt depicting a print of the Tyrannosaurus Rex chasing the car in the Jurassic Park film. Rakesh had made a hysterical scene, which resulted in their removal. On that occasion, Ravi had moved back in with his parents for a few weeks until things had calmed down. Rakesh had never forgiven him for showing him up like that in public.

The cocktails gave Rakesh a nice warm feeling. Something about a colourful drink and a garnish made him love life.

'Good evening. I'm assuming that isn't your first cocktail?' a deep voice thundered from behind.

Rakesh smiled without turning around. 'You know me so well.'

'How long have you been here?' the man asked.

'Just time enough for two cocktails, Edvin, I promise.' Rakesh placed his cheek on his shoulder, smiled and fluttered his eyelashes.

Originally from Porvoo, Finland, Edvin had relocated to London where he worked as a business executive for a prominent international finance company. This impressed Rakesh.

'Do you want another drink here?' he asked.

'Go on, I'll have a glass of Dom Pérignon, please.'

'I hope I have nothing to worry about when we get to our room,' Edvin said as he summoned a server.

'You never have,' was the boyish reply.

Edvin sat down and adjusted himself in the chair. The tight fit of his clothes showed off his immensely muscular body.

'However,' Rakesh said, self-absorbed, 'I have struggled lately. Ravi had a meltdown last night at his party. I don't know where it came from. Admittedly, I started moaning about our marriage and his cousin spending so much time at our place. Ravi is incredibly stingy with money, and if he would only relax his purse strings, our lives could be great. I don't mean like this,' Rakesh exclaimed as he looked around at the hotel's glamour. 'That would be too much to ask for, which is why I love spending time with you. I can relish the more exquisite aspects of life.' Rakesh leaned over, giving Edvin's knee a gentle rub and smiled back when Edvin mirrored the action. 'Meeting you was a dream come true. Ravi was OK at first. We've been together since 2011. It was great back then. We knew we were poor, so we did thrifty things. We went for walks by the river, ordered food in restaurants for one, and shared it. Friends came around, and somehow we made two bottles of wine last the entire night. But he's a qualified vet now. He has his own business and yet we still have to live like paupers. I know my retail work doesn't bring a huge amount of money in, but he needs to loosen up and let us enjoy life more. And, after what I heard from him last night…'

'Rakesh,' the business executive said, as he interrupted. 'I'm not paying you £500 for sex to listen to you droning on about your unimportant husband.' Edvin stood up. 'Are you coming with me to the room?'

'£500, plus the bar bill,' Rakesh replied, taking Edvin's hand and walking towards the lift with the occasional skip. They were unaware of the person watching them leave.

Once they were in their room, Rakesh noticed an odd look on Edvin's face, which worried him.

'Has more of your hair come out?' Edvin asked out of the blue. He appeared unaware of how cruel this question was.

'I don't think so,' Rakesh croaked with a quiver in his voice.

'If it does, I'll be searching for a younger model.'

'Please, don't do that. I need this part of my life to keep me sane.'

'I'm sorry, Rakesh, but a completely bald man just doesn't get me turned on. Maybe this should be our final encounter.'

'Where has this come from? Just now in the bar, you seemed as keen as always.' Rakesh sounded desperate.

'I think your moaning about your husband, and noticing your further receding hairline has made me rethink. It's time to end things. However, we can still enjoy tonight.'

'Ravi!' Rakesh hissed through gritted teeth.

9

Through the Eyes of a Murderer!

(Part Two)

24th September 2019

10:30 a.m.

The person stood on a busy street in Paris, peering into the café through an elaborately decorated window. This, along with the hoodie and dark glasses, would aid in concealing their identity. The man being watched was unaware of his impending danger. He was laughing and drinking his cappuccino, whilst oblivious to the fact that he was being stalked and his murder being plotted.

'Ravi Patel, I can see you, sitting there smugly with some of your conference chums, waiting patiently for 11 a.m. for the start of the event in the opposite building. Drinking your dull coffee with not a care in the world. Oh, I'm watching you and will be until the moment I put the scarf around your neck and pull. This is something for me to look forward to. You thought you'd been so clever with what you revealed at the party and then sent that text to say you couldn't remember exactly what you had said. You hadn't been that drunk. Ravi, you're to blame for what I'm going to do to you on 27th October.'

The individual laughed out loud, which brought some unwanted attention to them. One of the "chums" turned to stare into the street, but went back to her conversation just as quickly.

'There you go, rubbing both sides of your head again. That is such an annoying habit you've started doing recently. I don't suppose you even know you're doing it.'

'So, why that date you may ask yourself? It is the next official date the six of us are together again. Hopefully, it won't be a day full of arguments and unease like many before have been. In truth, I don't understand why we hang out together. But I want you to enjoy your closing hours on the planet. So, as you can tell, I'm not completely heartless. Your happiness is somewhat important to me.' Once again there was laughter, but this time to themselves. *'I'm going to wait until you all leave here, and then I'm going to go shopping and buy the murder weapon. Taking my time is important to me. It needs to be the correct colour and material. Don't worry, it'll be in good taste. I want only the best for Ravi. And if you think I'd be stupid enough to pay for it on a credit or debit card, you're wrong. I brought plenty of euros with me. Enjoy the conference and I will see you later at the restaurant.'*

10

Ravi

24th September 2019

7:30 p.m.

The restaurant, though expansive, successfully evoked the intimate ambience Ravi associated with Parisian establishments. Although there were already lots of diners, the noise level was perfect. A band was playing, but he couldn't see them from where he sat. However, he could recognise "Moon River," a song that held sentimental value. It had been the first dance at their wedding. A fast-paced Indian song called "Maahi Ve" which prompted people to get up and dance immediately followed it, even though it was still early in the evening. It had been a magical occasion.

Sitting by himself for so long, Ravi was beginning to feel self-conscious. Some people were looking over at him, making him feel uneasy. Conversations from others drifted across to him and their laughter dispersed through the air.

'Bonsoir, Monsieur,' said a server, making Ravi jump.

'Oh, sorry,' he sighed, a little flustered. 'I don't speak French.'

'I said, good evening, sir. That is all.' The server thought Ravi could have managed something as basic as that.

'Sorry, of course. I should have thought it through.'

'Can I get you a drink?'

'Yes.'

'I see you are waiting for three more guests. Would you prefer to wait for them to arrive and have a drink together?'

'No. That's OK. I'll have a…' Ravi pulled a face. 'I've forgotten what I like to drink. It's been a busy day at a conference. There were so many presentations, but you're not interested in that. Are you?'

'Not really, sir.' The server glared at his guest.

'I'll have a spiced dark rum with Coke, please.'

'Very good, sir.' The server walked away leaving Ravi feeling flustered. He rubbed his forehead.

Having finished his drink when Rakesh arrived, Ravi noticed that his husband was wearing a stylish new outfit and could instantly smell that he had on a new and expensive cologne. He had also had a manicure because his nails were perfect.

'Looks like you've been spending money again?' sneered Ravi.

'Well, it's not like you can't afford it!' was the harsh response. 'I like to look my best, darling,' he said as he leaned in to kiss his husband on his lips. 'It's nice to see you've left the dinosaurs at home.'

Ravi welcomed the intimacy, but the comment about his clothes aggravated him at the same time.

'Why are you late? And where are the other two?'

'I have no clue. I've been seeing the sights of this marvellous city and browsing the shops.' Rakesh raised his hand to request a server. 'Porn star Martini,' he demanded in an arrogant tone.

'Have you been spending money again?' Ravi hissed as he glared at Rakesh.

'You've just asked me that!' Rakesh snarled back.

'I assumed you'd be back earlier,' Ravi said. 'We could've spent some time together before this meal, which is bound to end in disaster.'

The two sat there in near silence, reading through the extravagant menu. Ravi tried to hold Rakesh's hand, but his attempt to show affection wasn't what his husband wanted. He didn't make another attempt. Finally, Norton and Parveena arrived, and so did another tray of drinks shortly afterwards.

'Where the hell were you this morning? You were at least two hours late for the start of the conference!' Ravi almost yelled these words to his work partner. 'It was so unprofessional.'

Parveena composed herself before offering a response. Her whisky had arrived and she swallowed it in one and then ordered another straight away. Rakesh smiled. He liked her style.

'If it has anything to do with you, I skipped this morning to do some shopping. I have to present tomorrow and I can't begin to tell you how nervous I am. Since our train leaves early tomorrow evening, I won't have time to go shopping after the conference, which as you know ends at 4 p.m. so I went today.'

Ravi wasn't happy with her answer. He had been dreading her presentation for weeks, letting her know this frequently.

'Are you prepared? If it goes as badly as I predict, we are going to end up humiliated. There'll be no coming back from this,' Ravi shouted as he rubbed his temples on both sides of his head.

'Oh, naff off, Ravi, and leave your head alone! These aren't the words I need to hear right now.' Parveena ordered another drink, as did Rakesh.

The atmosphere around the table was its usual stale thickness. How they were friends had often been the subject of conversation between them and others outside the group for a long time.

Norton had up to now spent his time on his phone, trying not to get involved.

'Reviewing your professional code of conduct?' Ravi asked.

'Don't start, just don't bloody start!' Norton scowled.

'What? Is this something to do with what we discovered at the birthday party?' asked Parveena.

'Let it go,' was all Norton said.

The food was served and set before them, accompanied by a fresh round of drinks. Ravi was concerned about the amount Parveena was drinking. Her presentation was going to be just before they went for lunch. His stomach tightened, and he flinched as he watched her knock back yet another one.

'How did you spend your day in the beautiful city, Norton?'

Slowly looking up from his phone, he answered Rakesh's question.

'I spent the morning having breakfast, then did some shopping. Then I went to see some paintings and spent the late afternoon in the spa at the hotel having a two-person massage. Two young things, one male and the other female. It was heavenly. I would wholeheartedly recommend it.'

'Is that appropriate under the circumstances?' Ravi asked.

Norton ignored the question.

'I planned to join you on this trip, knowing I'd be spending most of the time by myself. Furthermore, I have to say, I loved today. I am feeling refreshed and motivated. Time alone has given me room for thought.'

The table went back to silence. Everyone apart from Ravi was looking at their phones. People at other tables were staring across and then chatting with their friends. Ravi felt embarrassed.

'Hey,' a loud voice chimed from behind.

Rakesh pulled a face of disgust as the group turned around. Walking towards them were Dipen and Agatha.

'Hi guys,' Agatha bawled, as she gave an exaggerated wave. 'We thought we'd gatecrash. Dipen didn't like the idea of you enjoying yourselves without us, so here we are. We arrived early this morning on the Eurostar in first class. Dipen paid.' Ravi frowned at this information. 'We did our own thing for a few hours and met for a large lunch so we don't need dinner.'

Dipen called the server over to order more drinks.

'So,' he roared. 'Any news?'

11

Parveena

30th September 2019

5:30 p.m.

It had been a week since the veterinary conference and as Ravi had predicted, Parveena's presentation had been abysmal. From the moment she started, he saw how the other participants turned to each other and pulled faces, illustrating their disinterest in what was being presented.

Ravi also heard for himself how badly prepared Parveena had been, and had put his head into his hands. She had stuttered throughout, messed up her slide order, and when it came time for questions, she could not answer them. He knew the way the conversations were going to go during the break. He had also known Parveena would disappear straight after she left the stage, leaving him to take the backlash. The presentation made it clear to the whole conference that they worked together; he was named on the final slide.

They had barely exchanged words since their return from Paris. In truth, they did their best to avoid each other. Parveena because she was ashamed of herself and knew her partner was cross. Ravi because he was fully aware of how their practice was now viewed throughout Europe. He honestly didn't know if they could survive this, and it was taking its toll on his health.

Despite it being their late opening, there had been no bookings made as the day ended. Ravi had wanted to speak with Parveena and knew it would end in tears, and they would probably be his. The door to the operating room opened and an exhausted-looking woman emerged. She was wearing green scrubs, crocs on her feet and a blue surgical hat, which she was in the process of removing when she saw Ravi staring at her. She winced and went to pour herself a coffee.

'Coffee is dull. Why am I even drinking it? I'm not in the mood for you right now,' she shouted. 'I have just operated on Mr Blake's ferret.'

'Did it survive?' Ravi asked.

'Yes, it did,' she barked with annoyance.

'That's a novelty for you recently!' he snapped back.

'Fuck off, Ravi. Leave me alone. I'm exhausted.'

'And probably hungover,' he replied.

'You've changed. I don't think I like you, Ravi.'

'I'm not surprised you don't. No one likes to be pushed and questioned about their practice, but it's what you need. It's what I have to do if we have any chance of saving our jobs and reputation. You have all but destroyed us.'

Parveena downed her coffee and went to go back into the operating room to finish clearing up.

'We need to talk, Parv,' Ravi said, this time with some compassion in his voice.

'Please, just leave me alone. I have nothing to say to you. Being in the same room as you is causing me stress and upset. I know I messed up in Paris. The email you sent me was merciless and unnecessary. I thought I'd done my research and prepared for the perfect PowerPoint presentation. When I saw what others were delivering, I knew straight away how awful mine was.'

'It was dreadful. Embarrassing!'

'I know,' Parveena said wearily.

'We are an independent veterinary practice. We aren't part of a chain. What we do is vastly important. People in our business look to us. They want to see what we are achieving and the differences we are making to the healthcare of our animals. Did you check out Twitter?'

'Ravi, please,' she sounded desperate.

'#Parisvetconference2019, the worst presentation I have ever heard! #Parisvetconference2019, that practice should be ashamed of themselves! #Parisvetconference2019, avoid or your animals will be the ones to suffer!' he screamed at her.

'I know, you put it all in the email. There are only so many fucking hashtags a person can cope with. I made a mistake!'

'Yes, you did, drastically!' Ravi said. 'You also hardly attended the conference. Supporting every session is what we should've been doing. It didn't go unnoticed by the whole of sodding Europe that you were absent!'

'Don't bloody exaggerate, you imbecile!'

'I expect you were in a bar somewhere.'

The tension between the two of them was building to a crescendo. Their voices were getting louder with each sentence. Kwasi, their veterinary nurse came into the room, quickly put on his outdoor coat and slipped out the back to avoid getting involved in the confrontation, but not before giving Ravi a troubled look.

'I looked around but rarely saw you. You didn't even bother turning up the first morning. I know you intimated you'd been shopping, but we were paying to be there. It cost us a fortune, what with Eurostar, conference fees and the hotel. Not to mention food, and more noticeably, drinks. You, Rakesh and Dipen spent a colossal amount on alcohol. Why was Dipen even there?'

'I didn't bloody invite him. He's obsessed with you. Are you sure you're not slipping him your length?' Parveena said with a smirk.

'Don't be disgusting. He is my cousin, and besides, I have never cheated on Rakesh and never will!'

'Sadly, we can't say the same about your precious husband,' can we, she snapped.

'What is that supposed to mean?' Ravi asked.

'Just leave me alone,' was all she replied.

Parveena stood and glared at Ravi. A long time ago, she had been so fond of him. It had never been in a fancying or sexual way, because she was aware of his sexuality from very early on. Long before he even knew himself, or at least accepted it. She made a wise decision by not letting herself fall for someone who wouldn't feel the same. Sadly, for some time now the fondness was no longer present; instead, she loathed him.

She admired his work ethic and the love he showed for every animal he ever came in contact with. Parveena knew how much she had learnt from him and hoped along the way she had also taught him a few things. Their friendship had always been strong and the thought of a partnership was something they had worked towards from childhood. The past year had been difficult for her, and the whisky wasn't helping. She kept telling herself she was in control of it and could stop whenever she wanted. In truth, she didn't want to. However, each morning she woke up and promised herself she wouldn't ever drink again. By lunchtime, she convinced herself she'd only have one or two that evening, but by bedtime, she had downed more than she cared to remember.

Ravi's frustration was building up inside of him. He wanted to speak openly and address urgent concerns, but Parveena kept interrupting.

'So, what is going on between you and Rakesh? If it isn't Dipen, although I'm not convinced.'

Ravi let out a deep sigh. She had asked the one question he didn't want to face. It was also a clever question to move the conversation away from her.

'I don't know,' he said with a heavy heart.

'You must have some thoughts,' she said.

'Ever since my parents died he has been different. He seems to resent Dipen, and I don't know why. I know Dipen comes around a lot, but he's family. Rakesh wants to live a luxury life, which isn't what I want for us. I like plain and simple. Our differences affect our relationship, and he always seems angry with me, which hurts. We haven't had sex for about six months, maybe even longer. Also, I haven't felt great for quite a while now, which has impacted us. I did go to see my GP, but she says it's nothing to worry about. It's probably just stress-related, and I agree with her. However, Rakesh is taking it personally and won't talk to me about anything.'

Parveena hadn't expected this level of truth and couldn't care less about what he was saying. Her respect for him had vanished completely following the party and from what he had revealed. Nevertheless, as the conversation had already begun, she felt obligated to keep going.

'Why haven't you had sex? You don't need to answer if you don't want to. Sorry, I shouldn't have asked.'

'No, it's OK. To be honest, I can't maintain my erection. Sorry if that is too much information. I get a fuzzy feeling in my head and my stress levels are through the roof.' Ravi let out a heavy sigh. 'I also have things on my mind. I know things, and it is destroying my friendships.'

Parveena looked confused at this declaration.

'Do you know what you said to each of us at your birthday party?' Parveena asked. 'How upsetting it was?'

'I don't overly remember. Certain things, I think.'

'Ravi, you didn't have much to drink. Rakesh has a good reason for being angry with you, as do the rest of us. You were dreadfully inappropriate.'

'I don't want a post-mortem of events, Parv. We need to discuss you and what has been happening here for the past few months. Do you come to work drunk? Do you operate on animals when you've been drinking?'

'Screw you,' Parveena screeched as she walked away from him and shut herself away in the operating room.

Ravi rubbed the sides of his head and headed home.

12

Norton

1st October 2019

11:30 a.m.

Norton paced around his room, looking out the window and seeing where the sun was. Planning carefully where he would need to sit at this precise time of day had been his priority when he first arrived at work. It meant moving his chair at least one foot to the right. It was now angled at a slight diagonal to the space in which his patient would be sitting in her wheelchair. After completing some paperwork, he called her in.

Daisy Christmas was twenty-one and hated her surname. It had been the root cause of her bullying at school and the focus of much ridicule as a young adult. Norton had previously admitted his dislike for his name, which made her believe they had something in common. That was twelve months ago, and their sessions continued. Dr Greene seemed reluctant to bring them to a close. Daisy was lucky that her desperate parents paid for these extortionate sessions, but didn't once ask her how she was getting on. In Norton's experience, parents were just pleased that someone else was dealing with their child. Unfortunately, she had been involved in a life-changing road traffic accident a few years ago and was now a wheelchair user.

As Daisy continued talking about her deepest concerns, Norton delighted in the obvious movement of clouds, as the sun shone brightly into his office and directly onto her thin blouse. His plan had worked perfectly as he leered at his patient's small but pert breasts. Norton felt a movement in his pants, which he'd work on as soon as the woman droning on had left.

'I just can't help thinking my family would be better off if I wasn't around.' Daisy said, unaware of where her psychologist's eyes had focused. 'Their lives would go on, but I'd hope they'd miss me.'

Norton adjusted himself in the trouser area and shifted in his chair.

'Who would miss you the most?' he asked.

'My brother,' was her quick response.

'Brother? Why would that be? Has he ever sexualised you?' Norton spoke without thinking and instantly regretted his words.

'What?' she cried with a horrified expression on her face. 'Why would you ask that? You said something like this last time I was here.' Daisy was suddenly aware of where the sun was shining and felt uncomfortable. 'I don't like these questions. My brother is what stops me from taking my own life. He is not a pervert. I can't believe you'd ask me something like this.'

'I'm sorry, Daisy. I jumped in too soon with that statement and wasn't thinking straight. You've every right to be annoyed. I was trying to explore other possibilities for your mental health concerns.'

Norton observed the anger in his patient's demeanour as she went to leave. Since Ravi approached him a few weeks ago, his thoughts have been all over the place, and he is conscious of his slightly inappropriate behaviour with his patients. He went with Daisy to the reception desk, instructing her to book in again for next week, when he saw Ravi sitting by the window drinking a coffee that was usually only given to patients. As he approached him, he heard Daisy telling Sorel, the receptionist, that she'd prefer to find another therapist. Sorel nodded. This had been the fifth patient in the past few weeks to cancel future bookings. Norton glared at the man in front of him. He was to blame.

Sorel and Daisy watched the two men engage in a tête-à-tête. They couldn't hear what was being said as they'd lowered their voices but could tell by their body language it wasn't an affable exchange.

Norton turned to walk back into his office as Daisy left via the building's lift. Sorel watched as Ravi followed. She noticed how strikingly beautiful he was and at that moment had already planned their wedding and the names of their four children. The telephone rang and snapped her out of her dreamy trance.

'Hello, Dr Greene's practice. How can I help you?' she said with a renewed vigour to her voice. 'Oh, you want to cancel all future appointments?'

Norton and Ravi sat opposite each other. The sun had gone behind a cloud, so the room wasn't as bright. There was a thick tension between the two men, signalling a friendship on the verge of collapse.

'Just leave it, Ravi! I'm sick to death of you harping on about something which is of no concern to you. What happened was an error of judgement and I have put it behind me and moved on.'

'Has Stuart Schumann put it behind him?' Ravi hissed.

'LEAVE IT! As I told you at the party, I have dealt with the situation and it has gone away. Stop bringing it up.' Norton stood and moved towards the window.

'I've reported you,' Ravi said with an air of sadness in his tone. 'The Health and Care Professions Council and the British Psychological Society. I'm sorry, but you left me no choice.'

'You've done what?' snarled Norton.

A quietness descended the room as the sun broke through the clouds again, giving Norton a halo-like appearance. A contorted, violent expression on his face accompanied his visible trembling. Ravi watched the change in Norton and felt alarmed. In all the time they had known each other, Ravi had never seen the fierce expression on his friend's face before and stood ready to back away. Norton took his chance and lunged at Ravi, grabbing him by the throat, throwing him against the wall and punching him in the stomach. Ravi fell to the ground and put himself in the foetal position to protect himself. Norton took the opportunity to kick Ravi, paying no attention to the cries coming from him.

'Is everything OK in there?' Sorel called through the door.

'Yes,' yelled the psychologist.

'Stop! Please,' begged Ravi.

'PARVEENA,' shouted the psychologist. 'I assume you've reported her as well? HAVE YOU?'

Ravi shook his head.

'Of course, you haven't, because that would affect you.' Norton gave Ravi one last kick and then slumped into his chair as he watched Ravi crawl over to the door, using it to help himself stand. 'Get out.'

Ravi stood and looked over at Norton. He pressed his hand against his forehead, attempting to soothe the sharp pain that was causing his vision to blur.

'I've reported you,'

'What?' Norton gasped. 'You have just told me. Are you just taking the piss? Do you want me to hurt you again?'

Ravi shook his head. 'Did I?' he said. 'My mind is so mixed up. So many emotions are running back and forth.'

'Just get out. I am losing so much money lately. Patients are cancelling their appointments left, right and centre. Are you the cause of this? What you revealed at the party was bad enough, but I won't be responsible for my actions if you're trying to ruin my practice.'

'I did what any decent person would do in the circumstances,' Ravi expressed through gritted teeth.

'Just leave,' Norton said.

Ravi opened the door and saw Sorel staring at him with a pang of sadness. She noticed he was injured, with obvious bleeding where he seemed to have struck his head. Ravi was, however, clutching his stomach. Behind him, she could see her boss sitting with his head in his hands. Still catching his breath from the punches and kicks, Ravi limped out of the room and exited the building.

'Oh, my God! What happened?' she asked as she ran into the office.

'Nothing to fucking do with you,' Norton fired back.

13

Agatha

3rd October 2019

10:30 a.m.

Ravi walked along the street, nervous with trepidation. Agatha had sent him a message via Instagram.

"I need to speak to you. What you exposed at the party has been playing on my mind."

Why she didn't use a text or WhatsApp baffled Ravi. Social media wasn't his bag, so he had nearly missed her request. He was reluctant to meet her because he was still feeling uneasy after his recent conflict with Norton. Ravi had taken himself to his local A&E because of pain and issues with his breathing. He didn't want to face the questions of how his injuries had come about, so he told them he was mugged. They took a couple of X-rays and sent him home following a review with strong painkillers, and encouraged him to talk with the police, which he didn't do.

On the pavement opposite, he saw two women holding hands. Seeing people who were part of the LGBTQ+ community, and showing outward signs of affection always made him smile. Sadly, even in this day and age, it wasn't always the safest thing to do. Bigots could appear at any moment and cause physical harm. Ravi even felt uncomfortable holding hands with his husband in public.

'Why can't people just let others be who they were born to be?' he whispered.

As the café grew closer, Ravi's thoughts turned to Rakesh, who hadn't come home again last night. He contemplated where his husband might be having his breakfast. Ravi had retired to bed early because of another headache, yet found himself awake during the night needing to use the bathroom. Rakesh wasn't in their bed. This upset Ravi, and he had a restless sleep for the rest of the night. However, explaining his bruised body may have been difficult.

Ravi opened the door to the café. The smell of fried meat and coffee instantly struck him, making him feel nauseated. He scanned the room, eyeing up an empty table in the corner. This would be a good place to sit in case Agatha began getting aggressive. He was uncertain what kind of mood she would be in, so he needed to prepare himself the best he could. He sat with his back to the wall so he could look out over the café and take in the daily routines.

Three men were tucking into a full English breakfast. Two were looking at their phones, and the other appeared to be doing a crossword. At the furthest table from him, Ravi saw a young couple using sign language with each other. The man had his back to Ravi, but the woman periodically looked over at him and smiled. The speed at which their hands were moving fascinated him. Her facial expressions were also interesting, and Ravi assumed the young man was also pulling the same ones. Once, years ago, he had thought about learning a new language, but it never happened.

From the corner of his eye, Ravi saw the café door open with force. Standing in the doorway was Agatha. It had been just over a week since he had last seen her in Paris, but she appeared to have put on weight. Ravi sighed heavily when the woman, wearing overly tight bright red leggings and big purple glasses approached him and forcefully dumped her handbag on the table.

'Have you ordered yet?' she questioned, without bothering to say hello and speaking in an aggressive tone.

'Not yet. I was waiting for you.' Ravi sounded timid.

Agatha raised her hand to alert someone that they were ready to order. A young man with a wearied expression on his face slowly came over to them. He took out his pad and pencil and was ready.

'Full English, with extra bacon and sausage, a cup of tea and an orange juice, please.' Agatha said as if she only had moments to live. She then shot a piercing glare at the man sitting across from her and contorted her face in a way that instructed him to make his order quickly. Ravi was already sensing this was going to be a difficult meeting. Despite not being hungry, he grabbed the menu to avoid Agatha getting upset if he didn't get some food. He felt anxious and under pressure.

'Erm, apple juice and mushrooms on brown toast, please. Oh, and no butter. And mushrooms, please. Did I already say that?'

The server walked off without uttering a single word.

The two friends sat and gazed at each other. There was sadness in Agatha's eyes, and Ravi thought he saw a glistening in the corner of one of them. Had she been crying? He hoped not.

'How are you?' he asked.

'Not great, if I am being frank with you.'

'Sorry to hear that, Agatha. I can sense there is an atmosphere between us, and it makes me feel wretched. We've been friends for years. Surely we can talk about things and get back on track.'

Agatha scoffed, opened her handbag and took out a chocolate bar, which had already been half-eaten.

'You're about to eat breakfast,' Ravi said, instantly regretting it.

'This,' she vented, waving the chocolate bar in his face, 'is because of you and everything you have put me through over the years. How dare you question what I put in my mouth. It has zero to do with you.' Her cheeks were getting red. 'You have no authority over my life, so butt out.'

'You're right. I'm sorry.' Ravi felt embarrassed.

After some diluted chit-chat and awkward silence, the server wandered over with their food. He remained as uninterested as he had been when taking the order. The café was getting busier and Ravi knew this was a bad thing.

'You wanted to see me?' he asked. 'For anything in particular?'

'My God! Are you serious? The party! What you told everybody.'

'I'm not sure what I said. And you seemed fine with me in Paris.'

Agatha glared at him. Both of their breakfasts remained untouched. Ravi was feeling uncomfortable with her.

'Paris was Paris! I didn't want to get into arguments when we were away. It wouldn't have been fair to the others to have them watch me argue with you. Have you any idea what you have put me through? Is there any part of you that has compassion? It's like we are just pawns in your game of chess.'

'Agatha, what are you talking about?'

The infuriated woman threw her arms in the air, which gained the attention of the woman in the far part of the café.

'The party!' Her voice was getting louder. 'University, the hospital. Where do you want to start? You have destroyed me.'

Ravi noticed the signing couple. The woman was looking over at them and signing to her friend. They were blatantly talking about the situation erupting in the opposite corner, and he was mortified.

'Agatha, it's not my fault I'm gay. When we got together I was still figuring things out for myself. I am truly sorry you got hurt. I never meant to cause you pain.' Ravi had lowered his voice, hoping Agatha would as well; She didn't!

'YOU USED ME,' she screamed. 'Because of you, I've never been able to form lasting relationships. I'm struggling with a completely scrambled mind. Look at me! I'm obese and it's your fault.'

'Agatha, please don't do this. I can hear you're hurting, but you can't blame me for what's wrong in your life. We were together for only six months. It was so many years ago. You need to move on.'

'And what about the day in the hospital? You made me do that! I didn't want it to happen, but it was your decision.' Agatha was so loud the other customers were all staring over at her.

'No, Agatha! NO!' This was the first time Ravi raised his voice. 'You have misremembered. I am not to blame for what happened in the hospital. You're twisting things and I won't put up with it.'

He once again observed the signing couple who were glancing in his direction.

'You blurted out stuff at the party that the others had no right to know. You'd only had two glasses of wine, so you can't say it was because of the alcohol. Why did you do it? I need to know.'

'I don't know. I can't remember much about the evening. However, I will repeat myself. I am not to blame for your problems.'

'What about my suicide attempts? I wouldn't have done these if you hadn't treated me so badly.'

Ravi took a deep breath.

'I did not mistreat you, Agatha! I am not accountable for your attempts to kill yourself. You are! I am desperately sorry you have tried so many times, but I have and always will be here to listen and try to help.'

Agatha was now as purple in the face as the glasses she was wearing. She stood and threw her breakfast at Ravi.

'You've changed Ravi Patel. YOU'VE DESTROYED MY LIFE.'

Agatha leant forward and slapped Ravi hard across the face. She turned and stormed out. Ravi sat there, grabbed hold of his head rather than his face, and tears poured from his eyes. His ribs were still hurting and now, so was his face.

The woman in the far corner started signing to her friend as they watched Ravi get up and run from the café.

'So, what do you make of that, DC Faisal Asher?'

14

Dipen

5th October 2019

4:00 p.m.

The noise emanating from the big screen was going unheard by the frightened man sitting on the uncomfortable plastic chair. In his hand, he had already crumpled up his betting slip before the race had finished. Another wasted £300 on a horse named Midnight's Moon at 300/1. Dipen knew the nag didn't stand a chance of winning, but miracles can happen, and he needed one; desperately!

He fetched a coffee from the vending machine, yet it bore an uncanny resemblance in taste to a blend of tea and oxtail soup. As a Hindu, albeit not devout, he discarded the beverage, concerned it might contain traces of beef.

He was currently staying in his sister's house because he had been thrown out of his digs six months ago for being so far behind with his rent. His father had refused to lend him more money, and he had nowhere else to go. Beena had done well for herself and was working as a pensions specialist and had a four-bedroom house. He was permitted to stay on the condition that he was gone within the month. To her annoyance, he was still there, much to her husband's irritation.

Another race was due to start soon, and it took everything that he had to walk out of the betting shop and not place a wager. Dipen had tried to get himself a card game, but most clubs had barred him. There was an opportunity for an underground game in the Brockley area. However, Dipen couldn't get hold of the required cash, and it wasn't possible to make payments with a card at most games. Not that he had any credit left.

Ravi knew how much debt Dipen had got himself into, as the two had spoken about it several weeks ago. Dipen had begged for help, but his cousin just kept repeating that there wasn't anything left from his "insignificant" inheritance. The conversation had ended abruptly.

It had been bad enough when it had just been credit cards, store cards and bank loans, but now loan sharks were involved. His debts were shifting from one shark to another, with the interest and demands increasing daily. Dipen also deeply regretted getting involved with payday loans. They seemed the perfect solution when he saw them on TV, but before he realised it, they had become part of the sharks' calculations. Dipen could see no end to his debt that had snowballed so far out of control, that he knew eventually there was a bullet with his name on it.

He finally left the betting shop and walked along the street with his head exploding with anxiety. He had always been susceptible to mental health concerns and had come across as a highly anxious boy. His parents had taken him to a child psychiatrist from the age of six to ten, but it didn't help. As he approached his teenage years, when things usually started becoming more fragile and perturbing, Dipen flourished. He came out of his shell and began making the most of every situation presented to him. Having an older cousin like Ravi also helped to benefit and enrich his teenage years.

When he turned eighteen, he got his first proper job in an Indian restaurant. He was just the dishwasher at first, but he got a wage. Then, within a few months, he got promoted to help with the cooking. Little did he know that eleven years on, he would be doing the identical job in the same establishment. He was never good with budgets and planning, so got his first credit card when he turned twenty, and reached the credit limit of £1200 within a month. His financial troubles had begun.

Rain was now lashing from the sky as darkness encroached. Dipen quickened his steps and was just picking up some speed when a car pulled up at the kerbside, a tad erratically. A man dressed in black jumped out and grabbed a confused Dipen by his jacket and threw him into the car, bashing his forehead on the door frame before he landed on the back seat, scared out of his wits.

'What the fuck!' shouted Dipen. His hand touched the wound on his head and he could tell he was bleeding. 'Who the hell are you?' he demanded.

The man, now sitting next to him remained silent. The driver, who also said nothing, pulled away from the kerb and started driving. Dipen kept asking questions, but no answers came, which wasn't helping his fretfulness.

After driving for what felt like ages, the car pulled into a quarry-like environment, which appeared deserted. The rain was still coming down at a heavy pace and Dipen's apprehension was through the roof. Shaking visibly, he was about to ask another question he knew would go unanswered when another vehicle pulled up alongside theirs. Dipen was terrified when they manhandled him from one car to the other.

Sitting in the back seat was a woman in her mid to late fifties. She had a tidy, tight ponytail with black and grey streaks. This resulted in a slight lift at the sides of her eyes. She wore no make-up apart from pale orange lipstick. This woman had a rough-looking face which told an uncomfortable history. There was a two-inch scar on her left cheek and what Dipen thought were cigarette burns on the right. With a heavily tattooed neck and a raspy voice, she was quite distinctive.

'Do you know who I am?' she said.

'No,' he replied in a higher octave, which caused him concern.

The woman smiled. Dipen had prepared himself to see a mouthful full of gold teeth but was shocked by her flawless white ones.

'I'm Donna,' she revealed.

'What is going on?' Dipen questioned as if he hadn't heard what she had just said. 'Why am I sitting in your car?' He was finding his courage from somewhere, although he wasn't sure it would last long.

'I think that is a fair question,' she said with a deadpan expression. 'The life you've been leading has built up a debt. I have paid off your account from your previous lender, namely Mr Dimakos. You have been an incredibly stupid young man over the years, haven't you? Spending what you don't have and borrowing from the wrong sort of people. So now, you're mine to do what I want with! If you don't clear your substantial balance within the next month, I'm going to be expecting you to do modest jobs for me. Do you understand? And I don't mean doing my shopping or walking my dogs. There is the possibility you will get hurt as you do them, but that is a chance you'll have to take, Mr Patel.'

'I don't have that amount of money,' Dipen blurted out. 'You'll need to give me more time. I will get all the cash owed to you; I promise.'

He could hear the trembling in his voice, whilst aware the moisture on his cheeks was either the blood seeping down from his head, or the tears leaking from his eyes. Donna chuckled, which sounded sinister. Dipen couldn't shake off the feeling he was in a gangster film and a director was about to shout "cut."

Out of nowhere, Ravi popped into Dipen's thoughts along with the various heated conversations from a few weeks ago and the party. A growing bitterness towards his cousin had been simmering for a long time, and an idea grew in his head. Thunder cracked overhead, and this added an extra layer, which was making this whole situation horrendous.

'Mrs?'

'Donna, please,' she replied with a smirk.

'Donna, I have a plan in mind. In truth, I've had it in mind for several weeks, but I will need more than a month, and I promise I'll pay you.'

'One month,' Donna said, tapping Dipen's leg.

He peeked down to see that she was using a gun. He felt butterflies in his stomach and a dryness in his mouth.

Without warning, the car door burst open. Dipen was violently grabbed and tossed onto the gravel, causing his trousers to tear. The two cars drove off and left a broken man sobbing as he got drenched from the never-ending rain.

15

Rakesh

7th October 2019

2:00 p.m.

Rakesh stepped out of the luxurious hotel where he had spent the night in their most opulent suite, feeling like he was the richest man in the world. The sun was excessively bright, and it caught him off guard. The glare from it appeared to set off a round of sneezing. As Rakesh raised his hand to his nose, he could smell the delightful aromas of eucalyptus and lemongrass.

The hotel offered different spa treatments, and he had gone for the indulgence package. This included a ninety-minute full-body aromatherapy massage and a thirty-minute facial. A manicure and pedicure followed. Before the treatments, Rakesh had made use of the spa pool, steam, and sauna rooms, not to mention the swimming pool, complimentary champagne, and strawberries.

Edvin, the business executive Rakesh had recently stopped seeing, had told his friend about him. Last night was their first meeting, and as far as Rakesh was concerned, it couldn't have gone better. Ivan appeared to be even richer than Edvin, and this was exactly what Rakesh had wanted.

Upon their initial meeting at the hotel bar, Rakesh felt a twinge of apprehension. Ivan, with his deep Russian accent, wore a tailor-made suit and was nearly three times the size of Rakesh. He had a square jaw and deep-set grey eyes. His appearance gave Rakesh the impression of a 1950s London criminal.

After a couple of drinks the conversation had opened up and there were fewer awkward silences. However, they were one-sided most of the time. Ivan had refused to discuss anything about his work or private life and stated clearly it had nothing to do with the man he was paying for sex. Rakesh's role was to enjoy the times they would have together but to ask no questions. As they had finished their drinks and left the bar, a solitary figure had watched them leave.

Ivan had prearranged the reservation for the spa day, whilst payment for their intimate night was already in Rakesh's secret bank account. It was a working day, but Rakesh had called in sick when he saw the colossal breakfast arrive. With Ivan gone, this meal was now a solo affair.

Once he had finished eating and got himself ready for the day, Rakesh headed off into the city. He was feeling happy and wanted to give his credit card a bashing. He spent some time choosing the right venue to spend his money in, though already knew exactly where he was heading.

The concierge to the exorbitant department store saw Rakesh coming along the street and opened the grand entrance to welcome him in. The excited man walked straight through without bothering to say thank you. This was an everyday occurrence so the concierge just muttered "wanker" under his breath and wished him a crap day.

Rakesh had a passion for shoes, so headed to the correct department on the first floor and examined all the designer footwear. At one point, he even heard himself sighing as he lifted a pair with a £900 price tag. The smell of the leather was intoxicating, and he was now unaware of any other customers. This was heaven as far as he was concerned, and he didn't want it to end. He tried them on and walked about for a few minutes. They felt like they were made for him, and him alone. He eventually took them off but continued to look at the many other shoes. Finally, he took the expensive pair he was still holding over to the payment desk and handed over his card.

'I'm sorry, sir. It's been declined,' said the young man.

'Try it again,' Rakesh snapped back.

He was now fully aware of others in the surrounding area, as he could feel their eyes staring at him.

'Declined,' the man repeated.

'Oh, that's right,' Rakesh exclaimed in a voice unnecessarily too loud. 'I lowered the credit limit on this one.' He knew they would all know he was lying. 'I will come back for them later.'

Rakesh left the department store as fast as he could.

Once he had time to overcome his embarrassment, he called the credit card company and was told he'd reached his £15,000 limit. This information infuriated him, and he started shaking with anger.

'Fuck you, Ravi Patel!' he screamed.

'What's Ravi done?' a voice questioned from behind him.

Rakesh turned around sharply to find Dipen smiling at him. The two men looked at each other for a few moments without speaking and then the younger man spoke.

'Fancy going for a coffee?' Dipen noticed Rakesh's eyes peering down at the credit card he had been holding. 'It's OK. I'll pay.'

'I'm not going for a coffee. Coffee is dull, and I'm not going anywhere cheap. I'll tell you that for nothing!'

'How about the Savoy?'

Twenty-five minutes later, they were sitting and holding their drinks. Both had gone for a cocktail. Music played in the background and the ambience was just right for the occasion. The two men enjoyed their drinks as they engaged in small talk for a while.

'So, what has Mr Patel done that got you so angry you felt the need to yell his name out in public?' Dipen asked.

'If we are going to talk about him,' Rakesh grimaced, 'we need more drinks.'

'Hey, I'm not buying another round here. It's way too expensive.'

Rakesh opened up his wallet and took out a brand-new credit card. He had promised himself he wouldn't use it, but the need for another cocktail, or more, changed his mind. He had already decided to go back to purchase the leather shoes and a few other items once their drinking was done.

Although the two men spent a lot of time together, this was probably one of the few times they had been alone, and it felt fine. Maybe all this time the problem had been Ravi and not them.

'So?'

'OK. Ravi and I aren't getting on.'

'Obvious,' said Dipen.

'We haven't for ages, and it's getting to me. It must also be crap for him as well. Honestly, I miss the way it used to be, but he makes me so mad. I yearn for opulence. I want someone to pay attention to me and make me feel special by buying me expensive gifts and treating me to luxury holidays. Someone who thinks nothing of spending a fortune on me.'

'You sound like a total dick if I'm being completely honest,' Dipen said. 'Can't you just accept someone who loves you? I'd love to find a woman who truly gets me and wants to spend the rest of our lives together.'

'Ravi has changed during the past six months,' Rakesh declared, oblivious to what had just been said.

'How?' asked Dipen.

Rakesh shifted in his seat and caught the attention of the server.

'Oh, little things. He has started this thoroughly annoying habit of tapping the sides of his head, and I know it shouldn't, but it drives me mad. Why is he doing that?'

'Yeah, I have noticed that too, and it is slightly annoying.'

'We don't have sex anymore, well, barely. I need sex, I deserve wealth, and I crave another life. He makes me so angry with his penny-pinching ways. Especially after what we heard at the party. Ravi owes me, and I am going to make sure that he pays.'

Dipen noticed the expression on Rakesh's face was getting more and more contorted, and his hands were forming fists.

'Yes, the party was especially revealing, wasn't it?'

Rakesh relaxed slightly.

'Is it true what Ravi said about you?'

Dipen was now the one beginning to feel infuriated.

'Partly.'

'What does that mean?'

'I don't want to discuss it, especially with you, Rakesh!'

The tension between the two men was palpable for a moment, but it soon gave way to laughter as they signalled for another round of drinks. The conversation moved on to films, cars, sex, and money, but inevitably came back around to Ravi. Rakesh was now very drunk and started berating his husband, mostly through slurred speech.

'And another thing, he is constantly forgetting what I have told him, and that genuinely pisses me off!'

'Just so you know,' Dipen said, 'he's fully aware you frequently cheat on him.'

'He asked me just before the party if I was cheating. I said no.'

'We all know you do. It was quite surprising that he didn't bring it up during his rant at the party. You got off lightly compared to the rest of us. No wonder he forgets things. That man is going through hell thinking he is going to lose you.'

'Lose me? After what he told us, why would he lose me?' Rakesh was now standing and raising his voice. 'I'll tell you this. I may hate him, but there is no way he is getting rid of me, but I do want to hurt him.'

'Hate him?' Dipen replied with a confused frown. 'Why do you hate him?'

'Because he has money. You also acknowledged that you hated him at the party.'

'I know I did, but I could never hurt him. But don't worry about what I said. I have a plan.'

Rakesh passed out on the table as the server brought over their bill. With a scowl, Dipen took out his credit card, silently praying for it not to be declined.

16

Through the Eyes of a Murderer!

(Part Three)

10th October 2019

10:30 a.m.

The two people walked along the side of the river, both enjoying the slight breeze blowing across their faces. The usual sounds emanating from the unseen fox were shrieking through the air. There was a 747 darting through the sky, causing both of them to look up and wonder where the plane was heading. Ravi also pictured the cabin crew walking through the aisle, getting ready to start the drinks service.

They walked in silence, one lost in his thoughts, the other planning to kill. Ravi found the gentle ripple coming from the water relaxing. The autumnal leaves, some still attached to their branches, some scattered along the pathway, brought beautiful colours to the scene.

Ravi, who had told Parveena she'd have to manage by herself today as he didn't have the motivation to come to work, had his wireless headphones on as he listened to Eurovision winners. This was his guilty pleasure because Rakesh would not allow him to watch it when it was televised. His view was that it was outdated and farcical, therefore not something a person with any standing in life should be watching. This annoyed Ravi because he loved himself some camp Europop.

The two carried on with their walk. Ravi in front, and the other about thirty seconds behind, watching, tracking the doomed man in front. Ravi was completely unaware he was being followed.

'I can see you. Don't think for a moment that I can't. The day of your death is getting closer. Just over two weeks until I get to tie the scarf around your neck. I have been wanting to do this for ages. Your revelations at the party have increased the intensifying hunger, which is surging through my veins to carry out the deed. I won't rest until I see you dead! You have made me need to do this.'

Ravi continued along the pathway until a café came into sight.

'I could go for a coffee,' he murmured to himself.

17

Ravi

10th October 2019

11:00 a.m.

As Ravi pushed open the door to the Riverside Café, he heard the bell above chiming to alert the proprietor that another customer had arrived. He surveyed the establishment and noticed a significant amount of condensation on the windows, which hindered the view of the river. The café was busy, with only a few vacant seats available, but it had a cheerful vibe that he desperately needed.

The noise from the old-fashioned cash till rang out, breaking his trance-like state. Ravi enjoyed the sound as it was a sign of the past and he liked that. The signs on the door stated that although card payments were accepted, cash was the preferred method of payment. He put his hand into his pocket for coins and smiled when he touched some. He also knew there was £10 cash in his wallet. For a reason he couldn't name, he was feeling happy.

Over by the window was an empty seat, so he made his way over. Next to him were two older women who acknowledged his presence. Ravi picked up a menu and scanned through it, but nothing instantly jumped out at him. He looked about to see what others had ordered but saw nothing that tempted him.

'Hello. Can I get you something, my lovely?' asked a homely-looking woman.

'Can I please have an Americano with hot skinny milk, and…' Ravi scrutinised the menu again. His head was beginning to throb, and just for a few moments, the words in front of him became blurred. His body started to shake, so he put pressure on the sides of his head. A few moments passed.

'Are you OK?' the waitress enquired, sounding extremely concerned.

'Yes, yes, sorry. Can I just get some mushrooms on toast? Brown bread, and an Americano with hot skinny milk. Did I say mushrooms?'

The waitress nodded awkwardly and smiled as she walked away.

'Superb choice,' said a woman seated next to him. 'I enjoy mushrooms.'

'He's not interested in what you eat. We only come here for coffee and cake, don't we, Joyce?' Molly Ferres grinned at Ravi.

'Yes, that's correct. Every week, without fail, we have coffee and cake. Don't we sound boring?' Joyce laughed out loud.

Molly glared at her friend and looked angry.

'Oh, that's nice. You make it sound like a chore instead of a pleasant outing. That's typical of you, Joyce Latimer. I don't know why I bother, really I don't.'

'Oh, Molly,' said Joyce. 'Shut up!'

Ravi made polite facial expressions and picked up his phone, indicating to them that he wasn't interested in maintaining a further conversation. Instead, he started looking at hotel apps, as he thought treating his husband to a trip away might be a way to repair their fragile situation. As he studied his phone, he failed to see his stalker standing outside, staring at him with a venomous grin.

12:30 p.m.

With his bill paid in cash, Ravi waved goodbye to the gossiping ladies and the waitress who had served him. He left her a healthy tip, partly as an apology for frightening her. The air outside was cool and surprisingly refreshing after sitting in a stuffy café. The sounds of the river and the wind in the trees transported Ravi back to happier times in his life. He missed those days.

As he didn't want to go home yet, he continued with his walk. The pain in his head had improved, and the food seemed to have renewed his energy levels, so Ravi picked up his pace and walked further up the towpath, enjoying all the sounds of nature which surrounded him. Someone had once told him to use his arms as he walked briskly. This would help with his cardiovascular exercise and keep him trim. His friend Nichola said that when you walk, you should always get to the point when you "feel the burn" and therefore know that calories are being used.

In the distance, a bench slowly came into view. It was a welcome sight as Ravi had been walking for about an hour since leaving the café. Somebody was already sitting on it, but that didn't worry him. He was feeling exhausted and just wanted to sit and rest. Nevertheless, he regretted not bringing a bottle of water with him, as the breakfast had made him feel thirsty and dehydrated.

'Do you mind if I sit here?' he said to the unkempt man sitting on the bench.

The man, who was probably in his early sixties but appeared much older, glanced up and indicated with his hand he was happy for Ravi to sit.

'Thanks, I've been walking longer than I meant to and my legs are aching. I'm Ravi.'

'Pleased to meet you. I'm Basil. I won't shake hands because I'm a little grubby.'

Ravi noticed he was unclean and thought filthy would describe him better.

The two men sat in silence for a while. Watching the world go by and taking in the sounds. Ravi leant forward and rubbed the sides of his head.

'I shouldn't have said what I did. I realise that now.'

'What?' was Basil's reply, slightly surprised by the revelation.

'I had a party recently for my birthday. It was meant to be a quiet affair. Just my husband, cousin and three friends. I haven't been feeling well for a few months, so would have happily cancelled the whole thing. Rakesh, my husband insisted, so we had dinner at ours. The evening had started OK until Rakesh started winding people up. I'd already fallen out with everyone, either way back or recently, so hadn't had high expectations for the evening going well. I wasn't wrong! I made the situation so much worse. Unfortunately, I can't remember most of what happened. For about six months, I have been having stress-related headaches according to my GP and take codeine as pain relief. They make me feel quite spaced out.' Ravi looked over at Basil and smiled. 'Everybody was arguing, or I think they were. I don't overly remember. My GP says I have stress-related headaches. Did I tell you that already?' Not waiting for a response, Ravi continued. 'I know secrets about them all. Some I have known for many years, but most are fairly recent. Sadly, I lost my temper and told them all what I knew about each other. It didn't go down well, as I am sure you can imagine, but I don't remember how the evening ended. Rakesh was distant with me the following morning, but wouldn't say why. We are all meant to be meeting again on 27th October for a concert, but I don't think I want to go. No good can come from it. I love them all dearly, but three of them have done terrible things. Rakesh and, oh, you're not interested in their names, are you?' Again, there was no response from Basil, although he did look like he was taking in everything he was being told. 'The other two have issues which are massively impacting their lives and I believe blame me for them. Agatha is one, and the other is, oh, yes, I forgot, I'm not giving you names. Sorry. Over the past few months, I have been talking to each one about their issues, so I don't suppose I can blame them for hating me. I'm a nice person, though, and always try to do good. Everything has got out of hand, and it's genuinely affecting my health. I'm getting more forgetful, and struggle to get things sorted in my head. I'm tired most of the day and I've started getting blurred vision. Also, I have stress-related headaches. Each time I see one of them, I know it'll end either badly or with a falling out. I truly don't know what to do about the 27th. What do you think, Basil?'

The scruffy man appeared to be digesting the question and took his time in giving his response.

'Do you have £18, so I can get myself a room for the night?'

Ravi sighed and regretted paying for his café bill with cash instead of his card.

'No, I don't, and I'm truly sorry.'

He got up and walked away.

18

The Party

15th September 2019

7:00 p.m.

A "HAPPY BIRTHDAY RAVI" banner had been put up on the wall, along with orange, white and green balloons to represent the Indian flag. From the kitchen, there was a delicious fragrance wafting through the house. The dining table had been arranged exquisitely, and the house was cleaned thoroughly from top to bottom.

Ravi sat on the stairs with his head pressed against the wall. He was tired from all his domestic duties today and wanted to do nothing more than sleep. Rakesh kept on about hiring a cleaner, but Ravi usually enjoyed household chores. However, right now he felt low in mood and was aware of tears on his cheeks.

'Everybody will be here soon, so you'd better come up and finish getting ready.' Rakesh yelled from upstairs.

'I bloody wish they weren't coming.' Ravi mumbled. 'This has to be the worst birthday I have ever had.'

'What did you say?' Rakesh replied.

'Where were you until late this afternoon? TELL ME! I woke up by myself, on my birthday, and it stayed that way until you casually wandered in at 4 p.m.' Ravi sounded distraught. 'You promised we would make the food for tonight together. Instead, I have had to prepare everything myself. I have even made my bloody birthday cake and put up the party decorations. Is this because I refused point-blank to go out to one of your fancy restaurants? Is it? This is my birthday and I have never felt more alone.' More tears rolled down Ravi's cheeks, and he began to tremble. 'Are you cheating on me? Is that why you don't come home some nights?'

'No! I would never do that. I love you.' Rakesh lied as he came down the stairs and took his husband's face in his hands. 'I love you, Ravi. I'm sorry I was late home, but I got caught up with a few things.'

Ravi pushed his face into Rakesh's neck and sobbed.

'I love you too.'

8:00 p.m.

Everybody arrived at the requested time. Rakesh had put on some background music and drinks had been poured. Ravi was in the kitchen putting the final touches to his starters, a finger buffet of Indian specialities. For the main course, he had chosen to make lamb shanks, which he had marinated in a variety of herbs and spices. Dessert, which was also doubling up as a birthday cake, was made using blueberries with a cream cheese frosting on top and ice cream if desired.

The guests were gathered in the spacious living room and they chatted amicably. There was a calm and jovial atmosphere, and occasionally there was even some laughter. However, when Ravi appeared in the room to announce dinner was served in the dining room, Agatha, Parveena, and Norton all experienced a sudden sense of apprehension and felt their hackles rising.

The starters were being passed around the table, as were the specially made dips which accompanied them. Ravi had worked hard to get everything just right. The evening seemed to be going well so far, and Ravi started to relax, albeit slightly. He was determined to enjoy himself, despite it being the last place he wanted to be. He looked across the table and saw his husband in a deep conversation with Norton and the other three laughing at something funny that had been said. It was at this point Ravi realised he wasn't part of the discussions happening around the table, and no one seemed bothered even to try to include him. He looked at Rakesh and desperately wanted him to look back with affection in his eyes. Sadly, this didn't happen, but a sharp pain in his head did.

9:00 p.m.

With the Indian specialities finished, the guests were now starting their main course. There was a chorus of praise for the flavours and tenderness of the lamb, and Ravi felt he was being included a little more. Although he was aware of some tensions and the hard looks he had been receiving.

'On this special occasion, I want to wish my beloved but relentlessly unexciting husband a happy birthday.'

Rakesh's sudden announcement startled some around the table. They put down their knives and forks and raised their glass, and all awkwardly muttered, "Happy birthday" which lacked sincerity, apart from Dipen, who bellowed out the words; and then felt slightly embarrassed for doing so.

'Thank you,' was Ravi's only response, said with sadness.

'Why are we all here?' Rakesh questioned. 'Dipen, I don't understand why you are here so bloody often. We spend most of the time as a group arguing, and I'm not sure if I want to be doing it anymore. This evening would have been much better if we were all sitting enjoying exquisite wines and international delicacies at the incredible venue I had mentioned to Ravi a few weeks ago. However, he decided as he always does, that he'd prefer to put the evening together himself.'

'We were both meant to do it,' Ravi whispered.

Rakesh finished what was in his glass and grabbed the bottle of wine in front of him to refill his glass. It was then passed around the table and everyone apart from the birthday boy replenished their glass.

'Do you have anything else to say?' Ravi asked.

'Yes, as a matter of fact, I do. We are stuck here, eating food I'm not going to say is bad because it is acceptable, but we could have had so much better.'

'Rakesh,' Dipen said. 'Come on mate, you've drunk too much. There is no need to turn nasty.' He turned to Ravi. 'The food is really lovely, mate.'

'Why is it you never want to go out to fancy places?' asked Norton. 'You've changed recently, and I'm not sure I overly like who you're becoming.'

'Hear, hear! Are you ashamed of us?' probed Parveena.

'Some of you, yes,' mumbled Ravi.

'I just don't get you,' Rakesh expressed. 'Norton is correct. You've changed. We could be living a much better life than we do.'

'Better for whom, Rakesh?' Ravi asked. He took a deep breath as a method of trying to control the agonising pain that was shooting through his head. 'Please everyone, just stop having a go at me and continue eating your bloody dinner that I spent most of the day preparing for you.'

For a few moments, everyone got back to eating their food. More drinks were poured, but the atmosphere was getting thicker. Ravi struggled to eat because of his stress headache and the overwhelming sadness that was brewing inside. He was doing everything in his power to hold in the tears that wanted to break free and show all of those around the table how unhappy they made him. They had all been such great friends once upon a time, and Ravi longed for those times again.

With the main course finished and the dinner plates cleared away, Ravi brought in the cake and ice cream, placed it in the centre of the table and asked everyone to help themselves to what they wanted. There was a cheese board coming, he announced, once the dessert had been completed. Ravi sat back at the table and just wanted everybody to go home and leave him alone.

'Who are you ashamed of?' Agatha uttered, almost silently. Remembering Ravi's earlier words.

'An excellent point,' voiced Parveena. 'Who? Ravi.'

'Probably me,' laughed Rakesh as he grabbed the wine on the table and spilt a lot of it as he tried to refill his glass.

Norton glared over at his host, with a stare which said, "Don't you even think about it."

'I want to know what you meant by it,' stated Agatha, this time with more volume. 'I agree with the others. You're not the same.'

'Hey, leave him alone, it's his birthday,' Dipen declared.

'STOP THIS!' yelled Ravi. 'Why am I not the same? Someone tell me. I don't understand what you all mean.'

The room went silent and the only noise was the spoons against the pudding bowls. Even the music had stopped.

The evening was playing out like most had expected it would. Their toxic friendships were becoming more lethal with each meeting.

'Your forgetfulness is getting truly irritating,' said Parveena. 'It is also impacting work.'

'And what you've done isn't?' replied Ravi.

'Your personality is different, and you're so much more pedantic. You put your nose into other people's business where it isn't needed,' snapped Norton.

'You're just frantic because I found you out!' Ravi replied in a deadly tone to his voice.

At this statement, all eyes were now on Norton.

'Leave it!' ordered the psychologist.

'The damn rubbing of your head every few minutes is so annoying.'

Ravi looked at Rakesh and couldn't believe he had just broadcasted this. His eyes were full of sorrow.

'I can't help it. I get stress-related headaches.'

As the others chatted amongst themselves, the sorrow he had felt had changed to anger which was building up inside Ravi. This was his birthday, and he had put so much effort into trying to make it an enjoyable evening for everyone. However, he knew before the evening had even started, it would end in a disaster. Lately, they always did.

'OK,' Ravi said with a noxious edge to his tone. 'If you want to know who I am ashamed of, I'll tell you. All of you. One way or another.' Ravi took a sip of his wine. This was only his second glass of the evening. Everyone else had had much more. 'Let me start with you, Agatha.' She flinched and looked concerned. 'We dated for six months when we were at university.' Agatha went to speak, but Ravi put his hand up to stop her. 'I don't regret our relationship, but I understand it hurt you deeply. I was coming to terms with my sexuality and I now know I shouldn't have started things with you. But I won't take the blame for your countless attempts at taking your own life.' The others all turned to stare at Agatha. They knew of one attempt, but Ravi's revelation was massive. 'To be clear, I am also not to blame for the termination you had. I took you to the hospital for the procedure because you told me that I had to. I don't even think it was mine, but I can't be sure. You were part of the rugby team and I know there was a guy who liked you.'

'You arsehole!' Agatha shouted. 'Of course, it was yours. I love y... Loved,' she quickly corrected herself. 'I now loathe you so much.'

The tension in the room was mounting as they were all nervous about who would be next in Ravi's tirade. They didn't have long to wait.

'Let me do you next.'

'Ravi, don't. Please!' Norton said when he saw where the angry man was looking.

'You have all come at me this evening, and so I will be heard.'

'I haven't,' stated Dipen.

'Nevertheless, I will also get to you, but let me continue with Norton. A few weeks back, I came across a young man standing on London Bridge. I assumed he was drunk, but he wasn't. It was midnight, and I had been out with a friend. A loyal friend,' he said, glaring around the table. 'I asked if he was OK and if I could help him. He wouldn't get down, and I was so scared he was going to throw himself into the river. He told me his name was Stuart Schumann.'

'Ravi! DON'T!' yelled Norton.

'Stuart had been suffering from mental health concerns for years and went to see Dr Norton Greene for therapy. The so-called psychologist made sexual advances towards Stuart, who was eventually pushed to wanting to take his own life. Something you can relate to, Agatha!' Ravi hissed. 'I eventually got him down off the bridge. I haven't yet, but I will be reporting you, Norton.'

The group was shocked at this information, and there was muttering throughout. Rakesh had a smile on his face and enjoyed watching Ravi ranting at the others. He did, however, wonder what he was going to be told.

'Just so you know,' Ravi proclaimed. 'A murderer is sitting around the table.'

Everyone stared at each other, apart from one person who knew the words were directed in her direction. Parveena rose from her seat and went to the tray with the drinks, pouring herself a generous amount of whisky.

'I'll take it from here. If this has to be told, I'll do it myself. A few weeks or months ago, I had a run of bad luck when operating on a couple of animals. They were routine procedures I could have done with my eyes closed. Kwasi was assisting me. On two occasions…'

'Three,' interrupted Ravi.

'Unfortunately,' Parveena said, ignoring Ravi, 'the animals died on the operating table. These things happen and can't always be explained. Kwasi was with me the whole time and stated I did nothing wrong. I don't know why you have such an issue with it. Animals have died when you have operated on them.'

'I wasn't drunk when I did the surgery. Each time I smelt the alcohol on your breath when you were explaining what happened. I don't care what Kwasi thinks. He has been acting strangely recently. You killed those animals because you were under the influence of alcohol.'

'Are you reporting her to your professional body?' snapped Norton.

'I guess I will,' Ravi declared. 'I have to.'

Ravi picked up his glass and drained the remaining drops of wine. He contemplated pouring himself a third, but his headache put him off the idea.

'Do me,' shouted Rakesh, in a child-like voice. 'I can't wait to hear what you have to say about me.'

'This is an easy one,' Ravi chirped. 'I'm a millionaire about five times over, which is gaining large amounts of daily interest. I am therefore disgustingly rich.'

Rakesh's face went from a childish smirk as he had goaded his husband into saying something about him, to a dishevelled specimen of a man. His jaw dropped as he heard the gasps around the table.

Ravi was smiling, and bizarrely, he was finally enjoying himself.

'Which leaves you, Dipen. My ever-faithful cousin. I told you and Rakesh that my parents were useless in business and made poor decisions; I lied. They were both very successful and made millions. Like me, they preferred the simple life and didn't draw attention to their vast fortune. About a year before their fatal car accident, they told me they wanted to leave you and Beena the sum of £300,000 each. They knew your dad hadn't been successful and therefore wanted to provide for you. I convinced them not to do that. Dipen, we all know how bad you are with money. I agreed I would therefore give you both an allowance each month, and they thought it a great idea. That way you would hopefully have better control over your money. However, when they died, I decided not to give you any of the money because I knew you'd squander it. Beena is doing OK, so doesn't need it. So, when you came to me a few weeks ago asking for help with your debt of £200,000, I said I had nothing left from my inheritance. My parent's money will not pay your debts.'

'The money would have cleared what I owe and left me with £100,000 to start over again.' Dipen sounded emotional. 'I can't believe you'd do that to me. I'm your cousin. I am heartbroken, Ravi.'

'No wonder you started creeping around us five years ago. Rakesh hates you coming over so often. I assume you were sniffing out what money was around as your debts were escalating even back then.' Ravi glared intensely at Dipen. 'I have, stupidly, put you in my will, but I will not give you anything until the day I die.'

'You have a will?' Rakesh said in a deflated tone. 'You didn't tell me. Isn't that something we should have done together? Oh, wait, we couldn't, because you'd have had to tell me about your wealth. I assume your friend Bilam is the executor?'

The room was silent. The group was shocked that everyone's skeletons were being shared, and the new information they learned about each other also surprised them.

'You're rich?' mouthed Rakesh. 'I seriously can't believe it.'

'Disgustingly,' replied Ravi with a wide smile.

'I wish you were dead.' Rakesh snarled.

'Hear, hear,' whispered another voice in the room.

There was nervousness within the group, especially felt by Norton and Parveena.

'We are friends. What's said at this gathering stays within this gathering!' Norton pleaded. 'Things have been disclosed tonight which don't need repeating or reporting.' Norton looked at both Parveena and Ravi.

General murmurs of agreement were met around the table, apart from Ravi, who was seen leaving the room, holding his head in his hands, and heading upstairs to bed.

19

Parveena

14th October 2019

2:00 p.m.

Parveena sat in the trendy wine bar, nursing a glass of white wine. All around her were designer mirrors and up-styled lights using old pipes and enormous light bulbs with no shades. The artwork had a striking resemblance to pieces exhibited at the Tate Modern. Parveena hated it.

She began drinking wine instead of whisky since Ravi had reported her to the Royal College of Veterinary Surgeons on 2nd October. He called her just after he had done it. He had had a nasty argument with Norton the day before and felt guilty he had reported him to his governing body, but not her. Ravi had wanted to protect her, but Norton's anger forced him to realise he had no other option. It was obvious to both of them that their veterinary practice would inevitably collapse from that point onward. The business was suspended on 4th October, pending investigations.

In her head, she had tried to convince herself that wine was less destructive on her body and mind than whisky, hence making the change. She knew she was just kidding herself but needed something to *"take the edge"* off her day-to-day negative feelings about herself.

Sitting here waiting for Ravi to arrive, she had a hundred thoughts running around her head. At first, she thought meeting in a place where alcohol was served wasn't the smartest of venues, but she just thought *"To hell with it"* and agreed on a time and place. She wasn't sure there was much more they needed to talk about, but he had insisted.

'Like I should do what you want,' she hissed.

Bang on time, Ravi arrived. He came over and reluctantly asked if Parveena wanted another drink. She asked for tea to save her from being shamed, and he had the same.

'How are you doing?' Ravi asked but already knew the answer.

Parveena took her time to answer. She looked at him, and despite knowing this man for so many years, his attractiveness still blew her away. However, what he had done to her was hurting her deep inside. There was no forgiving or forgetting.

'Take a guess,' she eventually croaked.

'OK, stupid question. I'm sorry.'

'Sorry? For what? Reporting me? That action has caused the demise of the business we worked so hard for. We have spent a major part of our lives learning and setting up our practice.' She was so angry she was violently using her arms to help get her point across. Unfortunately, one of these gestures caused her to hit the server as he approached with their teas, and they went flying to the floor. Thankfully, there were no injuries. Apologies were made and fresh drinks were served.

'Parv, I'm sorry I didn't step in sooner. I could see your drinking was getting out of control, and I should've done more to help. Why didn't you come to me? Our friendship is long and I would have been there for you. If only you'd told me how bad it had got for you.'

'Really? I'm not so sure,' Parveena uttered.

The teas were delivered safely this time.

There were a vast amount of emotions being expressed at the table. However, Parveena's seething anger wasn't diminishing in the slightest.

'You've felt distant for the past few months,' she said. 'I didn't know how to reach out to you. I know you explained you and Rakesh had had your problems, but you weren't there for me. It reminded me of when we first started at university. The first day that we moved in, you were all over Agatha and Norton. You embraced these new friendships and forgot I even existed. I have never forgotten that.'

'That isn't true,' Ravi insisted.

'It is true. You have hurt me countless times throughout the years. Ravi, your actions carry significant weight and affect the people around you, despite your repeated insistence on being a "nice" person. Agatha is a complete mess and has been since you ended your relationship with her. You had no right telling us she had aborted your child. Did you see the impact it had on her? Her face told a terrifying picture. Have you checked up on her? I wouldn't be shocked if she tried to kill herself again.'

'Please, don't do this,' Ravi expressed. 'I'm not to blame for her issues.'

'You've ruined me and Norton. Your lies have devastated Rakesh, and we can only imagine what Dipen is experiencing. Do you see my point, Ravi? You're annihilating lives.'

The pressure of the meeting was proving too much for Parveena, and despite what Ravi might think, she ordered herself a large wine. As she did this, Ravi went to the toilets to take some codeine for a headache he could feel brewing. He didn't want to take the tablets in front of Parveena.

Once seated again, Ravi took a deep breath.

'Firstly, Dipen can't be trusted with money, therefore I hold no guilt for not bailing him out. How long do you think it would be before he was heavily in debt again? I will not subsidise his weakness. Rakesh just wants to live a luxurious life. If he knew I had that amount of money, I would have lost him forever. He would have been out constantly living a lavish life. The demands to move house, buy exclusive cars, designer clothes, exorbitant dinners, and expensive holidays, would have been too much for me. I want to live a quiet life. We already live in a lovely house and have nice cars. Why can't that be enough?' Ravi sighed. 'I know he cheats on me and has done for years, but I love him. If he had known I was rich it would have ultimately destroyed our relationship, even more so than it already is.' A single tear left Ravi's eye as he rubbed his head.

Parveena, who had been unmoved by what she had just heard, stared at him blankly. She waited for him to continue without speaking a word. She hoped he was feeling uncomfortable with the current situation and was suffering as badly as she was.

'Norton,' Ravi finally said, 'wrongly treated a young man. He was unprofessional and it nearly cost a life. He wasn't prepared to take responsibility, so I had to. I've also heard other rumours that he acts inappropriately. It sounds like he is abusing some of his patients. Parv, he had to be stopped.'

'And it was your job to do that?'

'I guess so. I don't know.'

'And what about me? We have been friends since we were kids. We used to run down the street after the ice cream van so we could either get a Fab ice lolly or a Zoom. Why was it never an ice cream?' She softly chuckled to herself. 'I loved the street games we played on the road with other children. Football or IT. You never did like playing football, did you?'

'Not really. A bit too butch for me.' They both laughed.

'Ravi, I so feel lost. I have no idea how I am going to recover from what you have done to me. My family has stopped talking to me. I have brought shame to our respected name and there is no going back from that. You know what they are like. I'm now seen as damaged goods! You have taken everything from me. I'm bereft and will never forgive you. Be scared, Ravi.'

'Parveena, you killed three animals. I honestly believe you were drunk when you operated on them. How am I meant to forget that and do nothing about it? I reported Norton, so I had to do the same with you. Don't you understand?'

'Kwasi has vouched for me. He told you there were complications during those surgeries. And he was there the whole time.'

'Kwasi? I don't trust him. There is something peculiar about the way he looks at me.'

'You're just being paranoid,' she said.

'Am I? I don't think that I am. Something just doesn't feel right. I need to investigate and try to put my finger on it. You're keeping things from me and I will get to the bottom of it.'

20

Kwasi

12th August 2019

(Five weeks before the Party)

11:00 a.m.

Mr Ripley's cat, Twix, was on the operating table. Surgery was necessary because of the internal bleeding from being hit by a car earlier in the day. Mr Ripley had been told not to worry, as it was a routine procedure and the practice would call him later and update him on Twix's progress.

Kwasi Moses was the veterinary nurse at the practice and had been working for Ravi and Parveena for about two years. He was originally from Uganda but came to the UK as a small child. He was bulky in build, always clean-shaven, had a kind but prematurely lined face, and liked to wear colourful shirts when off-duty. His eyes were a deep brown, and his flat nose had wide nostrils. His uniform was dark green and pristinely washed and ironed before each shift.

When Kwasi had gone into the reception area to collect Twix, he noticed Ravi was there talking with a little girl who was delighted to have her rabbit back following an overnight stay to have hydration and antibiotics. Ravi glanced over at the nurse. This made Kwasi feel uneasy, so he half-smiled and entered the operating room where he got ready to assist Parveena.

'I swear Ravi doesn't like me,' he said.

'You're overreacting,' Parveena replied.

'I'm not! He knows something is wrong. I just know he does.'

Parveena continued getting ready for the surgical procedure. There was a detailed checklist of things required to be in place before she could get started. Once everything had been ticked, she prepared the cat and got herself into her sterile scrubs. Kwasi assisted her with the gloves.

'Your hands are shaking,' he snapped. 'I'm not being part of this again.'

'Shut up and get on with what we are paying you for.'

'We've already lost two animals. I don't want it to be a third. I'm going to get Ravi.'

'STOP!' Parveena shouted. 'I am fine. Everything is great and I can complete this straightforward task. The last two were genuine errors and not my fault.'

'You'd been drinking.'

'I hadn't. Now let's just get on with the matters at hand.'

'Please, Parveena. I'm concerned about my registration. Let me get Ravi.'

Within a minute, the initial incision had been made into Twix. Kwasi now felt he had no alternative but to help. Parveena's hands were still shaking and sweat was pouring from him. His surgical mask was already damp and uncomfortable.

'Please, let this be OK,' he whispered to himself.

After what felt like a lifetime, the procedure appeared to be going well. Both of them had settled. Kwasi was now less concerned and Parveena's hands were steady. However, at that moment, the nurse noticed excess blood in the animal's cavity. He glared at the vet to see if she had noticed. She said nothing.

'She's bleeding,' he said.

'I can see that. Use the suction to clear the area, then I can see what is happening.'

Minutes later, the cat was dead. Parveena just stood there, still holding on to the pieces of equipment she had been using.

'Not again! My God! Please tell me you didn't do this for a third time. My registration will be taken from me. I have to earn money. My young daughter needs me to provide for her. I told you not to operate. Why didn't you listen to me?'

Parveena remained motionless. She could hear the nurse ranting but wasn't taking in everything he was saying until he said:

'I'm going to get Ravi.'

'STOP!' she yelled. 'Let me deal with this. It isn't your problem. Get out of your uniform and take yourself home.'

'No, I won't be treated like this. I have covered up two deaths because you threatened to report me. I can't risk losing my job. You're drunk! If I speak up now, maybe it won't be too bad.'

Parveena took her time to adjust her thoughts. She paced up and down.

'Will money help?'

Kwasi turned to look at her.

'What do you mean?'

'You require money for your daughter. I can give you extra each month. Ravi doesn't need to know. I will give it to you with my money and not through the company's books. We can say the internal bleeding was worse than I initially thought, and the cat just bled profusely, and I couldn't stop it.'

'How much?' Kwasi demanded in a rough tone.

'£200.'

'£300, each month.' Kwasi despised himself, but he was in dire need of money. 'I am still concerned. Ravi already mistrusts me. I know he does. I honestly like him. He is so nice and friendly and loves the animals that come to us. Please, God! How are we going to cover this up yet again?'

'Get yourself changed and leave Ravi to me. Go!' Parveena ordered.

Once the operating room had been cleaned and the relevant documentation had been doctored and finally completed, Parveena made her way to the main office. She was dreading what would come next. Ravi was at his desk.

Instead of proceeding with the necessary conversation, she hesitated. She began pacing, becoming a source of irritation to herself. Parveena made herself a cup of tea, which turned out to be lukewarm instead of hot.

'Would you like one?' she asked, pointing at the kettle.

'I'm fine, thanks,' he replied in a grumpy voice.

Parveena ambled over to the window and messed about with the shutters, trying to build up the courage to speak.

'So, I have some sad news,' she said. 'Mr Ripley's cat, Twix, died on the operating table. Kwasi and I did everything we could. The poor thing was hit by the car harder than we thought and she had a massive internal bleed. There was nothing to be done. I'll call him and break the news.'

Ravi stood and walked over to his partner.

'That's three animals, Parv.' He leant in towards her face. 'You're drunk, or at least you've been drinking.'

'Look, sometimes animals die,' she said, ignoring his comment. 'We can't save them all.'

'We equally don't have to kill them,' he snapped back. 'I can't turn a blind eye again. I have no choice but to report this.'

'Ravi, please don't. I'll make it up to you, I promise.'

'Too late, Parveena.'

'You'll regret it if you do,' she screamed at him.

'I'll call Mr Ripley. I don't want you going anywhere near that poor man.'

Ravi left to make the call from the reception. He didn't want to be near his partner.

'You're so full of yourself, Ravi Patel. Go on and report me. You'll be sorry. That I can promise you!' she said under her breath.

21

Norton

17th October 2019

3:00 p.m.

The noise from the traffic outside going about its usual business wasn't registering with the man, slumped in his leather, upright armchair. The chair opposite was empty, as it had been since his practice had been told to cease operating. Ravi, highlighting Norton's indiscretion to the governing body for psychologists had stopped Norton and his business in his tracks.

The question that haunted Norton was what Stuart Schumann had revealed about him to a stranger. Why had the young man got himself into such a state of mind that suicide was the only way out for him?

'Had I been that bad to him?' Norton questioned himself. 'He allowed those things to happen! I did nothing wrong.'

The office was ghostly as the late autumn coolness was circulating the room. As he pulled his cardigan tightly around his body, he got up to close the window. Outside, he watched the people going in and out of shops. Pedestrians were walking onto the road, oblivious to the slow-moving buses and cars. The decorative vase that had been unused on the cabinet near the window was angrily thrown to the ground and shattered into pieces. An exasperated cry followed this. Norton kicked the fragments of the vase on the floor and then violently upturned the armchair. The next to be thrown was the decanter of brandy that he often gave to the younger clients that he saw.

A sharp pain caught Norton's attention as he realised he had dug his nails into his palms, causing minor cuts that were now bleeding. This just added to his immense frustration at his current situation. A situation caused by Ravi Patel. Norton saw no concerns with his behaviour, or at least nothing he cared to reflect on. Ravi had gone a step too far and he would pay severely for his interference.

As the psychologist paced around his office, a noise from the reception area captured his attention. This startled him at first. Slowly, he opened the door and peeked into the other room. Standing there in a coat that was too thin for an autumn month was his secretary, Sorel. She was looking through the diaries on her desk. Norton opened the door forcefully and caused the young woman to scream.

'What the hell are you doing here?' he yelled.

'You scared the crap out of me.'

'Pathetic!' huffed Norton. 'I will repeat my question. What are you doing here?'

Sorel paused before responding. Surprised to encounter someone in the office, she found herself momentarily caught off guard.

'I just wanted to check the appointment book,' she said.

'Why?' he barked back.

'To ensure I had cancelled everyone.'

'How did you get in? The door was locked.'

'I have a set of keys, Dr Greene.'

Norton had forgotten he had given her a set about six months ago.

After a few moments, Norton walked back into his office, shouting.

'Do what you have to do and then get out. I see no point in you returning either. You're fired! Just go!'

Sorel, ignoring his words, followed him. She was visibly shocked when she saw the state of the office.

'What happened?'

This time it was Norton's turn to be startled.

'I said, go!'

Sorel, who had always been an inquisitive young woman, ignored her boss and took in the sight in front of her.

'You haven't told me why we aren't working. You just told me to cancel all future appointments and to leave. That was a couple of days ago, and I think I'm entitled to know why I don't appear to have a job anymore.'

'You,' hissed Norton. 'You're entitled to nothing. Now get the fuck out of my office, you stupid woman.'

'Is it because of what is being said about you all over social media?' Sorel said, acting like she hadn't heard his hurtful words.

There was a silence as Norton thought through what he had just been asked. His forehead tightened and he realised he was hurting his palm again.

'I don't use it. What is being said?'

Despite her embarrassment, Sorel took out her phone and shared some comments. '#nortongreeneavoid, #drnortongreenedisgrace. #drngreenepervert.'

Norton froze and looked confused.

'I don't understand. What does hashtag mean?'

'It helps what you want to put across to others, easier to find on platforms like Twitter and Instagram. Dr Greene, this is bad. You're hated. From what I can see, Stuart Schumann started them. He was followed by Daisy Christmas, who was engaging with others who have been through here, seeing you. They are all young patients. I recognise their names. Dr Greene, what have you done?'

'What are they saying?' Norton asked, trembling.

'Do you truly want me to read them out?'

'Just do it!' he yelled.

'OK, if you're sure. "*I was seeing Dr Norton Greene for a year. He was more interested in the sun shining on my blouse and my relationship with my brother. DM me for support.*" There are more.'

'DM?'

'Direct message.' Sorel said. 'Stuart Schumann next. "*I was a vulnerable young man who was seeing Norton Greene. Over time, he started to seduce me and offered me alcohol. It got so bad that I tried to end my life. I was lucky that a kind man came to my rescue.*" From what I can see, they have set up a support WhatsApp group. This is serious. They are coming after you.'

Norton said nothing but pushed a startled Sorel to the side, stormed out of the office and headed into the street. Just as the secretary tidied up, the reception desk phone rang. Sorel answered it.

'Dr Greene's practice. How can I help? Sorry, but we are currently closed because of an investigation. Can I ask your age, please? Twenty-three!' Sorel pulled a concerned expression. 'If I were you, I'd google social media and then decide if you want Dr Greene to help once he is working again.' She ended the call.

Norton darted through the streets to the nearest tube station, muttering to himself and getting strange looks from those he passed. His face was now puce and the veins on the side of his head were furiously pumping. Norton had one place to head towards and nothing was going to stop him.

Forty-five minutes later, Norton was hammering on a door and screaming. A nervous young man answered the door and immediately tried to close it again. Norton was quicker and pushed the door open wide.

'What the fuck did you tell Ravi Patel? I want answers!'

'I said nothing! Now go away.'

'Tell me what you said or I'll swear to God to get my revenge and make your life hell on earth. Now tell me!'

Stuart Schumann burst into tears. 'I just told the truth.'

'You consented, and you know you bloody did!'

22

Stuart

26th August 2019

(Three weeks before the Party)

11:45 p.m.

As Ravi walked through the streets following his evening with his friend, Bilam, he had a wide smile on his face. The evening had been just what he had needed. They had gone to their favourite restaurant, had too much food and a couple of mocktails. The two talked for hours, and she had shown interest in the things he had to say. Ravi, for a long time, had felt his other "friends" cared very little about him, especially Rakesh, and this was breaking his heart.

Across the street, sparsely clothed individuals were either on their way to a nightclub or going home. Not one of them was wearing a coat or even a jacket. Ravi could think of nothing worse than heading off to a club. They were too loud for him. On the rare occasions he had gone to one, he just wanted to talk and hear without straining.

The bright red night buses were going up and down the thoroughfare, and the city was lit up and looked stunning. It was nights like this that made him feel proud to be a Londoner. Ravi took out his phone and took a picture of The Shard, which was sparkling in the night sky. The top of it displayed a variety of colours. He was so pleased with the photo that he thought it was Instagram-worthy if he used the app.

Despite the hour, the air was still warm for the time of year and was wafting across his face. This was probably why no one was wearing coats. Ravi was wearing dark jeans, a black t-shirt, and a lightweight jacket. His smile was still present as he thought of Bilam. They had discussed work, relationships, and his pending trip to Paris. Ravi had spoken about his concerns with Parveena's presentation, but not about the matter with the animals. Bilam had also asked him about his new habit of rubbing the sides of his head. This meant a lot to him, as Rakesh and the others just got annoyed with him.

"*They are just stress-related headaches,*" he had said to her. *"My GP says they are nothing to worry about."*

Ravi had now reached London Bridge and began walking across it. In the distance, he thought he saw something of concern. The nearer he got; he realised it was a person standing on the metal frame of the bridge. His hand went to his mouth in shock and he yelled out, which made the person turn around. Ravi could see it was a young man, no older than in his early twenties.

'Don't jump,' Ravi heard himself shrieking.

'Get back! Don't come near me.'

'Please get down. You don't want to do this. I can help.'

'You can't,' the young man whispered. 'No one can.'

'I'm Ravi. What's your name?'

Moments seemed to pass without either of them speaking.

'Go on, jump,' said a voice.

Both Ravi and the man turned to see two girls holding up their phones and filming the scene playing out in front of them.

'Jump, you sad bastard. I'm putting this on YouTube. It'll go viral and I'll get millions of views and followers. Go on, JUMP!'

Ravi screamed at the two of them, but they just laughed and walked off.

A bus went along the road and Ravi could see a few gawping faces looking out.

'I'm Ravi,' he repeated with a tremble in his voice.

'Please, just leave me alone.'

'I don't want to do that. I want you to come down and talk to me. Will you do that?'

The young man turned and lost his footing and slipped. Ravi screamed and ran forward to grab the man's ankle.

'I'm Ravi.'

He vaguely recalled that when someone is contemplating jumping, you keep repeating your name to them. Or was that the name of the kidnapped person to the kidnapper to make them think of their victim as a loved person? Lots of thoughts were swirling around Ravi's head.

The young man had gently kicked Ravi away and looked down at the dark and merciless void.

'I'm Stuart,' he said with a frightened edge in his voice. 'Stuart Schumann.'

'That's a nice name, Stuart. Do you want me to help you down?'

The young man shook his head.

'I need to die.'

'Why do you?'

'Just because. I'm so messed up, and he is to blame.'

Ravi was feeling way out of his depth and looked around to see if there was anybody else who could come and help. A police constable would be incredibly handy right now. There were a couple of people going by, but they kept their heads down and hurried to where they wanted to be.

'The weather is getting cooler, Stuart,' Ravi lied. 'Are you feeling the cold? You haven't got a jacket on. Why don't you come down and let me buy you a hot drink? Are you hungry? Have you eaten? We could go for a coffee or a hot chocolate.'

Ravi could see that Stuart was contemplating the idea of food and drink.

'A hot chocolate would be good,' Stuart said in a childlike voice. 'I haven't eaten all day and I am feeling hungry.'

Ravi slowly approached the young man.

'Can I help you get down? We can grab a sandwich or something. You can choose whatever you want. It's my treat.'

Stuart looked at Ravi and smiled. He put his hand out and was then helped down. As his feet touched the ground, he grabbed and embraced Ravi and sobbed.

1:30 a.m.

The café was fairly busy for the time of night. It was full of a wide variety of people and had a lively feel about it. Ravi and Stuart sat in a quieter corner and had their refreshments.

'So, how long were you up there before I came along?'

'Not long.' Stuart sipped his hot drink.

'It was scary,' Ravi acknowledged, 'but it didn't genuinely take me that long to coax you down, did it? I don't think you wanted to kill yourself. I believe you're a vulnerable young man who has lost some direction in your life. Am I right?'

Stuart slowly nodded.

'You said "he" made you do it. Has someone been bad to you? You don't need to tell me, but I want to help.'

The young man finished his chicken sandwich and drained the last of the hot chocolate before speaking.

'For eighteen months, I have been seeing a psychologist. For as long as I can remember my head has been all over the place. I don't seem to fit in with anyone, so have very few friends. I guess I'm what they call "socially awkward" and it makes me sad. Not only that, but I struggle with the day-to-day running of my wellbeing. My parents are great, but they don't understand me. They either think I'm in a phase of something or just different from others. I'm OK with being different, but not with the constant sadness. I also think I might be gay. No, that's a stupid thing to say. I am gay.'

'It's not a stupid thing to say, Stuart. Coming to terms with our sexuality can be a hard aspect of our lives. I'm gay, and it's great, but it isn't a straightforward journey for some.'

The café remained busy with customers coming and going. Ravi ordered more hot drinks.

'I googled "psychologists" and reviewed who came up. My parents are wealthy, so they wanted me to have the best. I started seeing someone, and at first, it was going well. Opening up was much easier than I thought, and I could feel the darkness lifting from my thoughts. However, approximately six months later, he recommended hypnotherapy, and whilst I was eager to try something new, I had started feeling uneasy around him for no apparent reason, or so I thought. He used to place my seat at an odd angle, so the sun was right on my chest. He told me to only wear thin white shirts as a symbol of purity of body and mind. At first, I didn't think too much about this, but it's odd. Isn't it?'

Ravi nodded and wondered where this was going. The confusion which was evident on Stuart's face heightened his concern about the situations that he had been exposed to.

The fresh hot chocolates arrived and were gratefully received. Ravi waited for Stuart to continue, as he didn't want him to feel he was under any sort of pressure.

'The first couple of hypnotherapy sessions were OK, but I don't think they benefitted me. Then, during the third one, I thought I felt him touching me. It was just my arm at first, but then he felt me through my trousers. I was sure he did, but he denied it. By the fifth, it was obvious. I pretended I was still "under" but he was fully touching me. I felt embarrassed and wanted him to stop, but I also didn't want it to end. After that, the psychology part of the sessions ended and they were now just about sex. I was a virgin until him. I let him do things to me that I wasn't mentally ready for. It wasn't rape, or at least I don't think it was because, in a way, I consented. Not verbally, but I guess by letting him do those things to me. Every time I went home, I was ashamed of myself. He used toys on me. I hated myself. After about three months, my parents noticed a negative change in me. I was getting worse, so they stopped me going. They never asked why. My god! If only they had bothered to ask me why I was acting the way that I was. I know they care about me, but maybe just not enough.' Stuart sighed and had some of his drink. 'I fell into a deep depression and I thought that the only way to free myself of all the guilt and shame was to jump from a bridge. Thank you, Ravi. You saved me.'

'Did you involve the police?'

'No,' Stuart replied. 'I only had myself to blame.'

Ravi sat and looked at the man in front of him. He reached over to take hold of his hands but hovered near in case Stuart didn't want to be touched. He did and reached for Ravi.

'You're not to blame. That man was unprofessional and abusing his position of power. I am so sorry that he did those things to you, but I can help find you another psychologist. I have a friend who is one, so I am sure he could see you. What do you think?'

'I don't know. What happened to me was so awful and to be honest I can't bear the thought of it happening again.'

'I get that, but I can vouch for my friend, Dr Norton Greene.'

Stuart's eyes widened and he started to have difficulty breathing. Ravi became concerned.

'Get away from me,' Stuart yelled.

The customers in the café looked over and a few came over to their table.

'Stuart, what's wrong? What have I said?'

'That name. He's the person I was seeing. He's the one who did those things to me.'

Ravi sat there in shock and felt as if he was about to vomit. He didn't see Stuart run out of the café and into the street.

'My God!' Ravi said as he contemplated rushing after Stuart but thought that it might do more harm than good. Instead, he then took out his phone and made a call that went to voicemail. 'Norton, it's Ravi. I have just spoken with an incredibly fragile Stuart Schumann. If you can't give me a good account of what I have been told, then I'll have no option but to report you.'

23

Agatha

19th October 2019

9:00 p.m.

Screams echoed from every direction, some so chilling they could only be described as bloodcurdling. If you stood with your eyes closed, no one could blame you for thinking that your life was in danger. Then the sickly smell of deep-fried doughnuts, candy floss, and burgers alerted Agatha to the fact that she had arrived and was standing in the middle of a fairground.

There was a mix of petrol odours and booming music in the air, along with the infectious yet slightly annoying sound of children's laughter. Stallholders were yelling above the noise, encouraging people to "have a go and win a guaranteed prize." The food vans had long queues, but not as long as the beer tents that were scattered around the park. The Portaloos left a foul stench, and the heavy rain from the night before made walking slightly tricky.

Agatha was meeting her friend, Susie by the Ghost Train. This was a ride she certainly wouldn't be going on because of a nasty experience as a small child. The ride had broken down in the dark, just as a scary, shrieking clown had burst out of a wonky wardrobe covered in cobwebs and spiders. Initially, her father laughed, but she was later scolded for wetting herself and taken home in disgrace.

Just as Agatha was deliberating having a go on the "Hook-a-Duck," a hand tapped her shoulder, causing her to jump.

'Yo, babe,' Susie boomed.

Agatha's friend was of average height, slim and had bright ginger hair. Their mutual colouring was what brought the two of them together in the first place. She was always chipper and people enjoyed being around her.

'You're late,' was the reply.

'Sorry, I was with Freddie.'

'Oh, him,' Agatha said with little interest.

'I know you don't rate him, but he is good to me and the kids. It's not easy finding someone, especially on those shitty apps. He's the nicest bloke I've had as a boyfriend, so less of your attitude, Miss grumpy knickers.'

The two women erupted into laughter, embraced tightly, and then walked arm in arm to the nearest food truck for a burger with caramelised onions and brown sauce.

They walked around the fair soaking up the atmosphere. There was something quite special about these places. In some ways, there was a unique charm, but there could also be something of a spookiness.

'Wanna ride, ladies?' said a young man with greased-back hair, an arm full of tattoos and a cigarette hanging out the corner of his mouth. 'Only £3 each.'

'No ta,' Susie said. 'Bumper cars are more my thing. I can't stand Ferris Wheels; they scare the bejesus out of me.'

'Go on,' he persisted. 'That's what fairgrounds are all about. You know, taking yourself out of your comfort zone.'

'She said, NO!' snapped Agatha.

'Suit yourself,' the man said, watching them walk away.

There were vibrant, flashing lights all over the place. Some were white but mostly multicoloured. After going on a couple of rides and chancing their luck on a few gaming stalls, they headed off to a beer tent. Susie got the drinks and they sat at a white plastic table with two dodgy chairs, each with an annoying wobble. A few moments passed as they sat in silence, absorbing the excitement that could be heard from outside.

'You look miserable if you don't mind me saying.'

'Thanks for that,' said Agatha.

'Come on, out with it. What's happened?'

'It's nothing.'

'Ravi bloody Patel I expect!'

'I hate him!'

'Now we both know that isn't true. Don't we?' Susie said as she reached over and rubbed Agatha's arm.

With a shrug, Agatha shared the details of the party conversation with her friend and couldn't help getting upset.

After a few moments mulling things over, Susie spoke.

'So what! He didn't say anything you didn't already know. I agree he shouldn't have said it in front of the others, but they probably either knew or could have guessed. I genuinely don't know why you hang about with them. Whenever you all get together there is always drama and you come away feeling dreadful. Cut the ties and walk. You have to get over Ravi. You have wasted far too many years lusting after a gay man. Sorry, but you need some tough love.'

'That bastard has destroyed my life!'

'Has he? Really? Come on Agatha. I'm not taking his side, but he is a decent guy. In fact, he's lovely. Once he figured himself out, which probably wasn't easy for him, he has always been upfront with you. That man has been there when you've hurt yourself, or worse. You just need to reboot your friendship with him and realise that he is never going to be yours and move on with your life. Before it is too late.'

'You just don't understand what he has put me through.'

'Do you still have that box?' Susie asked.

'Box?'

'You know! The one you keep under your bed, which is full of memories of things you did together. Cinema tickets, restaurant receipts, pictures of him then and now. When you showed it to me, there was even a pair of his dinosaur pants.'

Agatha looked cross.

'I never showed you this stuff,' she said in a gruff voice.

'You did! You got drunk one evening and removed everything out of it.'

Susie looked around the tent and saw an opening in the bar queue. She jumped up and went to get more drinks. Agatha took out her phone and texted.

"I hate you. You have made my life a living nightmare. I should've kept our baby that you made me get rid of it. Our so-called friendship is over. I never want to see you again."

Susie sat back down and straight away saw the miserable expression on her friend's face, so tried to lift the atmosphere.

'Hey, it's your birthday soon. What shall we do for it?'

'I never asked to be born. Two people made that decision for me. I came into this world because of them, and yet I'm the one who has to endure this never-ending horrendous existence.'

Susie grabbed her drink and downed the whole thing in one.

'I hate birthdays,' Agatha continued. 'They aren't something to be celebrated, but a countdown to death. It can't come soon enough as far as I'm concerned.'

'Oh, my God! If you continue in this destructive mood,' said Susie, 'we may as well go home now. You seriously need to see either your GP or a counsellor. I'll come with you, but you need help.'

Agatha's head lolled forward as she reached out for her drink.

'You just don't understand, Susie.'

'What? Tell me! What don't I get?'

Agatha took a large mouthful of her drink, then wiped her lips with the back of her hand. The music from the fairground seemed to get louder. Agatha stood up sharply and swallowed the rest of her drink.

'I've been thinking about this for quite some time. For my life to have any chance of happiness, then Ravi Patel has to die!'

24

Agatha

July 2000

(19 years before the Party)

University

9:00 a.m.

The couple lay in bed with their duvet pulled up high. She had her eyes wide open, whereas his were tightly shut. Their breathing was also different from each other. Agatha's was slow and deep, and Ravi's was fast and shallow. They could both hear Norton in the adjoining room making sounds that neither one of them cared to know exactly what he was doing. Across the hall, Parveena was her usual quiet self.

Outside, a strong wind was blowing and howling noises did their best to drown out Norton.

'Why are you wearing them?' Agatha asked, knowing that although his eyes were closed, he was awake.

'What?'

'You know what! Your dinosaur pants.'

'Does it matter?' Ravi retorted.

Agatha stretched out her hand under the duvet and touched Ravi's thigh. He immediately twitched and moved himself a fraction away from her.

'You never used to wear them in bed. Has something changed between us?'

The wind sounded as if it was growing in ferocity and rain could be heard lashing against the window. Ravi flung back the covers and hurried out of the bedroom, heading into the bathroom that Norton or Parveena had just left. He sat on the toilet without putting the lid up, buried his head in his hands and gently sobbed as he rocked himself back and forth.

Half an hour later, Ravi was fully dressed and was putting on his winter coat.

'Where are you going?'

'Out.'

'I can see that,' Agatha snapped. 'The weather is awful. You'll get soaked.'

Ravi said nothing for a moment but continued preparing to leave.

'It's fine,' he eventually said. 'I like the rain.'

'Can I come with you? It won't take me long to get ready.'

'No! I'm sorry, Agatha. I need time to think and want to be by myself. I'll see you later.'

The door slammed shut, reducing the young woman to tears as she dashed back to their bedroom.

11:00 a.m.

The rain had settled and sunshine was breaking through the grey clouds. Ravi sat on a bench that he had attempted to dry with a few tissues from his pocket. He looked at his watch and a smile adorned his face. He looked left and right, and not seeing who he was expecting, took out his phone and played a game on one of his many apps.

'Hey, gorgeous,' came a voice from behind, accompanied by a kiss on Ravi's neck.

'Hey, back at you.' Ravi stood and hugged the man behind him. 'Chen, you also look pretty good.'

Chen was of Chinese descent and had thick black hair. His face was small, as was his pert nose, and his eyes were richly brown. He was roughly the same height as Ravi and had come dressed for late summer rather than mid-autumn. The two men kissed, then held hands and went in search of coffee.

'You think I can't see you?' Agatha said from behind a tree. 'No wonder you were wearing your pants in bed.'

The two men laughed as they walked to a coffee shop. Neither one had any idea that they were being followed. When they arrived at their destination, Chen went to the counter to order their hot drinks and Ravi took a table in the window. Across the street, Agatha paced around for a few minutes and then saw them holding hands and looking into each other's eyes as they waited for their drinks to arrive. As they moved their heads closer together and kissed, she turned and vomited into the gutter.

9:00 p.m.

Ravi walked up their garden path and noticed the house appeared to be in complete darkness. This pleased him. He was aware Parveena was out with her friends for a concert, and Norton had joined a dating agency so could be anywhere. However, he did speculate about where Agatha might be, but was content to have some alone time.

Sure enough, it was silent when he entered the house and no lights were on. He went through to the kitchen for a glass of water and then headed upstairs. Ideally, he wanted to be either asleep when Agatha came in, or at least be in a position to pretend that he was.

He opened the bedroom door and walked over to the wardrobe.

'Where have you been?'

'Fucking hell! Agatha, you scared the crap out of me.'

'Where have you been?' she repeated.

'Why are you in complete darkness?' Ravi asked as he switched on the main light, causing Agatha to squint.

'Answer my question, please,' she said in an acid tone.

'Why? What does it matter? I wanted a day to myself and that's what I had.'

Ravi went back out to the bathroom to brush his teeth and then crept back, hoping her questioning had stopped. He got into bed.

'Pants and a T-shirt tonight! What will it be tomorrow? Dressing gown and Wellington boots?'

'What are you going on about?' Ravi barked.

'So, what did you do with your "alone" day?'

'I just walked and had food. I saw a film and chilled. You?'

Agatha took a deep breath and could feel her heart racing.

'I went for a walk. I saw my boyfriend kiss a man in the park, and then I followed them as they had drinks and kissed in a café. Then I trailed them around for about two hours but left when they entered the Ackroyd Hotel.'

The silence that followed was unbearable for them both. Agatha was crying, but Ravi couldn't bring himself to touch her. He just looked at the wall opposite and had a million thoughts running through his head. Initially, he considered fabricating a lie to appease her but realised it was the wrong thing to do.

'I'm sorry.'

She didn't respond.

'Sorry,' he said again. 'Agatha, I should have told you I'm gay. I've been working on figuring things out for a long time and I was about to tell you soon. I met Chen…' Agatha grimaced at his name. 'I've been seeing someone else for a couple of months, so I know I've deceived you and you must hate me right now.'

No one spoke for ages. Ravi wanted to give Agatha time to compose herself and also get himself ready to answer the many questions he thought would be coming his way.

'I'm pregnant.'

This wasn't what he was expecting.

'You can't be,' he said in a state of shock. 'We've been together six months and only had sex twice, which we should both have used as a sign that things weren't as they should be. I've seen you hanging about with that lad you play rugby with.' Ravi regretted saying this as soon as the words left his mouth. Agatha turned and slapped him so hard across his face that it stung.

'Shit! That hurt.'

'GOOD!' she screamed.

Ravi jumped out of bed, stormed downstairs, and marched up and down the lounge. There were too many things rattling around in his head that he couldn't concentrate on any one thing. Agatha barged into the room.

'I've booked a termination for tomorrow morning.'

'You don't need to do that,' Ravi said. 'We can figure something out. I'll stand by you and help you; I promise.'

'Ravi, you're gay, and you have a…' She couldn't bring herself to say the word boyfriend. 'I don't want it, but you are coming with me tomorrow to get it done.'

'I don't want you to get rid of it. I'll think of something. Don't rush into this decision.'

Another silence fell on the couple. Ravi finally sat down but couldn't settle. His legs were shaking and his heart was racing.

'Are you sure that you're pregnant?'

Agatha pulled out the pregnancy test from her dressing gown. As she did, the sleeve rolled back slightly and Ravi noticed some marks on her arm. He grabbed her and looked shocked.

'What are these? What have you done to yourself?'

'I couldn't help myself. I wanted to feel pain.' She collapsed on the floor and was sobbing hysterically. 'I want to die! I'm going to kill myself.'

Ravi was at a complete loss as to what to do. He crouched down and patted her shoulder. Even now, he couldn't bring himself to show any more compassion than that.

'I will have the termination tomorrow and you won't be able to prevent it, but you will accompany me,' she hissed. 'Parveena and Norton must NEVER know about this. When we get back tomorrow, you can tell them whatever the fuck you want about you, but if you ever tell them about the baby, I will kill you!'

25

Dipen

21st October 2019

10:00 p.m.

It had been just over two weeks since his encounter with the woman he only knew as "Donna" and she frightened Dipen. If he didn't settle his £200,000 debt, she warned him he would need to take on some dubious tasks on her behalf. Even though it wasn't discussed during the initial car meeting, he believed that what he owed was gaining a huge amount of interest.

Dipen had always been a kind person. Some would call him a scallywag, rascal or rogue, which all meant the same, but much depended on who said which word and the tone in which it was uttered, to denote the seriousness of it. Despite his prankster tendencies, most people still liked him. The thought of being forced into carrying out questionable jobs petrified him. He wasn't the sort of man to do these types of things.

Getting into debt had been such a simple thing to do. Credit card companies just kept increasing his limit. Store cards had high APR percentages and betting shops were his nemesis. Dipen had never meant to let things get so out of hand, but before he knew it, £20,000 of debt had turned into £50,000, then £100,000, and before he knew it, he owed £200,000.

The frightened man had contemplated moving to another country, changing his identity and going underground. He had even thought about suicide, but none of these felt doable. He now had just under two weeks to find what he owed, plus the undoubtable interest or his life would go in a direction he was terrified of. Tears fell from his eyes as he reflected on his cousin's decisions.

'Ravi, I can't believe you have done this to family,' Dipen croaked. 'If you had only done what your parents had wanted I would be clear of debt and not scared for my life!'

The smell of chips emanating from the fish shop he was approaching was too much to resist. Dipen reached into his pocket and could feel a handful of coins that he hoped would be enough to buy some food. He hadn't eaten today as he had skipped breakfast and lunch because of the constant nausea caused by his current situation.

'Bag of your finest potato offerings, please,' he joked with the guy behind the counter.

'What?' the lad said back.

'Bag of chips, please,' Dipen said.

'Anything on them?'

'Lots of salt and vinegar.'

Walking along the street with the hot bag in his hands felt good. The aroma wafting up was intoxicating. A hand slapped him on the back as he placed a thick chip into his mouth. Dipen screamed and his food flew into the air and landed on the pavement and also in the filthy gutter.

'What the…!'

'Good evening, Mr Patel,' a menacing voice boomed from behind.

'You've made me drop my food. I haven't eaten all day, and I'm starv…'

Before he knew what was happening, Dipen had been kicked hard in the back of his knee and crumpled onto the pavement. The person behind him then pushed his face into the chips on the pavement.

'I'm not stopping you from eating. Eat as much as you want.'

Dipen was fighting hard to get his head up, but some food entered his mouth. He began choking and then vomited into his mouth and eventually had to swallow it.

A moment later, the frightened young man was sitting on the damp pavement. His nose felt incredibly sore. A quick check with his finger revealed blood. He knew it had scraped on the road so guessed it was badly grazed. His whole body was shaking. People were walking by, but each one put their heads down and hurriedly moved along the street, ensuring there was neither eye contact with the man sitting, nor with the large, foreboding hulk of a man still looming over him.

'I've still got two weeks to pay the money,' Dipen croaked. 'Please don't hurt me anymore.'

'Correction. You have just under two weeks.'

The man slapped Dipen hard across his head and then disappeared into the darkness of a nearby alleyway.

A few minutes went by, or it could have been hours. Dipen hugged his knees and gently rocked himself back and forth. The rain had been drizzling and made him damp.

'Hey, are you OK?'

Dipen jumped out of his skin, stood up too quickly and fell to the ground again. A kind-looking man was standing over him, holding out his hand. Dipen allowed this stranger to help him up.

'Thank you,' he said. 'Sorry, that must have looked very odd to you.'

'It's not my place to judge. I just saw you sitting there getting more and more wet. You looked like you were a million miles away. I wanted to ensure you were OK and not just walk by and say nothing.' The man had a warm smile.

'If only more people did that, the world would be much nicer,' replied Dipen.

'Can I help in any way?' the man asked.

'No, but thank you. I was thinking to myself and forgot where I was. It's been a tough few weeks, but I'll get through it. I am very appreciative of you stopping to check, though. Have a nice night.'

The man smiled and walked off.

Dipen, still feeling shaky and scared, headed off toward his home. As he walked, he glimpsed his reflection in a shop window; he shuddered. The graze on his nose looked worse than he thought and he knew instinctively that it would leave a nasty scar. His face was gaunt and his hair was in a mess. The awareness of his plight grew unbearable, and he collapsed against the window. Initially, his sobs were quiet, but as his shoulders started to shake, they grew louder.

'You could have saved me, Ravi,' he wailed as his sobs intensified and he once again fell to the ground.

26

Dipen

13th August 2019

(Five weeks before the Party)

7:00 a.m.

The stiff fire exit doors burst open and Dipen stepped out into the quiet alleyway. He took in a deep breath and felt instantly ill. There was an overwhelming, obnoxious smell of bins that turned his stomach. Two rats were making themselves at home, scampering through the rubbish strewn over the floor. A couple of crows were also seizing the opportunity to scavenge.

Dipen had entered the nightclub around 1 a.m. knowing that he would be spending the entire night there. The place was called *"Depravity"* and lived up to its name. When he first arrived, he kept to himself by ordering a drink, and then he stood in a corner watching a couple of partying girls. The younger of the two, with long black hair, exaggerated eyelashes, too much make-up and a tight glittery top that was revealing a satisfactory amount of cleavage, caught his eye.

As much as he wanted to go over and engage in conversation, he needed them to replenish their drinks first so that he didn't end up paying out. Unfortunately, they didn't go to the bar, so Dipen gave up waiting and went over to introduce himself.

'Good evening, ladies.'

Both turned and the younger one liked what she saw.

'Hello,' she said.

'I'm Dipen.'

'Rose,' she smiled. 'Imogen,' she then said, indicating her bored-looking friend, who was already looking around the club for something more interesting than what was occurring in front of her.

The two chatted as the friend walked off in a sulk. The dance music was deafening, so they had to lean into each other. Dipen liked Rose's perfume and told her so. With Imogen gone, they got more drinks and their conversation flowed, despite the need to shout and lip-read.

'Am I going to get your number before I leave tonight?' Dipen cheekily asked.

'Depends if you carry on buying me drinks,' laughed Rose.

The time was going well. After another round of drinks and a couple of dances under their belt, Dipen asked for a kiss. Rose was happy to oblige. Then, before he knew what was happening, the friend was back and pulling Rose towards her.

'The Uber will be here soon. Come on!'

'Go without me,' Rose screamed above the noise.

'We don't do that. We arrive and leave together.'

'I can take you home,' Dipen volunteered.

'No,' Imogen snapped.

With only moments left, Dipen asked for Rose's number. She took his phone and entered her details.

'You sure you're giving me the right one? Twice I have been stitched up. Once, she entered only ten digits, leaving me unable to determine which number was missing or its correct position. The other time, when I called her number the next day, I got a builders firm that had never heard of someone called Shivani.'

'It's my number, I promise.' Rose kissed him and then followed her friend.

Dipen had planned to meet with Ravi to discuss his precarious financial situation, but that was hours away. He was too nervous to sleep, so going home wasn't a choice, but it was still only 4 a.m.

Then, by chance, he spotted an acquaintance of his from school. He knew he wasn't the most trustworthy of characters, but he kind of liked him.

'Craig,' Dipen shouted.

The pair shook hands and before Dipen knew what was happening; he was being taken to a back room where a poker game was about to start.

'Oh, no,' he protested. 'I can't get involved in a game. My cousin is meeting me later to discuss money. I can't afford to take part.'

Seconds later, Dipen's coat was on the back of the chair and he was sitting with cards in his hand. The bids were taking place with the stakes were being added to the pot and the adrenaline was pumping around his body.

The game continued until just before 7 a.m. with victories and defeats marking the night and money changing hands through bank transfers facilitated by apps. Dipen was up £10,000 when he declared he was walking away on top.

'You need to play fair,' a gruff woman demanded. 'We have a right to try to win our money back.'

'I have the right to leave,' he protested. 'But I'm a nice guy, so one last game?' The players all nodded.

As Dipen stood in the alleyway, his £10,000 was now in someone else's bank account. His bluffing, which had been working for most of the games, failed him in the end. He felt sick to the pit of his stomach.

It was still too early to meet with Ravi, so he took himself to Tooting for what he considered the best Indian breakfast. He jumped onto a bus and headed off to "Darchini's" where he ate a dosa, mooli paratha, upma and had a masala chai to drink.

Dipen had just about the correct change to pay for his food. Mr Dimakos had made him take more money to help him along until he could sort out his situation. The last thing he wanted to do was take it, as he knew the interest would be astronomical, but he had no choice. He needed money. Mr Dimakos, his loan shark, was playing on his vulnerabilities and Dipen was afraid. He also knew what would eventually happen. Another shark would purchase his debt, and the more you progressed through the chain, the more ruthless they became. This terrified him.

'I need your help, Ravi,' he said to himself. 'Please don't let me down. I promise I'll pay it all back eventually.'

11:00 a.m.

Dipen paced outside the veterinary surgery for longer than he meant to. The panic was building up inside, and his head was near exploding point. He needed to get inside and say what he needed to, but courage was required and that was severely lacking at this precise moment.

Through the window he could just make out someone sitting at a desk who he assumed was Ravi. His arms were flying all over the place so he guessed that something had angered him. This wasn't a good sign.

Dipen pushed open the main door and crept in. Loud voices were emanating from the office. Luckily, the waiting room, which doubled up as the reception was empty.

'What did you do?' Ravi cried out.

'Nothing,' said Parveena. 'It was a complication during the procedure. There wasn't anything I could do. I told you all this yesterday when Twix died.'

The two vets stormed off in different directions, and neither of them noticed the scared man by the door. Dipen, unsure what to do, sat quietly and waited. Coming from the door marked *"operating room,"* he could hear raised voices. The male's wasn't Ravi's but one he didn't recognise. Its owner was soon revealed when the door flung open.

'I'll have to leave,' Kwasi shouted. 'If you and Ravi can't sort this out, then what hope is there for me?'

'Don't leave,' Dipen heard Parveena shout from inside the room.

'It's no good. I have to move on, but don't stop those extra payments.'

The nurse left the building and Parveena slammed her door shut. Dipen sat for a few more minutes when Ravi entered the reception and saw his cousin.

'Does this have to be now?'

'Ravi, please. I need to speak to you. Something has happened here, I can see that, but I must speak with you today. Please, I won't take too much of your time.'

The disgruntled vet walked into his office and beckoned Dipen to follow.

The establishment was immaculately clean and there was only a slight whiff of surgical solutions. Dipen wondered why no animals and their owners were waiting to be seen. He entered the office and immediately witnessed how Ravi and Parveena worked. Her desk was in a chaotic state. There were papers and journals scattered and a heavily stained coffee mug. She had a picture of her parents and her computer needed a thorough good clean. Ravi's was the complete opposite. The professional journals were stored away, leaving only the current issue on display. The picture of Rakesh was in a stylish frame and his computer was almost sparkling. Dipen smiled at the contrasting desks.

Ravi motioned for his cousin to sit down.

'Does this have to be now?' he said.

'You've just said that,' Dipen said.

'Coffee?'

'No, it's a boring drink,' Dipen replied. The shake in his voice was obvious to them both.

'Well? What do you want? I'm dreadfully busy.'

Dipen thought of the empty waiting room but ignored the comment.

'I've been stupid,' he said. 'I may need some help, cuz.'

Ravi, who was still thinking of the mess that Parveena had created, looked perplexed.

'What?'

'Money, mate. I have to ask you to lend me some.'

'How much do you want? I've got £100 in my wallet. Will that do?'

Dipen inwardly laughed. He didn't want to aggravate his cousin.

'This is exceptionally hard for me, Ravi.' He placed his head into his hands and began crying.

Ravi sat and watched the performance playing out in front of him. Dipen stood and began pacing.

'I need money, and plenty of it. I'm an idiot. It has been getting worse, but started with my first credit card. Ravi, I'm sick.'

'Sick? Are you dying? Do you need money for treatment?'

'No, nothing like that. Gambling. I play poker tables; sometimes win, but mostly lose. I've been betting large amounts on horses, and I have countless credit cards, store cards, bank loans and advances with so many companies, most being illegal. Ravi, I am in so much trouble, and I'm deeply ashamed of myself.'

'Why? Are you dying? Do you need money for treatment?'

'No,' Dipen repeated with frustration. 'You have just asked me that.'

'Oh, did I? Sorry.' Ravi said, confused.

'Please, listen. I am terrified of what could happen to me.'

Ravi got up and went over to his cousin and embraced him in a warm hug. He held his face in his hands and kissed him on the tip of his nose.

'How much do you owe?'

'£200,000.'

Ravi sat back down in utter disbelief, and it took him a while to speak.

'Oh, Dipen. You silly, silly man.'

'It's going to get worse, Ravi. And I mean dangerously bad. My debt will soon get moved on to another loan shark. It is how these things work. If I can't pay them back, they will make me do terrible things; or kill me!'

Ravi, standing again, joined his cousin in pacing the room. He brushed his hand through his thick hair and then fingered his beard.

'Why do you think I can help you with that amount of money?'

'Your inheritance?'

'You sound like Rakesh! There wasn't much of one, I promise. Once all the debts, funeral expenses, and miscellaneous costs were settled, hardly any money was left.'

'But my dad said his brother was a wealthy man.' Dipen sounded desperate.

'If only that were true. My parents were awful in business. At the time of their accident and subsequent deaths, they owed so much money. Thankfully, their mortgage had been paid off, so once I sold their home, the money was used to pay things off. I'm so sorry, Dipen.' Ravi hugged his cousin and felt his whole body shaking.

They stood like that for a few moments and then Dipen pulled away. He wiped his eyes and sniffed loudly. The room was a blur, and it took him a short time to centre himself again.

'I'm truly sorry, Dipen.'

'Ah, that's OK, cuz. I was wrong to have asked. You shouldn't have to save me from my situation. I'm alright. It'll all be OK. Don't worry about me.'

Ravi watched as Dipen left with drooping shoulders. He then went to find Parveena.

Outside, Dipen took out his phone to call Rose from the nightclub and truly hoped she had given him her correct number as he needed cheering up. The number connected.

'Hello. Pegasus decorating services.'

Dipen ended the call and headed off to the betting shop.

27

Rakesh

22nd October 2019

10:00 a.m.

The sky was as dark as midnight and rumbles of thunder could be heard in the distance. With the next flash of lightning, Rakesh began counting. He got to eight. As a child, he had been told that this meant the thunder was eight miles away. He chuckled as he flicked up the collar on his coat, hurried along the street and headed for the river.

The night before he had stayed at a high-end opulent hotel at the courtesy of Ivan. The executive had been called away to Luxembourg at the last minute but allowed Rakesh to stay and enjoy the splendour of the establishment.

The sudden crack of noise above his head caused him to jump.

'So, not eight miles away,' he said with a slight laugh.

The rain started to pour, and within moments it was causing havoc. Bodies were running for cover and getting in each other's way. Rakesh opted to embrace the weather and carry on with his walk.

As he reached the river there was now just a slight drizzle. The heavy rain came and went leaving behind an enhanced smell of nature and it was an enjoyable walk. In the distance, Rakesh could see the Riverside Café and contemplated nipping in for a snack. However, his full belly following his sumptuous breakfast caused him to change his mind and get home before another shower started.

When he turned onto his road, his heart sank. On their driveway was his husband's car. Rakesh had hoped to have the place to himself for a few hours giving him time to prepare something to say about his night away. Ravi probably wouldn't believe anything he had to say as the hotel stays had become increasingly frequent. Rakesh felt nervous. Something was telling him that the next half an hour wouldn't be very pleasant and it started causing him some anxiety.

Tentatively, he put his key into the lock and slowly turned it. He tried to make as little noise as possible. With a slight nudge, the door silently opened and Rakesh stepped in. There wasn't a sound so his anxiety level diminished slightly.

He cautiously entered each room on the ground floor. They were all gleaming. There wasn't a speck of dust to be seen and the glassware was sparkling.

'Ravi?' he called gently.

No answer came back.

'Ravi?' he tried again with more volume.

With no answer, he climbed the stairs. He could feel his heart pumping in his chest and he was also experiencing some shortness of breath because of the anxiety which had escalated.

'Ravi? Sweetheart?'

Rakesh entered their modest bedroom. Like downstairs, it was immaculate, as were all the other rooms on this level. Assuming his husband wasn't at home despite the car out front, he returned to their bedroom to get changed. In the corner was a suitcase he had missed on his first room inspection. It was Ravi's. Rakesh had a sudden sensation of guilt. He lifted the case and it was heavy.

Wanting to steady his nerves, he headed to the kitchen where there was a bottle of brandy. Although it was early, he knew he needed a drink. When he opened the cupboard, he heard a noise behind him. He turned, but nothing was there. Then he heard it again, but this time it was someone whimpering.

'Ravi?' he called out.

No reply came, but the noise emanated from their utility room, which he hadn't checked earlier. He opened the door, and sitting on the floor propped up against the wall in just his underwear was Ravi. The rubber gloves he had used to clean the entire house were lying beside him. He had his knees up to his chest and was holding his head and crying as he slowly rocked back and forth.

Rakesh just stood and looked at the pitiful sight in front of him. He knew he had caused this and his heart was breaking. He crouched down and touched his husband's shoulder. Ravi shrugged it away and carried on crying. Undeterred, Rakesh tried to hug Ravi. This time the distressed man fell against the open arms and his crying became jerky sobs. They stayed like this for what felt like an eternity. Plagued with shame, Rakesh couldn't bring himself to look at his husband. He just held him tight and allowed him to cry.

Finally, as Ravi's sobs abated, Rakesh released his grip and helped the man to his feet.

'Why were you cleaning the house wearing just your pants?'

'Didn't feel right doing housework in the nude.' They both smiled. 'Why aren't you at work?'

'Why aren't you?' Rakesh snapped and instantly regretted doing so.

'Do I look in a fit state to be operating on animals?'

'No, I guess not. I've taken a sick day.'

The two men stood and gazed at each other.

'Where were you last night?' asked Ravi.

Rakesh took a breath and saw the sadness on the face of the broken man before him.

'You've done this to him,' he said in his head.

Ravi looked pleadingly for an answer.

'I was in a hotel.'

Tears appeared again in the corner of Ravi's eyes. He was now the one taking in a deep breath. Fearful of what he was about to hear.

'Why?' he asked.

'I like hotels. Things haven't been great between us, so I like to treat myself. It makes me feel better about things.'

'And why do you think we haven't been getting on? I'm not the one that stays away.'

'Come on, Ravi. Let's not do this. You know I love you.'

'Do you? Do you honestly still love me?'

'Of course.'

Rakesh moved to embrace Ravi, only to be stopped by a firm hand against his chest. The atmosphere was growing darker between the two men. A weird expression appeared on Ravi's face, giving off a "Jekyll and Hyde" vibe. Rakesh became concerned. Despite his typically calm nature, Ravi's face took on an almost demonic appearance.

'We have been drifting apart like two unanchored boats on the sea. I have been trying to ignore things that I know about you; just to be able to hold on to you, Rakesh. You see, the love in this relationship is going in one direction only, from me to you. Nothing is coming back except empty words. I've asked you time and time again if anything is wrong, and you always say that there isn't.' Ravi, suddenly aware of his near-nakedness, grabbed a T-shirt from the washing basket in the utility room. 'Is there someone else that I should know about?'

'No! Of course not. I love you.'

Ravi sighed and tried to hold back the tears that were fighting to get out. Nevertheless, he wanted to remain focused for as long as he could.

'Who's Edvin?' he demanded.

'I don't know anyone called that,' lied Rakesh.

'Who's Ivan?'

Rakesh, knowing that further lying wasn't going to be productive, burst into tears. A sense of accomplishment appeared on Ravi's face as he watched his husband dissolve in front of him.

'Did Dipen tell you?' Rakesh said.

'He may have mentioned your numerous indiscretions. He is family and I trust what he tells me. Dipen would never hurt me. However, I've followed you. The hotels you have been staying at are well beyond your price bracket. The drinks alone cost more than you earn in a day.' Ravi was almost enjoying himself. 'I was there when you met these two men and I watched you go into a lift and head for your room.' Ravi started to rub his head.

'Why haven't you said anything before?' Rakesh shamefully asked. 'Why did you just ask why I stayed in hotels if you already knew?'

'I was curious to see if you would eventually confess, and I would then embrace the moment you grovelingly start begging for my forgiveness. I would also sleep in your lavish hotels overnight and follow you the next day. As you now know, money is not an issue for me. I can happily spend as much as I want.'

'But you DON'T,' yelled Rakesh. 'You have so much money and yet we do nothing. I want the life I have with Ivan. You utterly bore me!'

With these words resonating with Ravi, Rakesh started pacing back and forth. He then ran to the front door and out into the street. Ravi followed, forgetting he had no trousers on.

'I HATE YOU!' screamed Rakesh. 'You only want to live a quiet, humble life. I want riches, expensive holidays and everything the husband of a millionaire should have. I'm being held back by you! We could be living a life of luxury! You were so lucky to have parents who loved and accepted you for who you are. My parents were different. They despised me for being gay.'

'It isn't your money. It's MINE!' Ravi shouted back as he went back towards the front door. 'Do you think I'd give you anything now? If you do, then you are very much mistaken. You may hate me, but I LOATHE you. You're a SLUT!'

Before he knew what was happening, Rakesh slapped Ravi so hard across the face that he fell and hit his head hard on the door frame. Rakesh stepped over the crying man, who was holding his head, and walked back into the house.

Slowly, Ravi got up and looked up and down the street for any sign that they had been seen.

'I can't believe we just did that. I'm disgusted with us. Screaming at each other on our own doorstep. We were like fishwives.' Ravi said. 'Why on earth did you have to run out into the street?'

'I don't know. I felt caged in and needed some space.' Rakesh hissed as he ran upstairs.

'I hope no one witnessed that fight. I'm so ashamed.'

'Oh, shut the fuck up, Ravi.' The angry voice shouted from the bedroom. 'No one gives a shit about what goes on in this house.'

Ravi thundered up the stairs and stormed into their bedroom. He grabbed the suitcase he had already packed and went to leave. Rakesh grabbed his arm.

'What are you doing?'

'I'm leaving you, Rakesh. You have broken me, and I can't be where I'm unloved. I want a divorce. Now, please get out of my way.'

Rakesh refused to let go of his husband.

'Ravi, I love you. Please don't go.'

'How can you look me in the eye and lie?'

'I'm not lying. I have been so stupid and can see that now. Please let me make it up to you. PLEASE!'

'You're just worried that you won't get any of my money, which will enable you to lead the life you are so desperate to have. I'd rather give it all to charity than see you benefit from a single penny,' Ravi growled. 'Why are you so obsessed with money? What happened in your childhood that has made you this way? You have never told me.'

'Where will you go?' Rakesh said, ignoring the questions his husband asked.

'A posh hotel. You know the type. Expensive drinks, spas and rich men getting their kicks from pathetic male prostitutes.'

'I don't want you to go. Hating me right now is the right thing, but please forgive me. I can't imagine my life without you.'

'I always assumed that we would grow old together and see out our lives side by side. Loving each other until the day we died,' Ravi croaked.

'I want that too. I honestly do.'

'I believe you no longer have feelings for me, despite what you may think, and it's been that way for a while.'

Ravi's gaze at his husband revealed that despite everything, he still loved him. He wanted to embrace him, and for them to tell each other that everything would be OK. That the bad times could be forgotten.

'Please, please, don't leave me,' Rakesh begged.

'I need some space,' Ravi said. 'I want to process what I have to do next. It's not just you, Rakesh. Dipen's debt is causing me sleepless nights, as are the issues with Parveena and Norton. They all hate me, and I'm sure that they wish I was dead.'

'Don't say that,' snapped Rakesh.

'It's true. And Agatha, I believe, has gone mad. She truly petrifies me.'

'Please don't go,' pleaded Rakesh.

'I need time.'

'Will you still come to the concert on the 27th? I want you there.'

'I'll think about it.'

'Please,' Rakesh softly mouthed.

Ravi then pushed his husband out of the way and as he walked down the stairs he could hear him crying in the bedroom. It took everything he had not to run back and comfort him. Upstairs, Rakesh was standing by the window with a smile etched on his face. He watched as Ravi climbed into his car without his trousers on and drove off down the street.

28

Rakesh aged 18

November 1999

5:00 p.m.

There were rows and rows of people with exaggerated headphones fixed on their heads, and mouthpieces that curved around to just the right position. Computer screens dominated the room and voices echoed throughout the building. The tap-tap-tapping of keyboards was as annoying as the mixed tones all trying to confirm if the person they had called had been in an accident in the past five years.

Rakesh had only been working in the call centre for six months, but the monotony of the place was driving him mad. Its only saving grace was that it got him out of the house and away from his parents. His boss, a woman slightly older than him and quite arrogant, ensured they met the daily call targets. Failing to do so would lead to reporting to higher-up, which would have negative effects on their pay.

With his shift ending, Rakesh was keen to see if anyone would go out with him for a few drinks. Anything was better than going home. His parents disapproved of alcohol, and Rakesh had been at the other end of his father's fist on more than one occasion when he had smelt it on his son's breath. This had made Rakesh crave it even more. No one was going to dictate how he would live his life. Not his parents, religion or society. Money was his driving force, and he knew that being stuck in this dead-end job wouldn't make him the millionaire he desired.

'Who is up for a drink?' he asked loudly.

'Shush,' a few people said, who were still taking calls.

'Can't, I'm brassic, mate,' said the guy in the next booth.

'Anyone?' pleaded Rakesh.

With no response and feeling deflated, he switched off his computer and put on his coat, which he had owned since he was at school, and it was looking tatty. He wrapped his arms around the holes hoping no one could see them.

'Bye,' he called out.

A few arms waved, but on the whole, he was unseen by most.

The slow walk home gave him time to think and plan his future. His home environment was depressing and he needed to get out as soon as he could afford to. Unfortunately, this would probably be years and this thought lowered his mood. Rakesh was an only child and frequently told that he was an enormous disappointment. Complications during his birth had prevented his parents from having more children. Rakesh was blamed for this, as well as many other things out of his control.

As he arrived at his front door, he put in his key as quietly as possible. He aimed to get up to his bedroom, unheard, before the usual questions, put-downs, and demands could be heard coming from the lounge.

"Rakesh, you're late. You need to get dinner ready."

"You are such a disappointment to this family."

"When are you getting a wife?"

"You need to help your father have his shower."

"You need to be more like my friend's sons."

The worst of these tasks was washing his overweight dad. The man barely moved and spent most of the time sitting in his chair demanding food and attention. He had type two diabetes, which was poorly controlled, and there were three ulcers on his legs. A district nurse dressed the largest one every other day, and the smell that came through the bandage turned Rakesh's stomach. The day the inevitable amputation happened would be the day that Rakesh left the house forever. Seeing his father naked once a week was awful enough, but with only one leg was something he wouldn't do. However, he prayed that he would be long gone by the time that happened. Although knowing how awful his father's health was, that day was possibly fast approaching.

Without his parents noticing, Rakesh skilfully made his way up to his room and now sat on his bed, admiring the posters of Britney Spears, Madonna, and Backstreet Boys hanging on his wall. Underneath his mattress, he had safely stowed away the adult magazines given to him by a colleague. Rakesh knew his parents would vehemently disapprove of Vulcan, Colt, BoyZ and Playgirl.

8:00 p.m.

Rakesh slowly made his way down the stairs because he felt hungry. The thought of eating anything from their disgusting kitchen turned his stomach, but he usually found something he could eat. As he reached the bottom, the final step creaked.

'Is that you, Rakesh?' his father called out.

'Heat some food. We have been waiting for you. Why are you so late home?' shouted his mother.

Every time Rakesh opened the lounge door, he felt repulsed, just like he had done thousands of times before. He had seen rooms like this on the television when programmes set in the 1970s were being shown. The wallpaper was peeling off the walls in a few places around the room, and it was tired-looking and covered in geometrical shapes. They had been bright orange and lime green when first put up, but now were faded and to Rakesh, it looked like someone had vomited against the wall. The carpet wasn't any better. It was threadbare, and the washed-out colours clashed with everything else in the room. Even the curtains were hanging off from the rails. The entire room needed to be demolished.

The next sight that met his eyes was his parents. Wedged into his armchair was his father, wearing the same clothes he had been in since last week when he had been washed. Rakesh could see the greenish ooze from his ulcer seeping through the bandage. His mother, who looked like she barely ate anything, sat in the chair nearest the fire. A Bollywood film was playing on the television, but the sound was off and neither one was looking at it. A wave of hopelessness swept over the young man. His shoulders slumped and he headed through into the equally depressing kitchen.

There was clutter everywhere. It gave the impression that it hadn't been cleaned in years, which was probably true. As a young teenager, Rakesh used to come home from school and tried his best to keep things clean. This was usually at the expense of being able to do his homework. He was constantly told off and put in detention. He never explained to the teachers why he seldom finished his work because he thought they wouldn't believe him. After a couple of years, he stopped. Despite his attempts to keep things clean, his parents never acknowledged his efforts and instead scolded him for interfering or touching things he shouldn't.

On the stove was a pan of something he couldn't describe. He just knew he wouldn't be eating any of it. He heated it through at the same time as making some fresh rice. When both were ready, he took it through to his parents who would eat it from trays. Their dining room table was covered in junk and hadn't been used for its intended purpose for years. Rakesh ate only the rice that he had made. On his way to work the following morning, he would eat again when he could buy from the local shops.

His father was a noisy eater and slurps and chomping were regular sounds. His mother put tiny amounts in her mouth and hardly made a sound.

'Why were you late?' she suddenly demanded.

'I wasn't. I was listening to music in my room.'

'Hiding from your parents? That is disrespectful,' his father snapped, spraying food from his mouth. 'Since you live in my house, I expect you to let me know your whereabouts. It is your duty.'

Rakesh, ignoring his dad, looked down at the bowl he was using. He counted three chips on the edges. The stains were deep-set, but every piece of crockery in the house was like this, and it caused him distress.

'When are you getting yourself a wife? Your father has spoken to a couple of respectable families. Mrs Singh's daughter, Neha, was interested.'

'I'm gay,' the exhausted young man said back to his mother.

'Don't speak of such an abomination in this house,' his father yelled. 'It is our Diwali celebration in two days and I expect you to make an effort. I will be at the temple giving out your photograph. I will not have a queer under my roof!'

'Tough, Dad,' Rakesh sneered, 'because you do. I am gay and nothing you can do or say is ever going to change that! I want to get out of this sickening house and start living my life. The two of you repulse me. I need to be somewhere clean and full of splendour.'

Rakesh's father tried to pull himself out of his chair. His hand, stretched out, was ready to slap his son. However, his colossal weight stopped him from being able to move quickly enough.

'You are a disappointment and bring nothing but shame to my family,' he roared. 'You don't tell us who you hang out with, and we have a right to know. We wish you hadn't been born to us!'

'Don't say that to the boy,' Rakesh's mother said in barely a whisper.

'My friend's son has already started doing his medical training, and his brother wants to be a lawyer.' Rakesh's father ranted. 'Your cousin, Manish, is halfway to becoming a pharmacist! These are the sons I wanted and deserved. They are respectable men who recognise the importance of financial success and hold an impressive social status. I disown you! You are no child of mine.'

'Do you honestly think that I am bothered by anything that you have to say?' Rakesh growled. 'You are an obese, bone-idle tyrant with a rancid leg. How can you speak of success when you have achieved nothing in your life? You sit wallowing in this room surrounded by pictures and statues of your Indian gods and Sai Baba. I have the foul job of washing you once a week and I can't begin to tell you how much that makes me feel sick. I am not the one that brings shame to this family. It is you. Oh, and yes, I love cock!'

The words had the desired effect on the bloated man. His face turned a darker shade, and he was showing signs that he was having difficulty with his breathing. Rakesh stood and happily watched as his mother became frantic at seeing her husband in such a state.

'Do something!' she screamed. 'You should not talk to your father in that disrespectful manner. Why we had a son like you, I will never know.'

'You just told him not to say things like that. It will settle. Give it a few moments,' Rakesh replied nonchalantly.

'Why are you like this?' she said as she helped her husband.

'Maybe something to do with how you have treated me since I was born. Your failure to recognise who I truly am.'

This wasn't the first instance of things playing out like this. It was a regular occurrence ever since Rakesh had told his parents that he was gay when he was fifteen. He had omitted the detail that his first experience with a male had been with his father's best friend's son; the one training to be a medic.

Over the years, Rakesh had got used to the constant negative attitudes towards him. The hurtful words spoken by his parents daily motivated his decision to leave and better his life. He knew that once he left this vile pit of a home, he would never see his parents again. This feeling brought him not only joy but peace.

After a short period, things became settled. His dad's face had returned to his usual colour and his breathing calmed. Rakesh rose from his chair and headed over to the door. He then turned back to look at his parents.

'Today was my eighteenth birthday,' he uttered with sadness.

'Rakesh,' his father sneered. 'Is your hair beginning to thin?'

29

Through the Eyes of a Murderer!

(Part Four)

26th October 2019

12:30 p.m.

Although it was late October, it was another day of sunshine and showers. The weather forecast explained that this was happening because of the high pressure that had built up to the north. A splattering of rain had come early this morning and had left a freshness in the air. Damp leaves lying abandoned on the pathway were slippery but glistened with moisture that almost gave them new life. There were only a few puddles scattered about despite the rain. Children were jumping in the bigger ones and howling with their childish glee.

At a little past midday, the sun glared brightly in the sky. Its heat, now weaker in the autumn months, still brought comfort and joy. There were lots of people out enjoying the day. Some were only wearing light jackets to keep the slight coolness from bothering them. Others were bundled up in heavy coats, scarves, and hats. Dogs ran freely around the park and the sound of laughter sprang from the children's play area. Taken at face value, this could be a perfect day.

Situated on the outskirts of the park was a gym and spa centre. It was fairly new having been completed the previous summer, following years of planning permission issues. It was a modern building in its appearance but didn't blend so well into its surroundings. Some had even called it an eyesore, whilst others embraced its multitude of glassworks and yellowish walls.

Sitting on a bench, an individual watched a man in the distance walking towards the yellow building. He appeared to be enjoying his time and taking in the wonder of the beautiful autumnal day.

'Nice to see you enjoying yourself, Ravi,' hissed the figure on the bench. 'Today is your last full day, so I want you to enjoy every minute of it. By tomorrow evening you will no longer exist in this world. You'll be but a memory for those who wish to think about you. I won't be doing that.'

Coming along the path was an older man hoping to find someone to start a conversation with. The winter months would bring him isolation, and loneliness was becoming harder to deal with each passing year. Days like this were perfect for social interactions. He approached the bench with the person sitting exactly in the middle of it, who was intensely watching Ravi enter the health centre.

'Good afternoon,' the man called out with enthusiasm. 'Do you mind if I sit?'

'Yes, I absolutely do mind,' was the aggressive answer, causing the shocked man to walk away in disgust.

As the time approached early afternoon, the sun was feeling warmer. The individual left the bench and started walking towards the yellowish building.

'What are you doing in there, Ravi? I hope it isn't a new gym membership because you won't be getting value for your money. Oh, guess what? You can't? Well, I will tell you. I got myself a gun. It was worryingly easy to get hold of. I was surprised. It is such a dangerous thing, but a few questions in the right areas got me what I wanted. Sometimes I feel like I'm in a film. Why a gun? That is an extremely understandable and worthwhile question. My weapon of

choice is the scarf I bought in Paris, but if something goes wrong, I thought it would be good to have a backup. I'm understandably hoping that I don't need to use it. I think it would scare the crap out of me if the thing went off. Why have I ended up like this? I always thought that my psychological state of mind was great. Having these murderous thoughts has been taking its toll on me as well. I honestly can't believe the person I have become. You have done this to me, Ravi. That is why you have to die. I need to get my everyday thoughts back to normal. Although, what is normal?'

Arriving at the building, the individual looked through the many windows. There in a waiting area was Ravi. He held a cup in his hand, and close to where he sat there was a vivid blue sign displaying the word "Spa."

'Good for you. I approve. Are you treating yourself to something special? I hope you have booked yourself in for the full works. I want you nice and relaxed for when we all meet up tomorrow for the concert. However, why we are still getting together baffles me, but it will serve a purpose. I hate you, Ravi Patel.'

30

Ravi

26th October 2019

12:30 p.m.

Ravi entered the park and slowly made his way along the path. He enjoyed looking at the trees and how the sun shone through the gaps and warmed his face. Numerous people were dotted around, revelling in their enjoyment, which brought a smile to his face. Seeing others happy cheered his soul. Then, thinking of his current situation generated a sadness that deeply upset him.

Ravi continued with his walk, taking in his surroundings and looking forward to his spa treatments. It had been ages since he last had a full body massage, and he was excited. When they were first together and for at least a couple of years following this, he and Rakesh used to take turns to massage each other. Sadly, those days were long gone.

In front of him, a yellow building came into view. Ravi quickened his pace, like a child on the way to buy sweets. He found the main door very heavy when he tried to open it. It felt like he had no strength in his arms. Then someone from within signalled that it was necessary to take a step back. As Ravi followed the instructions, the automatic doors opened.

'You were standing too close,' the receptionist said. 'It won't work if the magic eye or something like that can't see you.'

Ravi lingered, observing the door's mechanisms longer than necessary as they began to close on him. He made a jumping movement and went over to book himself in.

'Hey,' he smiled. 'I am a fraction early, but I have a booking in the name of Ravi Patel.'

The receptionist, with a badge saying Greg, looked at his computer and a puzzled expression formed on his face.

'I can't see anything on my screen. Was it for the gym or spa?'

'I'm booked in at 1 p.m. for a full body massage.'

The receptionist searched for a while longer, yet nothing appeared.

'There is no booking for a Mr Patel. Not for today, or during the next month. I'm sorry, sir, but I think you've made a mistake.'

'You're wrong,' Ravi grunted. 'I have a confirmation email I can show you.'

'That would be useful, thank you.'

Ravi scrolled through his emails; regretting that he never deleted any of them. When he found nothing, his frustration increased.

'I'm sure it's here somewhere.'

'Let me go and speak with one of the therapists and see what can be done.'

Ravi was hardly listening to what was being said to him. The situation was causing him some anxiety and the pain in the front of his head was beginning to start up, as was the blurred vision. Ravi's legs started shaking, which worried the receptionist, who came from behind his desk and helped him to a chair. He then brought him a cup of tea.

'I'll be back soon.'

As Ravi sipped his drink, he took in his surroundings. For a fairly new business, the place appeared empty. He looked towards the windows and stopped.

'Is that…' he began to say. His impaired vision still causing him an issue.

'Mr Patel?' a voice said loudly, which made him look away from the person at the window.

'Yes,' he replied.

'Hi, I'm Jade-Marie,' a woman said in a standard black uniform with a gold motif. 'Greg tells me you're here for some treatments but haven't made a booking, is that right?'

Ravi could smell aromatherapy oils in the air that he assumed were coming from the therapist. His eyes were clear once more. He couldn't help himself look back at the window to confirm if he saw who he thought was there, but they had gone.

'Mr Patel,' Jade-Marie said, getting slightly irritated.

'I did have a booking. I'm sure I did, but I can't find the booking in my emails. It must have been deleted.'

There was something slightly pathetic about the man standing in front of her, and she instinctively knew she wanted to help him. Jade-Marie excused herself, saying she would be straight back, and encouraged Ravi to sit and finish his tea. Greg went back to reception as the telephone was ringing.

A short time passed, and the therapist returned with an exaggerated grin.

'Good news! We've had a cancellation and I can fit you in. It's a half an hour wait, so I hope you don't mind.'

Ravi just nodded and smiled. He wasn't sure if it had been their error or his, but he was pleased he was getting his massage. Jade-Marie then went over to the main desk.

'I thought you were due off soon?' Greg said.

'I am,' she whispered, 'but look at him. There is something so sad about that man. I can't just leave him. If a treatment will make him happy, I'm pleased to do it.'

1.30 p.m.

Twenty-five minutes later, Ravi was sitting on a massage table with a hole for his face, wearing just his Jurassic Park pants. The moment he had removed his trousers and saw them, he groaned. When he got dressed this morning in his hotel room, it hadn't occurred to him that a therapist would see them.

As he waited for Jade-Marie to arrive, he picked up some aromatherapy bottles. He knew from previous massages in other places that he'd be asked to choose one. Lemongrass was his favourite, followed by eucalyptus and then lavender. Picking one would be difficult. The usual type of spa music was playing, which gave him a moderate zen-like feeling. However, he was still anxious about the people in his life and what he was going to do about them all.

The door slowly opened, and Jade-Marie glided in. When she saw Ravi sitting in his themed pants, her heart went out to him, especially when she saw the sadness on his face.

'Mr Patel, are you OK?'

'You can call me Ravi,' he smiled. 'It was my fault; wasn't it? I didn't make this booking, did I?'

'No, you didn't,' she said. 'Why do you look so sad?'

Ravi took in a deep breath and looked at her.

'Sure you want to know?'

'Look, Ravi. You're my last client for the day. I suggest that if you want to, you tell me why you're feeling this way. Then, once you've got it off your chest, you can relax and enjoy your massage. Deal?'

'Deal,' the grateful man said.

Ravi sat for a few moments to get his thoughts in some kind of order. The therapist could see he was trying to work out things in his head.

'I get stress-related headaches. The pain can be bad, and lately, I have also been getting blurred vision. My GP thinks they are nothing to worry about, but I have also noticed that my memory is getting worse, and at times my limbs are shaky. I know that the other things going on in my life cause these symptoms, for want of a better word. My partner, family and friends have all been doing some incredibly stupid things and I have been the one to point them out and try to make some sort of sense out of them. That, as I am sure you can imagine, has not been welcomed with open arms.' Ravi looked at Jade-Marie to see if he still had her attention; he did. 'Rakesh, my husband, thought we were of slightly higher than average income. He is desperate for the grander things in life, but I stand in his way. This has meant many affairs. I know for sure about two men: Edvin and Ivan. I'm truly convinced of many more. He hates me rubbing my head but doesn't ask me about the intense pain that I get. I recently revealed to them all that I was a multi-millionaire with no interest in money. Rakesh, I think feels betrayed by me. Possibly making his affairs justifiable to him.'

Suddenly aware that he was still just sitting in his pants, he picked up a towel and wrapped it around himself.

'OK to continue?' he asked.

'If you're happy to,' was the reply.

'Dipen is my younger cousin and I love him to pieces. However, he recently asked me for money to help him out of debt. When he asked, he wasn't at that time aware of my fortune. He just assumed that following the death of my parents, I had more than I was letting on. He owes

£200,000. I turned him down because I believe he needs to find his own way out of this mess, or he'll never learn. I can only imagine his shock at my reveal. Then there's Norton. He is a psychologist and a nasty man. He has been seducing his clients in the name of therapy. One young man tried to take his own life, but I stopped him.'

Jade-Marie sat open-mouthed opposite Ravi. When she had asked him to get things off his chest, she hadn't been prepared for what he would say.

'Parveena,' Ravi continued, 'is my business partner in our veterinary surgery. She is a drinker, and sadly a few animals have recently died under her care. I have reported them both to the relevant governing bodies, so our practice and Norton's are under investigation. We can't continue with our work until after they have been completed. Then lastly, we have Agatha. I think she has severe mental health problems and she scares me. She and I were an item so many years ago. I was coming to terms with being gay and at the same time, we were dating. She caught me with a guy called Chen and all hell broke loose. She told me she was pregnant and still says that I insisted that she terminate it. Agatha remembers this all wrong. I said I would stand by her. Her behaviour worries me the most. Do you think she might hurt me? Why do people have to be so messed up and wrong? I'm a nice person, or at least I think I am. Sorry, I don't know why I have just blurted this all out to you.'

Jade-Marie waited until she was sure Ravi had finished and then sat next to him.

'I'm not sure what to say, Ravi. How can one person be dealing with so much? You wouldn't believe it if it was written in a book.'

Ravi sat with his head looking down.

'You said that Agatha worries you the most. Are you also worried that the others might hurt you?'

'Good question,' he muttered. 'Honestly, I think that they all hate me. I'm not sure if I can put them in any order of hatred, but I guess that "hate" comes in many different ways. Dipen wouldn't hurt me, but I think the others might. I can't believe I'm even thinking this about my husband. What has my life come to? I am meeting them all tomorrow at a concert. We have had it planned for ages. I wasn't going to go, but both Rakesh and Norton have sent me messages saying that I should.'

Jade-Marie reached over to a table and handed Ravi a glass of water, then rubbed his back briefly.

'You sound like a lovely guy, Ravi. You have done the right thing. People need to face up to their own mistakes. You ready for that massage?'

'Yes,' he smiled. 'I can't make my mind up about the oils. Shall I go with lemongrass?'

'How about a blended concoction of my own? It's designed to help with relaxation, reduce anxiety and help you have a better sleep. They are warming and enriching oils of Mandarin, Juniper, Ylang-Ylang and Ginger.'

'That sounds like exactly what I need.'

Ravi removed his towel and lay face down on the table with his face in the hole. He could tell that Jade-Marie was preparing to start his massage. She pulled his pants halfway down his bottom and then tucked a towel inside. He could hear her putting the oils on her hands and then felt her gentle touch on his shoulders and back.

'I'm hoping that tomorrow will be a good day, and friendships will be repaired once those who have done wrong recognise I was only doing the right thing; and that the evening will end well. Then maybe I can walk away with closure. Did I tell you that I get stress-related headaches?'

'Shush,' the therapist said. 'Enjoy your massage.'

31

The Murder!

27th October 2019

7:30 a.m.

This was Ravi's fifth morning waking up in the Seaview Hotel. Why it had this name he couldn't work out, as there wasn't any sea to view. The only thing he could see from his window was the backyard belonging to the pub next door. He had deliberated checking himself into a luxury hotel; like Rakesh would have, but decided against it. There was something about this type of establishment that appealed to him. Ravi had never been one for decadence. His favourite thing about this place was the tea and coffee in sachets and the cheap versions of custard creams and bourbon biscuits on a side plate.

Ravi lay with his head on the pillow and frowned. He had woken with a splitting headache and regretted the two red wines he had enjoyed with his dinner last night. Eating alone for the past few nights was something that he had come to enjoy. He had never really done this outside of his home and initially felt apprehensive. However, he soon realised there was nothing to fear. He had prepared by downloading several TV shows onto his smartphone and had also brought along a new book titled "The Murder of Debbie Byrd" to read at the hotel's bar.

After his hot shower and third cup of tea with UHT semi-skimmed milk, he was finally feeling slightly better. The pain in his head was now dull rather than sharp.

When he had seen his GP about his headaches quite a few months ago, this was how he was asked to describe them; sharp or dull. Then after a short consultation, he was told they were stress-related.

The concert wasn't until the evening. It was a mixed indoor and outdoor venue, so pleasant weather was vital but not guaranteed in October. There would be beer tents and food vans, but Ravi wasn't keen on going following all the arguments. He was unsure whether he would be welcomed, but as he had showered, his phone buzzed with three new messages.

Rakesh: "*We will meet you there. Text when you arrive.*"

Norton: "*Let's put things behind us, at least for tonight. I want you to come.*"

Parveena: "I'm still incredibly upset with you, but this has been planned for a long time and I hope you come."

Ravi sent no replies, but the texts had given him an overwhelming sense of guilt that swept over him. He felt it was no longer a decision to make; he had to go!

4:00 p.m.

The most direct route to the train station was via the pathway along the river. As he ambled, taking in the late autumn sun, Ravi thought that doing this walk in reverse tonight, when it was dark, wasn't something he was looking forward to. The lighting would be poor and the crime rates in this area had increased recently.

'Maybe get a taxi,' he mumbled.

Upon arriving at the platform, the first thing he saw was the digital display announcing the train's cancellation due to a shortage of train crew. Ravi perched on the corner of a raised flower bed and soaked up the autumn sun. The summer flowers, now pretty much dead, were still in the pots. Taking his phone out, Ravi was relieved that no further messages had come through. He just wanted to get this day over with. During the past few days he had made some life-altering decisions that would come into play, starting tomorrow.

His next train finally arrived, but not without its own delay. Thankfully, it was only a short one. Shocked to see that it was half empty, Ravi had somehow expected it to be full of standing room only. He settled into a window seat facing the direction of travel.

'Can't be heading to a concert without an alcoholic beverage.'

Startled, Ravi saw Dipen smiling down at him and handing him a ready-mixed cocktail in a can.

'No thanks, I don't want that,' he said. 'I've still got a dull ache in my head from two drinks last night. Wasn't I meeting you all there?'

'Yes, that was the plan. Then I saw you walking through the park and by the river and thought I'd travel with you. When the train was cancelled, I went to the shops to get these drinks. Go on, have one.'

Ravi reluctantly took the drink. Its sweetness tasted good. Dipen plonked himself down next to his cousin.

'Why are you only wearing a thin T-shirt and a lightweight jacket? It's October. You'll be cold on the journey home.'

'Yeah, I didn't think it through,' Ravi said. 'I was having a muzzy head.'

'How are you feeling about today?' Dipen asked.

Ravi took a deep breath and exhaled slowly. He then took a swig from his can, for which he was grateful for the slight delay in answering.

'Being completely honest, I'm dreading it. I don't want to go. You all hate me, so what is the point? Why are Rakesh, Parveena and Norton sending me texts encouraging me to come? It doesn't make any sense to me. They despise me. At least Agatha is being honest in her absence of messages. Something just doesn't add up, Dipen. Maybe I'm intrigued, and that's why I'm going.'

His cousin was unsure how to respond. He understood where Ravi was coming from, but had no answers.

'I don't hate you,' he said as he nudged shoulders.

'Well, that is also strange. You owe £200,000 and know I could wipe that debt, but won't. I might have thought that you would despise me more than the others. Why were you following me along by the river this morning? If you knew it was me, why didn't you call out and walk with me?'

'Oh, don't worry about that. You looked deep in thought and I didn't want to disturb you. As for the debt, yes, I'm deeply troubled by your refusal to help me. Is it worth me begging you now? Ravi, they have given me my first task. I don't know what they are getting me to do, but I have to meet my loan shark's heavies on Tuesday next week to be told. It won't be good. I have the feeling that either I'm going to get hurt, or I'm going to have to hurt some poor person. Ravi, please can you help me? I'll pay you back. Ravi! PLEASE!'

The rest of their journey went in silence. Ravi didn't answer the plea, so Dipen remained quiet. When they entered the concert arena, they parted company, each saying they needed to use the toilet, grab a drink or investigate the food vans.

7:30 p.m.

The place was slowly filling up. There had been a couple of support acts playing that were largely going unheard as people were meeting up with friends and sorting out refreshments. Ravi hadn't seen Dipen since they arrived.

He looked at his phone and had no messages. He texted the WhatsApp group.

"Hey, I've been here for an hour. I can't see any of you. Are you here? I am standing by the Lovetts beer stall."

It took a while before he got a response, telling him where to find them. When he arrived, it was obvious they had been here for quite a while. Dipen was missing. However, the other four had a full drink and two empty glasses in front of them.

'Been here long?' Ravi sarcastically said, pointing at the table.

'Yes. And we are getting on just fine. Strange that when you're not here, we do just fine,' Rakesh sneered.

'Where's Dipen?' Ravi asked.

'Haven't seen him,' replied Norton.

'What have you done to your face? Did you cut yourself shaving?'

Norton looked at Ravi and pulled a disinterested face.

'Well, if that's what it looks like, then I guess that is what I did!'

'I see you all have a drink and chose to ignore me from the very beginning of the evening, so I'll get myself one.'

From his place at the bar, Ravi observed the group of four huddled close, then burst into raucous laughter, their heads thrown back in unison. He scanned the vicinity for his cousin but couldn't see him. With his drink, he walked back to their table. They hadn't bothered to get him a chair, so he had to ask a few other tables if they had a spare one before getting lucky.

'So, is this how the rest of the day is going to go? Ignoring me? Making me feel unwanted? I can go home if that's what you'd prefer?'

'Oh, chill out,' Parveena croaked. 'We texted and asked you to come.'

Ravi sighed.

'OK,' he said. 'So, are we looking forward to the concert?'

'We've already done that question,' Norton snorted.

After about twenty minutes, it was clear to Ravi that the intention behind his presence this evening was to isolate him and make him feel bad. They didn't want him here. Agatha hadn't even acknowledged his arrival, even though he was sitting next to her. She had flinched when he barely touched her when taking his seat.

'I can't wait for this day to end,' he whispered. 'Does anyone want another drink?'

Orders were shouted out and Ravi got up.

'I'll help you,' Parveena said.

As they waited their turn to be served, there was an uncomfortable tension between them.

'Why am I even here?' Ravi asked with sadness.

Parveena could see that his eyes were moist.

'We've had these tickets booked for ages. I suppose we thought we shouldn't let them go to waste.'

'I get that. But why am I here? I'm not wanted. I know that our practice is never going to recover from this. Kwasi is now out of a job and hates me as well. Bloody hell, everybody hates me.'

'We all have good reason to, Ravi. We grew up together and shared dreams. I was going through a rough patch, and you threw me to the dogs. Because of you, my life, career and future have been destroyed. And for what? A couple of dead animals. We could have worked through this together. It didn't need to end with you reporting me.'

'But don't you get it? That's exactly how it had to end, otherwise you wouldn't have stopped. More animals would have died because of your excessive drinking.'

'What's the delay?' a voice boomed from behind.

Norton made them both jump. He noticed the troubled expression on Parveena's face.

'Have you been upsetting her?' he said, jabbing Ravi's shoulder with his finger.

'Stop that,' Ravi said as he stepped backwards.

Norton grabbed him and pulled their faces together.

'Leave her alone,' he snapped. Ravi felt Norton's spit on his lips. 'Haven't you done enough to both of us? You set out to ruin our lives, and you did a good job.' Norton started to shake Ravi. 'I can't think of a person I hate more right now.'

'Why the text, Norton? Why did you say you wanted me here?'

'I wish I knew.'

'Because that's what you do, isn't it?' Ravi vented. 'You bully people into doing what you want. I've seen the way you speak with your receptionist, Sorel. Stuart Schumann was so badly coerced by you that you manipulated him into having sex that he wasn't ready for. The online hashtags going around. All of them say what you have done to so many young people. You're a monster. Then the passive-aggressive text to me, making me believe you all possibly wanted me, only for you all to treat me so dreadfully.'

Norton punched the ranting man in the stomach. Ravi fell to the ground clutching his side as his attacker walked off, shaking out his fist. Parveena glanced downwards and deliberately emptied the pint of beer she had just received from the bartender on Ravi before walking away. From their table, Agatha looked on and laughed, and her laughter then turned to hysterics.

9:00 p.m.

After about twenty minutes, Ravi pushed himself over to a wall and sat, bringing his legs to his chest. He held his knees and lowered his head. He was in too much discomfort to move any further.

'You've only got yourself to blame,' Rakesh said as he walked over.

'Really?'

Rakesh sat down and put his arm around his husband.

'They are all leaving. None of us want to stay for the concert now. I've texted Dipen, as we have no idea where he is.'

'Has the concert started?'

'Yes, they went on a few minutes ago, but the night is ruined and that's because of you, Ravi.'

'I don't see how any of this is my fault. I'm a nice person.'

'You should have heard the things Agatha was saying about you.'

'Just leave me alone, Rakesh. I'm going back to the hotel.'

'Why don't you come home? I miss you being there.'

'No. It isn't what I want. Or at least I don't think it is. You've lied and cheated on me countless times. How do I even know where to begin to forgive you for that? You have broken my heart. I loved you so much, Rakesh.'

'Loved? Past tense?'

Ravi looked into his husband's eyes and saw the tears beginning to form, slowly trickling down his cheeks. Ravi used his thumbs to wipe them away.

'Yes, Rakesh; Loved. I have nothing left to give. You have destroyed me and I need a fresh start. I'm thinking of going to live in India. I have some family there, so it would be good for me. It's not my fault. I'm a nice person.' Ravi started to massage his head.

'Stop that rubbing! It gets on my bloody nerves. And stop repeating yourself. You're constantly saying the same things over and over again for the past few months and it drives me mad! Are you really such a nice person?'

'I want a divorce,' Ravi blurted out.

'I'll get half your fortune in a settlement. So go on, divorce me,' sneered Rakesh.

'Not if I give it all away before heading off. There are lots of charities I could give it to. I have decided to give Dipen the money that he owes. Also, some other people would benefit. Stuart Schumann, my friend Bilam. I'd make sure I even gave some to Jade-Marie.'

'Who the bloody hell is Jade-Marie?' shouted Rakesh.

'A kind person, that's who.'

Rakesh got up and started to pace. The noise coming from the concert had until this moment gone unnoticed. His other friends had all gone their separate ways, and only the staff were milling around as they cleared up. Rakesh crouched down and whispered in his husband's ear.

'You're dead to me, Ravi Patel. I have hated you for such a long time; as have all the others.' Rakesh stood and then kicked Ravi so hard in the stomach that it caused his husband's head to turn as he vomited. If any of the staff witnessed this, they chose not to get involved and just carried out their duties. However, someone was watching.

Half an hour after Rakesh had left him, Ravi finally got himself to his feet and stumbled out of the venue and eventually onto the train home. When he arrived at his station, there were no taxis to be seen. Ravi took out his phone to call for an Uber, but his phone had run out of battery.

11:30 p.m.

The riverside path was shrouded in darkness. The moon struggled to illuminate the way; only streetlights could have truly made a difference. Despite repeated appeals to the council, the request for lighting was always rejected as it was not considered a priority.

Ravi staggered along the path. No one else seemed to be around. He could have done without the spooky animal noises. The fox calls were the most chilling, as was the hidden owl. As he walked, he held onto his stomach and his side where he had been attacked earlier. Tears were falling down his face. All Ravi wanted was to be back in his hotel.

'I'm a nice person,' he sobbed.

A noise from behind startled him, and he instinctively and abruptly turned. This resulted in a sharp pain that caused him to shout out. He then continued to walk until he heard something else.

'Is there someone there?' he said with fear.

Getting no answer, Ravi walked faster in the hotel's direction. He tripped on a large branch and banged his head as he fell. Standing up was proving difficult because of the pain coming from all over his body. His head had started to pound.

Once again, walking quickly, Ravi thought he heard footsteps and heavy breathing.

'Is someone there?' he repeated, but without stopping.

'Yes,' uttered a voice that sent chills down Ravi's spine.

He went to scream, but before he could release any noise, he felt a scarf wrap around his neck. His assailant was pulling the material tighter and tighter. Ravi, whilst making choking noises, was trying as hard as he could to get his fingers under the scarf and pull it away from his neck. The pain in his head was ready to explode.

'Please don't,' he choked.

The scarf was getting tighter and Ravi thought his eyes were getting ready to explode out of his head.

'Stop,' was Ravi's final word as the life was just about taken out of him.

The killer pulled tightly once more and brought their mouth to the victim's ear. Then, just before Ravi took his final breath, they whispered their name. Once the body dropped to the ground, it was rolled and pushed into the river. The killer started to laugh, which then turned into hysterics as they watched the silhouetted body drift away.

32

Isaac

29th October 2019

06:00 a.m.

Detective Chief Inspector Isaac Davidson was forty-three but looked much younger. His crystal-blue eyes were always what people first noticed about him, followed by his strikingly handsome features.

Thanks to his personal trainer, Edward, he was now in the best physical shape he had ever been in. Even as a teenager, his body was never the same from one year to the next. He had never been overweight, but he had love handles beginning to form at times. Upon joining the police force, his exercise routine enhanced significantly, leading to his twenties being marked by a robust and enviable figure. When he reached his late thirties or early forties, he had the slight beginnings of a protruding belly. Edward had put together an exhausting but effective workout plan, and it was this that gave him his current physique.

For the past eighteen months, Isaac had been learning Swedish. During the recent summer, he had been able to put into practice what he had learnt. After taking some time off from work, he spent a week in Stockholm and got along well. He had been impressed with himself. Unlike previous holidays, he had gone alone. His brother, Alan, who usually went on trips with him, had met someone at a singles Valentine's event and was spending most of the time at hers. Isaac was pleased for his brother but missed him.

Today, he was meeting someone for a late breakfast, so when he finally crawled out of bed, he made himself a coffee and two slices of toast. This would be enough to see him through until he met his friend.

Breakfast had always been a big part of the day for them both. His brother typically cooked breakfast and Isaac sorted out dinner. The DCI sat at the kitchen table and looked through his emails and various apps. There wasn't much of interest, so he headed for a shower. The hot water felt great. He had the head selected to an intense setting, which meant it powered down on his shoulders where he had some pain following his workout last night.

Leaving the bathroom, he walked back to his bedroom, but not before opening the door to Alan's room. Everything was neat and tidy.

'Happy for you, mate,' he said out loud.

Once dressed and ready for the day, he made a conscious effort to ensure he had both sets of keys, wallet and phone. Alan had habitually shouted out these items when he had been here, as Isaac usually forgot at least one of them. Then, not understanding why, he turned to look back at his hallway and let out a deep sigh before closing the door and heading off to work.

10:30 a.m.

Isaac sat in the café by the river and waited for his former colleague to join him for breakfast. He rarely took time out of a working day to meet friends, but Emily was only here in London for a conference and would be heading back up north later today.

Emily Morgans, his previous detective sergeant, had moved to Manchester when she had been promoted to Detective Inspector. She was a tall woman of slim build, and when Isaac had last seen her, she had mousey hair that sat just above her shoulders. The woman who was now walking through the door had long blonde hair and looked a force to be reckoned with. They both clocked each other and smiled.

Isaac stood with open arms, and she embraced him as hard as she could. They had always worked well together and respected each other's professionalism.

'You look bloody amazing,' Isaac said when they finally broke free from each other.

'Not looking too bad yourself, DCI Davidson. In fact, dare I say it, you're looking hot!' They both chuckled and then hugged again.

They sat and perused the menu. Isaac decided on a regular coffee, and Emily a decaffeinated one. Both chose a bacon and sausage sandwich, Isaac's with brown sauce and mustard, and Emily's with mayonnaise.

'Decaffeinated coffee and mayonnaise on a bacon butty?'

Emily blushed.

'You're pregnant. Aren't you? They don't call me a DCI for nothing.'

'Four months,' she replied.

'That's wonderful. I'm so happy for you. Tell me everything.'

The food and drinks arrived, and the two former colleagues chatted with a new vigour. When Isaac had been her boss, personal information was rarely spoken about, but today was different.

'I met Chris at our first social gathering a few months after starting as a DI. He was, and still is the proprietor of the restaurant we were eating in. Short version, we hooked up, and within six months we had moved in together. This little monster,' she said as she rubbed her tummy, 'wasn't planned, but we are both so excited.'

'Sounds great, Emily. I am so pleased for you.'

'Thanks.'

'How is work? Do you have a nice team working with you?'

'Most of them are great,' she replied. 'I have moulded my management style based on yours if I'm being completely honest. We all respected you so much. I do have one detective constable, Angus, who plays me up. I can't work out if he resents me, likes me, or hates being a police officer. He is a strange one. But enough about me. How's the team? Anne?'

The mention of his DC brought a smirk to his face.

'As much as she drives me mad, she is doing well. She was the one who solved the Sally Raines murder I was texting you about. She is still slovenly and has bits of Danish pastries on her clothes, not to mention coffee stains. Sadly, her dad died recently, but it seems to have had a positive outcome for her. Since she returned from compassionate leave she hasn't been late.'

'Wow, that is something special.' They both laughed.

'Hamish,' Isaac continued, 'doesn't appear to be doing great. I've noticed he's not been the same and always looks low in mood. I have tried asking him about it, but he shrugs and says it's nothing to worry about. Jian and Faisal are dating and have been for about eighteen months. It's actually quite cute. They think we don't know, but we do.'

'That is adorable. I can totally see them together,' Emily said with a smile.

'That leaves Lily. She has turned out to be a fantastic DC. Sadly, she is putting Hamish to shame.'

A server came over and asked if they wanted more drinks. Isaac did, and Emily was happy with the bottle of water she brought with her.

'How's Alan?' she asked.

'He is all loved up. He met Daisy about six months ago. She also uses a wheelchair, so her bungalow is fully adapted. Alan spends most of his time over there now. He does come home periodically. I'm so happy for him.'

'Do you miss him?' Emily asked.

'I really do,' he said with a sigh. 'Oh, guess what Daisy's surname is? Christmas. Alan is dating Daisy Christmas.'

Enjoying each other's company, they laughed and shared all their news.

'So, any romances in your life, DCI Davidson?'

'No,' he replied quickly. 'I came out as asexual last year. Then joined a social group for LGBTQ+ people, and I will admit, I have a great time. I have one close friend who is also a member. Her name is Jane, and she is trans. We get on so well, and she makes me smile on a daily basis.'

Emily reached over and held Isaac's hand.

'That sounds brilliant,' she said as Isaac's phone alerted him to a text.

He read the message and then looked over to his former DS.

'It's from Jian. *"Body of a man found in the river. A scarf around his neck. Forensics on the scene. Call me."* Oh, Emily. Looks like I need to go. It was so lovely seeing you today. I'll be in touch.'

They embraced, and Emily couldn't help herself from smiling as she watched DCI Davidson heading off to solve another murder.

33

Crime Scene

29th October 2019

12:30 p.m.

It transpired that Isaac was only half a mile from where the body had been found, so he left his car where it was and walked along the towpath. The past eighteen months had been fairly quiet on murders. There had been a few, but they had been solved fairly quickly and had not utilised too many resources. They had mainly been gang-related and obvious perpetrators. Towards the end of 2018, Isaac and his team had a long case they worked on alongside the fraud squad. A couple of dead people had been found under suspicious circumstances, but it was concluded that they had both taken their own lives. That had kept his boss silent for a few months, however since that had been concluded, Superintendent Chandra was constantly asking Isaac to think about making staff cuts. The department had to save money, and quickly. He had been told that by the end of this year, someone would have to go.

Further along the path, he could see a small gathering of people. This was never a good thing, as small soon swelled to large. Large meant there was a potential for crime scene disturbance. Isaac could already see uniformed police trying to control the area. However, a body in the river was always going to attract attention.

The forensic team members were noticeable in their white suits and blue shoe coverings. As he came closer, Isaac could see that the crowds were far enough from the crime scene not to be causing any concerns; and this pleased the DCI. Jian was talking with a woman who he assumed was the person who came across the poor man.

Isaac always thought deeply about the murder victims he had investigated and wondered what had led them to the point that they were killed. This was the part of the investigation that he relished the most. Not in a ghoulish way but to get the victim justice. In the past, he had delved into the most depraved of minds. It was statistically correct that the murderer was more often than not known to the victim.

The DCI arrived at the point where the crowds had formed, took out his badge and waved it around in a superior manner. He then asked everyone to step further back and let him through. Predictably people had their mobile phones out filming the macabre scene. He found this an abhorrent human quality and wished they would all go away and get on with their day and let him do his job.

Through the hordes, Isaac could see the forensic tent had been erected, shielding the body from the onlookers. At least this meant the poor man would not end up on YouTube or other social media platforms.

Isaac signalled his arrival with an overstated wave and put on the required protective equipment. He always struggled with the shoe coverings as balancing on one leg was never easy for him. Once prepared, he approached the forensic lead, Alex.

'It's been a while. How have you been, Mr Poole?'

'Good, thanks.' Alex replied. 'Yourself?'

'Plodding, as they say. What do we have here?' Isaac looked at the body and an upsurge of sadness washed over him. 'Poor bugger.'

Alex took his time to prepare his initial thoughts. He possessed remarkable skills within his chosen profession and had received high praise throughout his extensive career. His team was occupied with capturing the required photographs, collecting swabs, and obtaining ground and water samples. Isaac noticed how bloated the man looked. There was a piece of material tied around his neck and one eye was open, but it appeared to have been ravaged by creatures in the river. Isaac never got used to seeing things like this.

'So,' Alex started. 'The state of the body is going to make things awfully difficult for me. He has been in the water for a considerable amount of time, but I can't say exactly how long. Maybe two to five days. As you can see, he is bloated and has been a food source for whatever lives in the murky depths of this river. Initial thoughts are that he was strangled, but I can't rule out that he drowned. There are no other obvious signs of injury that could cause death. A brief examination does show some bruising to his torso. However, it is still difficult to say when these occurred, but they look extensive from what I can see by lifting his T-shirt. Once we remove his clothes, we will get a proper look.'

'Any demographics? I can tell by the state of the body it might not be easy to confirm right now but do your best,' Isaac enquired.

'We have an adult male of probable Indian descent. At a guess, I would say mid-thirties to mid-fifties. The bloating isn't helping me call it any closer at the moment and neither is the post-death damage to his face thanks to the parasites and fish in the water. Strangulation is my first thought. He is wearing good quality clothes, his nails are nicely cared for, and his teeth are in perfect condition, so he is not a vagrant. We will know much more when we transfer him to the department.'

Isaac expressed his gratitude to Alex, then took some time to examine the scene and the body, beginning to piece together his thoughts. The poor man was horribly disfigured. Isaac then looked up and saw that Jian was finishing with the woman.

'Why would someone want to kill you, my friend?'

'Sir,' Jian called out. 'That is Alison Rambles,' he said, pointing to a woman being comforted by a uniformed officer. 'Out for a walk in her lunchtime when she came across the body. She said it was quiet along the pathway, which is surprising for the time of day. Then she stood gazing into the river and something caught her eye. She said that he was tucked under or caught under some weeds. It was his legs that she first saw. By the sounds of it, she handled things well. She told me that she knew if she screamed it would attract attention, so she calmly called the police and then stood blocking him so that others walking by didn't get involved.'

'Sensible woman. I wish they all acted like her,' Isaac said. 'If you're happy with her statement and don't think she can tell us anything more, get her details and then thank her on my behalf and tell her she can go. Please make sure she has someone to go to and let her know that one of us from the team will call her tomorrow to check and see how she is getting on. Oh, Jian, make sure she has the relevant support numbers as I'm sure this was a dreadful shock for her.'

'Will do,' Jian replied.

Isaac watched as Alex and his team finished all that they could. He then looked at the crowd to see if anything, or anyone stood out as suspicious. Nothing and no one did.

'Can we ID him?' Isaac called out.

'Bank cards say he is called Ravi Patel,' shouted Alex. 'However, his driving licence states that he is Ravi Patel-Kumar.'

The DCI went back over to the body and crouched down.

'I'm so sorry this happened to you, Ravi. I will find out who did this to you and they will spend an exceptionally long time behind bars.'

34

Crime Board

30th October 2019

06:30 a.m.

With no one at home to keep him company over breakfast, Isaac had quickly eaten a piece of toast and then headed into work via a café to get himself a large coffee and bacon roll. He hadn't got used to Alan not being at home, so work was the next best place. At this time in the morning it was fairly quiet. Isaac had already placed a photo of the victim onto the crime board and it didn't make for pleasant viewing.

In the next room a vacuum cleaner could be heard. This would be Glenn, their cleaner. He would be coming into this office soon, so the DCI did what he always did and made two cups of tea. Last year Isaac found out that Bourbons were Glenn's favourite biscuits, so he put a couple on a plate. As the tea was brewing, this gave time for some emails to be checked. When he arrived back in the office yesterday, he had sent messages asking about missing people of Indian background. No answers had come back yet.

As he waited for Glenn's arrival, a text came through to his phone.

"Sorry bro, I can't make our dinner plans tonight. Daisy isn't feeling great. I'll be in touch with you soon for a catch-up. Love you."

'Love you too,' Isaac whispered.

The main door burst open and in came Glenn, struggling with his equipment; he was also breathless. He was a lovely man, but had too many health conditions to be working at his age. Last month he turned seventy and the team had taken him out to his favourite restaurant as a treat.

'I won't tell you again. You need to retire.'

Glenn looked at the DCI and laughed a whole-hearted cackle.

'I have years left in me; don't you worry about that.'

Isaac brought over the tea and biscuits and they chatted.

'Seriously, Glenn, I'm concerned about you.'

'It's OK, boss man,' the cleaner said. 'I leave in December. My family has been going on and on at me. *"Dad, you don't need the money,"* or *"Dad, your health is more important."* So, I have listened and will be leaving soon. This job was never about the money for me. I did it for this,' Glenn said, indicating Isaac and the tea. 'I love talking with people and having a sense of purpose; helping out.'

'You're truly an amazing man, and we will all miss you. However, you can call in and see us at a decent time of day.' They both laughed.

09:30 a.m.

The rest of the team had arrived and were waiting for their boss to start the meeting. He was, however, on the telephone in his office.

'New case, judging by the board,' Hamish remarked.

'Strangulation,' Jian volunteered.

'Picture is grim,' Lily said.

'Bloody hell,' shouted DC Anne Michaels. 'Why all the small talk? Get lively, people.'

Laughter filled the air as Anne polished off her sausage roll, scattering flakes of puff pastry across her dress.

DCI Davidson finally left his office and addressed his team.

'As you can see by the famous crime board, we have a murder to investigate. I was just on the phone with our colleagues about missing people. This poor person,' he said, pointing at the gruesome picture, 'is Ravi Patel or Ravi Patel-Kumar. There have been no reports of individuals missing under those names. We have identified the body using his driving licence, but we need his next of kin to come in. That is going to be extremely upsetting for them. We have these details as Mr Rakesh Kumar, which fits with the double-barrelled name. Hamish and I are going to see Mr Kumar this morning.'

'Me? Why me?' DC Potter asked, sounding surprised. 'You usually take DS Wong.'

Hamish was on the wrong side of thirty-five and had recently shaved off his bountiful ginger hair without ever giving a reason why. His body was of an Olympian statue, but he had recently stopped going to the gym, which used to be an everyday occurrence. He had remained single for quite some time, even though he had tried various dating apps.

'I thought it would be good to spend some time with you,' Isaac said.

'Am I in trouble?'

'No,' was the curt reply.

Focusing back on the near-empty board, Isaac continued.

'We are still waiting for Alex's findings, but what we know so far is that the body had been in the river for at least a couple of days. You can tell it was mauled at by whatever lurks in the river. He was hugely bloated and does have some extensive bruises. There was a scarf tied around his neck, so current thoughts are that he was strangled and then pushed into the water.'

'Who found the body?' asked Lily, who was the newest member of the team. She was tall with flowing blonde hair that now had a few streaks of pink running through it. The extra weight she carried around her tummy remained, despite trying to exercise more.

'A woman called Alison Rambles,' Jian said. 'I called her this morning to ask how she was doing after such an ordeal and she said all was good. I've given her the support line numbers if she needs them.'

Isaac scanned the room.

'Sir, are there any thoughts on whether this was a targeted crime or a random one?' asked Faisal. Jian couldn't help smiling at his partner of eighteen months.

'Crime rates, as we all know have shot up in recent years. However, the victim had on a modest-looking watch. He had some money in his wallet. We haven't found a phone, but this is probably lying at the bottom of the river. We also don't know where he was killed. He may have floated for quite some time or got tangled in weeds and not floated that far. Hopefully, these are all things we can start to unpick as we go along. Any more questions?'

The room remained silent, then DC Michaels raised her hand. Anne was forty-four, plump, with a hooked nose and rather large ears. Her hair was as messy as her desk was and in the past year she had started engaging more with the team.

'Sir, so he knew his killer? If he still had his valuables on him, then this suggests a targeted attack.'

She started writing something into her notebook and the rest of the team scattered back to their desks or into the kitchen.

'Guys,' the DCI called out. 'Usual request. Please finalise other work you have on the go so you're ready to start this new investigation. Start seeing what you can find on a Ravi Patel or Patel-Kumar.'

Isaac entered his office to grab his coat and headed for the exit.

'Ready, DC Potter?'

'Ready, sir,' was the reluctant reply.

35

Rakesh

30th October 2019

09:00 a.m.

The day was dry and sunny, with isolated showers. However, the naked body lying on his front in bed, spread-eagled, was unaware of the weather outside his window. His arms were tucked under the pillows, and the volume of his snoring was extraordinarily high. This likely stemmed from the bottle of red wine he had indulged in after returning from a catastrophic evening with Ivan.

The evening had started as they always do. An expensive hotel, drinks in the bar, then back to the room and money hopefully transferred into Rakesh's secret bank account. However, he had got too cocky and thought that a night with him was worth more than Ivan was willing to pay. Rakesh had been lucky to leave with just a punch to the face. His leg was still hurting from kicking Ravi three nights ago. As he limped into reception and asked them to call him a taxi, they couldn't help but notice his bruised face.

As he began stirring from his slumber, Rakesh was instantly aware of a mouth that tasted disgusting, but equally tuned to having a clear head. This surprised him, as red wine wasn't usually that kind to him. Resting on the bedside cabinet was an empty Merlot bottle and a glass containing traces of red liquid. Rakesh smiled to himself.

He knew that if Ravi was here, he'd be furious. He always hated alcohol in the bedroom.

'Well screw you, Ravi,' Rakesh laughed.

After a few stretches, yawns, breaking wind and nose-picking, Rakesh was under a cascading waterfall. When they had renovated the bathroom, they had both agreed on a power shower. This one even had a massaging setting. As he turned and placed his face under the jet of water, Rakesh was rapidly alerted to the injury to his face. The forceful stream of hot water was painful.

'Wanker,' he shouted. 'You'd better have paid me.'

Downstairs in the kitchen, the bread was in the toaster and an orange juice was on the worktop. Sitting in just his designer underwear, Rakesh was reviewing his banking app.

'You total bastard!'

Ivan hadn't paid the latest fee. Seeing as no sex took place, Rakesh wasn't shocked but thought he might have paid, as a parting gesture of an apology for the brutal attack on his face. However, what was causing him more distress was the account balance. With money having come from both Edvin and Ivan over the past few months, Rakesh anticipated a minimum of £10,000. There was, nonetheless, a list of expensive transactions and a total left of £1500. His expenditure had been through the roof lately.

'To hell with it! I'm going back to bed.'

10:45 a.m.

The DCI's car pulled up outside the required house. DC Potter immediately released his seatbelt and went to open the car door.

'Hang on,' Isaac said. 'I just wanted to check in with you.'

'I knew there was a reason you chose me to come with you today, sir. You have never done that.'

'I just want to check that you're doing OK.'

'I'm fine.'

The two men sat in silence for a few moments.

'How's the gym?' Isaac asked.

'Why are you asking that, sir?'

'You usually talk to us about your workouts; lately, we haven't heard anything from you. Is everything OK? I'm not just your boss, Hamish. I'm here if you ever need to talk.'

'Has someone said something?'

'Not at all, Hamish. I have just noticed a subtle change to your demeanour and wanted to speak with you.'

'Was it Lily?'

'Hamish, stop. Nobody has said anything.'

'I'm fine,' DC Potter said as he pushed open his door and got out.

11:00 a.m.

As he lay half asleep, Rakesh could hear someone knocking at the front door. He dragged himself out of bed and went to answer it.

'Mr Patel-Kumar?'

'Yeah,' he replied.

'Can we come in, please? I'm DCI Davidson and this is DC Potter.' Both men presented their identification badges.

Rakesh rubbed his eyes, clasped his hands together, turned them inside out and stretched.

'Why?'

'Please, sir,' Isaac said. 'It is important.'

'OK, I'll go and get some clothes on.'

Rakesh turned and headed upstairs, leaving the detectives to shut the door and take themselves into the living room.

They wandered around and took in the smart décor.

'Sir,' Hamish said, holding up a wedding photograph. 'I know the body is grossly disfigured, but look; It's him.'

'Oh, so sad. Look how happy he is,' Isaac said. 'They both look so content.'

Fifteen minutes went by when Rakesh eventually came down the stairs looking like he was about to go out clubbing, but also with a noticeable limp.

'I believe one should always look fabulous when entertaining. Can I get you men a drink?'

They both politely declined.

'Please can I confirm that you are, Rakesh Patel-Kumar?'

'I am. But I tend to only use Kumar.' he replied, looking straight at the DCI. 'Why do you need to know that?'

'Please ready yourself for some distressing news, Mr Kumar. A body was found yesterday in the river. The man had bank cards and a driving licence in his wallet. The names on these were both Ravi Patel and Ravi Patel-Kumar.'

Silence fell upon them all. DC Potter watched the reaction on Rakesh's face. The bravado he had first exhibited to the detectives was now gone.

'But he's currently in a hotel. I only saw him a few days ago.'

'We need you to come and identify the body. I'm so sorry to do this to you,' Isaac said.

'No,' Rakesh responded. Tears fell down his cheeks.

DCI Davidson and DC Potter gave time for Rakesh to process what he was being told. He was clearly distraught. Hamish was jotting things down in his notebook.

'It won't be Ravi,' Rakesh finally said. 'I know we've been fighting, but couples do that. Don't they? We all left the concert separately, and Ravi was going back to his hotel. It won't be my Ravi.'

'I hope you're correct, Mr Kumar, but we require your presence at the police station to view the body. I must caution you; it has been submerged for a while, and I regret to inform you, he does not appear peaceful,' Isaac said, trying to express as much tact as he could.

Rakesh looked numb and was gently rocking himself back and forth.

'I'm not sure if I can do it.'

'We will be with you the whole time.'

'Patel-Kumar is our married name. For ease, we both kept using our surnames given to us at birth. I'll get my coat.'

36

Viewing the Body!

30th October 2019

1:00 p.m.

Rakesh sat on a cold bench in a corridor somewhere inside the police station. He was asked to wait so they could prepare the body for viewing. DC Potter had offered to stay and keep him company, but Rakesh had wanted time alone to help compose himself for what he was about to see. A large window was in front of him but with a pulled curtain on the other side. Even though he knew there was activity going on, there wasn't a sound to be heard.

Rakesh had contemplated texting the others but thought it best to verify if this was going to be his husband or not. Or at least, this is what DCI Davidson had advised him to do when he had asked him in the car about what he should do. DC Potter had echoed his boss's words.

Time seemed to be moving slowly. Rakesh had been only waiting ten or so minutes but it felt like a lifetime. Then, making him jump, the side door opened and both detectives walked in. The atmosphere was chilling, as to be expected, and he couldn't help shuddering as the men approached him.

'Mr Kumar,' Isaac said.

'Just Rakesh, please. Mr Kumar feels weird.' He then hesitated. 'I don't want to do this. If it is my husband, I can't face seeing him like this.' Tears trickled down his cheeks.

'Is there anyone else we can ask?'

Rakesh looked at Isaac, and half smiled.

'His cousin, Dipen. Maybe he would do it.'

A hush fell as the three men pondered on the next move. Rakesh was fighting with his tears to keep them from falling off his cheeks.

'Do you want us to ask his cousin?'

Rakesh thought long and hard, and then he awkwardly stood up, which caused some pain in his leg.

'No, I can do this. If it is Ravi, then I should be the one to call it.'

'This is what is going to happen,' Isaac calmly said. 'The curtain will slowly open. There will be a long silver table with a covered body on it. Someone will then gently lower the sheet so you can see the man's face. Once you're ready, let us know if he is your husband. Is that clear?'

Rakesh nodded and then braced himself. Isaac pushed a button on the wall and the curtain slowly drew back. The scene in front was exactly as described. The sheet was pulled back.

'Oh, my darling Ravi,' was all Rakesh said before he fainted and fell into DC Potter.

37

Rakesh

31st October 2019

08:00 a.m.

Following his morning beverage with Glenn, Isaac sat in his small office preparing for the morning briefing. He had been impressed that DC Anne Michaels had been the first to arrive. As always, she was clutching a coffee from a chain rather than buying from an independent local shop. Although he was irritated, he remained silent.

Isaac rose and made his way to the central area of the crime room, pausing to gaze out the window. It was the best place to get a signal on his phone. He had hoped that Alan would have texted, but nothing came through. Outside overlooked the main car park and he saw Jian and Faisal getting out of the same car. He knew what would happen next as it had been happening for so many months. Jian would come into the room first, and then a few minutes later DC Asher would appear. They would then say good morning to each other, pretending this was the first time they had seen each other since leaving work the previous day. Isaac couldn't help but smile. Everyone knew exactly what was going on but they all allowed the loved-up couple to play out their game.

DCI Davidson busied himself around the crime board, and everyone else was either logging on to their computers or catching up on what others had done last night. There was a good vibe being created.

'I've decided to get myself "out there" and join a dating agency.'

Everyone stopped what they were doing and looked around the room to see where these words had come from. Without turning, Isaac had a broad grin on his face. He knew exactly who had said this, and it made him so happy.

'I think that is a brilliant idea, Anne,' he said, finally twisting around.

'Thanks, sir,' DC Michaels said. 'Dad has gone, and I do miss him, but I can finally live and be me. So, I want loads of advice. What dating apps are good? Also, do I pay on the first date or do we go Dutch?'

'Fantastic, Anne. Boys? Girls?' asked Lily.

'Let me start with the men, but if I can't find "the one" then watch out girls!'

Everybody burst out laughing, except one.

'Dating is nothing to laugh about,' Hamish vented, before heading off to the toilet.

'What's got on his gonads?' exclaimed Anne.

08:30 a.m.

They all sat around the pretty empty crime board. Placed at the top was the picture of Ravi taken at the scene where his body had been found.

'This is our victim, Ravi Patel-Kumar,' Isaac stated. 'He was thirty-eight and mostly went by the name Ravi Patel. We are still waiting for Alex to come and give us a detailed account of what actually happened, but initial thoughts as we have previously discussed, are that he was strangled. His husband has identified the body and will be interviewed this morning. He was too distressed to answer anything yesterday. I don't have much more to go on. Did any of you find anything out?'

'Sir,' Lily said, still wearing her odd socks in memory of her father. 'I did google and search social media for Ravi Patel. Do you have any idea how many results I got?'

'Three,' he joked.

'I wish. I then tried Patel-Kumar, but I still got several results. This is going to be a hard search.'

There was a general conversation going on between them all. No one had found anything of significance.

'I think once we speak again with his husband, we will get more of an insight into our victim,' Isaac told the group. 'We will then hopefully be able to streamline our searches. We need to know if he can think of anyone who would hurt Ravi.'

'Is his husband a suspect?' voiced Faisal.

'Not sure,' DCI Davidson said. 'Why don't you do some digging? See what you can find out about him. In the meantime, Hamish and I will go back and speak with Mr Kumar.'

DC Potter pulled an irritated face.

10:00 a.m.

The drive over to interview Rakesh started in near silence. Isaac had tried to engage his DC in conversation, but Hamish looked out the window and responded with one-word answers each time. This wasn't like the jovial Scotsman, and DCI Davidson was concerned. Yesterday evening, as they were all leaving the office, he had heard the DC snapping at Anne and Lily. He hadn't heard exactly what it was about, but they both appeared annoyed. Then he barked earlier at Anne.

'How do you find the dating apps?'

DC Potter looked around at his boss.

'Sir?' he uttered, his tone a mix of confusion and concern about the direction of the conversation.

'I noticed you slightly reacted this morning to Anne mentioning them.'

'It doesn't matter.'

'OK,' Isaac said.

'Actually, it does matter,' Hamish said, becoming animated in his movements. 'They destroy your soul. You match with someone and get chatting, and then the following day you're ghosted. I am sick to death of being treated like I don't matter. It's all my fault. I probably haven't used the right profile pictures. Most are either of me at the gym or with my top off, which I thought is what they'd want to see. That is probably going to attract a certain kind of woman, I suppose. I guess it gives them the impression that I'm all beef with no substance. Last year, I dated Amanda for a couple of months. She works at the front desk, but she ended up telling me I was monotonous. That all I could speak of was how many repetitions I did at the gym, and how much protein I needed to consume in a day. So, of course, she dumped me. I'm boring.' Hamish said as he let out a deep sigh.

'You're anything but boring,' volunteered Isaac.

'I'm single, shit at my job and have no friends. I love the gym, but that isn't enough for me. I've lost direction in my life, and why the hell am I telling you all of this? Please, just forget I said anything. There's the house we want.'

Rakesh had seen their car arrive and was standing on the doorstep to greet them and then he showed them into the lounge. The first thing Hamish noticed were more pictures.

'I see you're displaying more photos than last time.'

'Yeah, I wanted more of Ravi on show. I still can't believe that he's gone and in such a horrific way.'

'When did you last see your husband?'

DCI Davidson was pleased his DC was taking the lead.

'27th October. We had all been to a concert.'

'What time was this?'

'9 p.m. I would say. We all left separately to get trains home.'

'Why weren't you travelling with your husband?' DC Potter asked.

'Ravi had moved out for a while. We hadn't been getting on. I guess there is no point hiding stuff from you.' Rakesh flounced over to the sofa and practically threw himself onto it. 'The thing is, I was having an affair. I know it was a stupid thing to do, but Ravi found out and wanted to get away for a few nights. However, we did talk at the concert and I hoped he would eventually come home.'

'You said "we" all left the concert?' Hamish said. 'Who are "we"?'

'Well, I was waiting for you to ask me if there was anyone I thought would harm Ravi,' Rakesh said with an air of superiority.

Hamish raised his eyebrows and stood poised with his pen and notebook.

'Please go on.'

'Dipen Patel is, or should I say was, Ravi's cousin. Norton Greene and Agatha Hawksworth were his friends, and Parveena Johal was his business partner.'

'And why do you suspect these four people?'

'They were all at the concert, although I didn't see Dipen. In fact, apart from Ravi, none of us saw him. He must have left earlier than we all did.'

'So,' Hamish said. 'Why is them being at the concert important? And why do you believe they would want to hurt your husband?'

'That is something you'll need to discuss with them,' Rakesh said frostily. 'Can we call it a day? I have a headache coming on. I was up half the night crying and I kept reaching out to Ravi's side of the bed. Please catch whoever did this horrible thing. He was such a nice person and didn't deserve to die in this dreadful way.'

'Just one more thing, Mr Kumar,' Hamish said. 'You've been limping and have a nasty bruise on your face. How did that occur?'

'A guy I was seeing decided he wanted things to end and beat me up as a goodbye present.'

'There will be a family liaison officer coming to meet you today,' Isaac voiced. 'He will stay with you to give support as you come to terms with what has happened. His name is Joseph.'

The detectives got back into their car and headed back to the station. The silence between them had returned until they were almost at their destination when DC Potter finally spoke.

'What a rat-like man. I neither like nor trust him.'

38

Cause of Death!

4th November 2019

08:00 a.m.

The team sat in their usual seats except for Anne who had sent a group text asking everyone what they wanted from the coffee shop as it was her treat. The message had promised her DCI that she'd get them from a local business.

'Morning, campers. Hi-de-Hi,' she yelled out as she came in with drinks and refreshments.

'Someone is happy,' Lily all but shouted, as she rushed over to help her colleague.

'It's pouring from the heavens, I got splashed by cars three times, but all is right with the world.'

'You got a match on a dating app,' Faisal surmised.

'His name is Nathan, he's fifty-two, works in finance, amateur cook and loves detective shows! Thank you very much!'

For the next few moments, DC Michaels held court and the others were loving this new version of somebody who was already rather wonderful. Even DC Potter seemed pleased for her.

'Right,' bellowed DCI Davidson, making them all jump.

'Lavender and orange tea, sir,' Anne said, passing his drink to him.

'Creep,' Jian whispered from the side of his mouth as they both giggled.

'We have had a couple of days to focus on the death of this man,' Isaac said as he tapped the picture on the crime board. 'I have also given you the names of people his husband told us about.'

As Isaac spoke, a call came through to the room. Jian answered it.

'Sir, Alex has requested your presence. The final report is through for the cause of death.'

'Thanks, Jian. I'll be back soon and update you all. Faisal, with me, please.'

DS Wong beamed a smile as he watched his boyfriend heading off with their boss. Lily witnessed.

'You two make such a gorgeous couple,' she said.

'Shush,' Jian said, winking. 'No one else knows.'

'Thought I was his favourite on this case,' whispered Hamish.

Mortuary

Five minutes later, the DCI and DC Asher were in the mortuary. The smell of chemicals was overpowering. The post-mortem examination room was further down the corridor to the left. As they went through the door, Faisal saw two bodies waiting to be dissected. One was covered, but the other was naked and looked like she had died from a gunshot judging by the hole in her chest.

Faisal, captivated by the room, felt compelled to move closer for a better look at the woman. She could have only been in her late teens. Something about the bullet hole intrigued him.

'So young,' he sighed.

At the next table, Alex was calling them over. Their victim was still having the last parts of the examination done.

'Morning,' Isaac said.

'Back at ya,' Alex replied, at the same time smiling at Faisal. 'Asphyxiation, which I believe were your first thoughts. Although the scarf was a giveaway, we needed to verify. Come over for a closer look.'

DC Asher didn't need to be asked twice. He shot over and took in the entire scene.

'His Hyoid bone is fractured.'

'His what?' both detectives said in unison.

'It's a bone that is held in place by muscles and helps with the movement of his tongue and swallowing. This was a tight strangulation. He was asphyxiated with the scarf, which we have sent off to be analysed. Can you see the bruising on the muscles?'

They both nodded.

'The right side is slightly more damaged than the left. This might, and I say might, mean the person who did this was right-handed. However, that may not be the case. Mr Patel-Kumar was dead before he went into the water, but he would have known he was being killed as it would have taken around five to seven minutes for death to occur. He would have got weaker with each passing minute. The poor man would have been in terrible pain and likely frightened beyond understanding. This was a horrible way to die.'

The detectives spent some more time looking over the body, trying to imagine what he went through in his last moments.

'I can see a lot of bruising on the rest of his body. What do you think happened?' Isaac asked.

Alex made some mouth movements from side to side as he thought about the question. He wanted to give a systematic answer.

'He has some faded discolouring to his stomach, which tells me he took a beating about a month ago, probably a punch. This was a nasty attack, so if I were you I'd check local A&E departments to see if he got himself checked out. The other marks you can see are more recent indicating they were most likely from the night of the murder. We can make out a contusion that came from a left-handed punch into the stomach. The mark made by this attack shows the thumb on the right side, making it a left-handed person. Whoever did this will have a very painful and bruised hand. The victim also sustained a kick to the lower abdomen, evidenced by the imprint of a shoe's toe. Again, this was a powerful assault and Mr Patel-Kumar would have been in great pain as one of these assaults also broke his ribs. I can't tell whether the same person did the punch and the kick. There also isn't enough of an imprint of the shoe to tell us the make or size.'

'The poor man,' sighed Faisal.

'You can see the deep purple marks on his fingers,' Alex continued. 'These were made as he tried to pull the scarf away from his throat. There is even small amounts of his blood. He definitely fought back because the discolouration was widespread, and I say good for him.'

Silence enveloped the three men. As Faisal reflected on the victim's last hours, he felt a growing sense of distress.

'Alex, anything more?' Isaac asked.

'Well, I haven't looked at his brain yet, but that is next. I wanted to get you down here once I knew the cause of death. The absence of defensive marks, apart from those on his fingers suggests he was strangled from behind. The additional marks and bruises likely resulted from the time that his body was in the water, colliding with riverbanks and walls.'

'Where is his left eye?' asked DC Asher.

'Eaten by fish,' Alex replied.

09:30 a.m.

With everyone back by the crime board, DC Asher gave them a detailed account of what they had just heard.

'So we are looking for a right-handed male?' DC Potter suggested.

'Why does it have to be a male?' asked DC Tovey.

'Because,' huffed Hamish, 'to kill a male over five to seven minutes, you'd need to be strong.'

'Woman can be strong. Also, in extreme circumstances, the weakest can overcome the near impossible,' barked Lily.

'Look,' Isaac groaned. 'Alex just gave us some suggestions, which may or may not prove correct. A TV report is scheduled for 1 p.m. today, seeking potential witnesses. Due to the state of the body after being in the water, the time of death is not accurate so we are hoping some people come forward. But remember there will also be the cranks. Lily, Faisal, and Anne keep looking at the names Mr Kumar gave us, go through Ravi's social media and bank accounts and try to find out where his veterinary practice is. We forgot to ask his husband.'

Hamish took this last comment as a direct dig at him as he had led the questions at that interview.

'What do you want me to do, sir?' he asked.

'DC Potter, contact local A&Es. Get in touch with his GP. Jian, get ready and then you and I will visit his cousin, Dipen Patel.'

39

Jian & Faisal

4th November 2019

11:30 a.m.

Jian was thirty-one, originally from China and was considered a nine in the gay world. His black hair seemed to get thicker each year, and his youthful looks never appeared to diminish. Standing in the changing room waiting for Faisal to appear, he adjusted his clothes in the mirror. Ever since he started dating DC Asher, his life felt complete.

Faisal, a mixed-raced twenty-eight-year-old with a strong East London accent, came into the room and embraced his boyfriend.

'We need to be careful,' DS Wong said, but couldn't let go.

'It's fine, no one suspects,' was the innocent reply. 'Are we OK?'

Jian was stunned by the question.

'What do you mean? Everything was great this morning over breakfast. Has something happened?'

'Oh, no! Sorry. I mean, are we OK at work? You're a DS. If it gets awkward for us, then I'd be happy to move to a different department. That's all I meant.'

DS Wong looked relieved.

'I have loved living with you for the past year. I never expected to fall in love with someone from work.'

'But you're a nine,' Faisal croaked, 'and I'm barely a six!'

'Is this about your acne scars? You are beautiful exactly the way you are. I'd score you a ten.'

They kissed.

'Is it wrong that I'm so fascinated by seeing dead bodies?' Faisal asked, parting from DS Wong.

'There was a young woman with a bullet hole in her chest and I couldn't stop looking at it. How can such a tiny piece of metal cause death? Don't get me started on our victim's body without an eye.'

'You're proving to be an excellent detective. You consider the smallest details, which many of us often overlook.'

'Who is cooking tonight?'

'I'll make us a Chinese chicken, roast potatoes and a salad with my special lemon and mayonnaise dressing,' Jian said as he held Faisal's face and gently kissed him on the tip of his nose.

'I love you, DS Wong,' Faisal whispered.

'Ditto, DC Asher. Now let me go and meet Dipen Patel with the boss.'

40

Dipen

4th November 2019

12:00 p.m.

The noon race from Newmarket had just started. Dipen had £250 on Lame Duck to win. The odds were in his favour, despite the horse's name. He was up on his feet, screaming at the TV and acting like he was the jockey. The bottle of water that he had in his hand went flying and nearly hit a guy sitting in the corner. The horse won! Securing his first victory in weeks, he was overjoyed as he proceeded to the counter to collect his winnings.

The main door opened and the detectives walked in. Customers couldn't help but take a second glance at their confident demeanour. Some felt incredibly uncomfortable. Over by the counter was the only Indian man in the establishment.

'Mr Dipen Patel?' Isaac asked, showing his identification.

'Who is asking?' he replied before seeing the badge.

'Your sister let us know where she thought you'd be. Can we please talk?'

'Why? What about?'

The other punters were now relieved that they weren't the ones being spoken with.

Dipen took them over to a quiet corner.

'Is here OK?' he asked.

'It is of a sensitive nature, Mr Patel.'

'I'll ask if there is a room we can use out the back,' volunteered DS Wong.

A few moments later, they were sitting in a dank room with blue paint peeling from the walls. The carpet was heavily stained and the yellowish ceiling showed signs that it hadn't been repainted since a smoking ban had come into force. Screams could be heard from the shop as the next race had evidently started.

'Can you please confirm your name?'

'You just called me by it, outside,' he replied to the DCI. 'It's Dipen Patel.'

'Mr Patel, I have some bad news. Your cousin Ravi Patel has been murdered. We believe in the past few days, but after he was killed, he was dumped in a river so precise dating is proving difficult.'

'I saw him on the 27th. We went to a concert together. It can't be him. Why would someone want to hurt him?' Dipen closed his eyes and lowered his head.

'We don't have the answers yet, but we will.'

'How do you know it's him?'

'His husband has identified the body, plus he had things in his wallet. I'm sorry for your loss.'

Dipen sat and kept shaking his head in utter disbelief. The stuffiness of the small room was beginning to suffocate him.

'Can you please tell us more about when you last saw your cousin?' asked Jian.

'Yeah, we travelled to a concert together. Sorry, I think I'm going to be sick,' Dipen said as he rushed to grab the wastepaper bin in the corner of the room.

Jian gagged and retched as Dipen emptied his stomach contents. Isaac had momentarily left to get the young man some fresh water.

Once he had been able to compose himself, the detectives continued with their questions.

'How was he on the journey?'

'OK, I guess,' Dipen said, staring back at DCI Davidson.

'Did you stay with him at the concert?'

'I did, yes.' Jian looked at his boss with a quizzical expression.

'Are you sure, Mr Patel?'

'Why are you questioning me?'

'Because Mr Kumar told us that although he knew you had arrived with Mr Patel, no one else saw you.'

Dipen took some time to gather his thoughts.

'Oh, that's right. Sorry, the news of Ravi has messed with my thoughts. I stayed for about half an hour but left, as I wasn't getting the vibe. I texted Ravi to let him know.'

Feeling slightly perplexed by his answer, Isaac tried a different angle.

'What was your relationship like with your cousin?'

'Great, we were really close. Hey, wait, am I a suspect?'

'We are just gathering facts at the moment. Can you think of anyone who would do this to him?' asked Isaac.

'No. Who would do something so horrible as to kill another human being? How was he murdered?'

'Asphyxiation. He was strangled and then his body was disposed of into the river.'

Dipen grabbed the bin and vomited again.

'I've noticed,' DCI Davidson said, 'that you have a nasty scar on your nose that still looks reasonably fresh. How did that happen?'

'Nothing to do with Ravi,' was the only answer given.

'We will need to speak with you again,' Isaac said as the two men left.

Upon returning to the car, they both sat in silence, lost in thought for a short while.

'So, DS Wong, what are your thoughts on Dipen Patel?'

Jian rubbed his chin and screwed up his face.

'He looked genuinely distraught, and you can't fake vomiting. I don't believe he killed his cousin. Trust me, I'm never wrong.'

41

New Information

5th November 2019

08:30 a.m.

The morning routine was in place. On the crime board were now three faces: Ravi, Rakesh and Dipen.

'So is the husband a suspect?' asked Faisal.

'Yes,' answered Hamish in a slightly aggressive tone.

'DC Potter has picked up a feeling about Mr Kumar, hence he is on the board. However, we need to remain open-minded for both men. They aren't officially suspects yet, but as they say in all the good police dramas, "they are helping us with our enquiries," and I have a fancy to trust his thoughts,' DCI Davidson said.

Jian then gave the team a rundown of their meeting with Dipen Patel.

'I liked him,' he stated. 'He seemed genuinely shocked to hear about his cousin.'

'Decent actor?' volunteered Lily.

'Maybe,' replied Jian.

'How is everyone getting on with scouring the internet for information about our victim?'

'Sir,' Anne said in response to her boss. 'I have requested his mobile phone records from his provider. They said it could take a few days. I phoned Mr Kumar to get the number as no sign of the actual phone yet. I also got bank details, which Faisal was working on.'

'I have had an initial look through his accounts,' DC Asher said. 'There are personal and business ones, but they all look in appropriate order. There are regular payments from his business account, the usual direct debits and standing orders from his personal one. They are all within the same banking group. I will do some more digging. I noticed that there wasn't a joint account with his husband. Also, I saw that the last transaction made on his debit card was on 27th October at 8:27 p.m. I googled the name on the receipt and it's the venue where the concert was held.'

DC Tovey waited to make sure that Faisal had finished before starting her turn.

'I'm going through his laptop which we collected from his house, and will be going over to his workplace tomorrow to look through his computer and diaries and also speak with the staff there,' said Lily. 'Oh, and still not much to find on social media.'

'Good work, team,' acknowledged Isaac. 'Jian and I will go and speak with Norton Greene. This was another person our victim's husband alluded to.'

As the team started to disperse and begin their tasks for the day, Alex came through the main doors and beckoned everyone to sit back by the crime board.

'Hey, sorry to interrupt,' he announced. 'I just want to give you an update.'

'Great,' said Isaac. 'Let's hear it.'

'Firstly, nothing back on the scarf yet, but it may take a few days due to strike action within the department. I'll let you know as soon as I hear anything. I'm calling the time of death late on 27th October or early on the 28th. That is as close as I can get it. Sorry, I know that isn't ideal.'

'That fits with the final payment on his cards,' Faisal chipped in.

'However, what I wanted to say was that our victim was an incredibly sick man.'

These words caused the detectives to all look at each other with raised eyebrows and exaggerated eye movements.

'How so?' asked Lily.

'Mr Patel had a brain tumour, and a particularly nasty one. I have dispatched samples to a hospital specialising in neuro-oncology to confirm the precise type; It was large. It was remarkable how this man was able to function on a daily basis. He would definitely have had symptoms such as blurred vision, memory loss, confusion, headaches and potentially other symptoms as well. I want to wait to hear back from neurology, but in my experience of these types of tumour, which is limited, he would probably have had four to six months to live; maybe even shorter. If the person who killed Mr Patel had only waited a little while longer, the tumour would have done the job for them.'

Alex's words profoundly impacted the team, particularly Faisal who appeared visibly upset.

'This is too sad for words,' he croaked. 'He was going to die anyway, so why did he have to be murdered in such a brutal manner?'

Jian wanted to go over and put his arms around him, but instead indicated with his eyes to Lily, who took the hint and went to Faisal to comfort him.

'Hamish,' bellowed Isaac, 'Did you go to the hospitals and speak with the GP about Ravi's potential visit following his beating a month ago?'

'Shit! I forgot.'

'Do it today, but now also try to find out if his tumour was known about. Also, team, please don't mention this new piece of information to anyone. Let's get the details back first from the neuro team. Also, before you all go, can someone contact the train company that operates between his home station and the closest to the venue of the concert? Ask for their CCTV. Let's see if we can spot Mr Patel and his assailant if we're lucky.'

'I'll do that,' DC Michaels said.

Alex left the room, and the team scattered to their desks to begin their searches. DC Potter grabbed his coat and headed off without saying goodbye to anyone. Isaac watched him leave.

42

Norton

5th November 2019

10:30 a.m.

The drive over to Dr Greene's practice was an interesting one. Jian had googled the man to find his working address, as they assumed he'd be at his office on a Tuesday. What had come up was a barrage of complaints and accusations against him. Quotes from Twitter and Instagram were front and foremost. They were damning.

DS Wong read a few from each site, and DCI Davidson listened curiously.

'Nothing there to link him to Ravi,' Isaac said. 'Remember, we are just talking to him today based on what Mr Kumar told us. He is not currently a suspect.'

Jian nodded.

The weather outside was gloomy. The pleasant October had turned into a wet and windy November. Storm clouds were gathering and the temperature had dropped.

'Tell me your thoughts on DC Potter,' Isaac asked.

'Woah, where did that come from?'

'I'm concerned about him. You might have picked up on something I haven't. Do you talk?'

Jian thought for a moment.

'Yeah, I've noticed a change in him, but not sure if I could pinpoint what has triggered it. I mean, he is unlucky in love, but is that enough? We all go through crap in our lives from time to time. Maybe it's just Hamish's turn. I'll keep an eye on him.'

'I'd appreciate that,' Isaac said. 'Anyhow, any news from you about things happening in your life?'

'No, sir,' Jian lied. 'All quiet.'

DCI Davidson smiled broadly as he turned the car into the street they needed.

'Jian, we all know.'

'Know what?' he cautiously replied.

'That you and Faisal are dating, and have been for quite some time. And as long as it doesn't get in the way of your work, then I think it's fantastic that you have found each other. Some people never find the right person.'

'Hamish?'

'Maybe.'

'I can't believe you all know. We were so careful to keep it from you all.'

'Really?' laughed the DCI.

11:00 a.m.

Norton sat in his armchair, holding a glass of brandy. The fourth since he had arrived. His left hand, wrapped in bandages, throbbed with significant pain, while his face bore a patchwork of stubble and bits of tissue stuck to the nicks from shaving too quickly. His body odour had got to the pungent stage, and he was wearing the same clothes for the past three days.

He had stopped looking at social media as it was depressing him, and he hadn't spoken with anyone for days. Therefore, when a voice called out from the reception area, it startled him and he knocked over his glass.

'Who's there?' he called out. 'How did you get in?'

'Mr Norton Greene?' Isaac enquired, taken aback by the state of the man standing in front of him. 'The door was open.'

'Who are you?'

Introductions were made, but Norton didn't get any more welcoming.

'Mr Greene, we are here because of a death that happened on 27th October.'

'I know. Someone murdered Ravi. His husband called me, but I also saw the news report on the television yesterday.'

'Did you know the victim well?' Jian asked, trying to read Norton's facial expressions and body language.

'I knew him exceptionally well. I guess you'd say we were best friends. We met on the first day of university and have been in each other's lives ever since. Rakesh's call has devastated me. I was already feeling down, but to hear about Ravi was shattering. He was such a kind soul, and didn't deserve to die in that awful way.'

'When did you last see him?' continued DS Wong.

'Erm… It would have been around 9 p.m. on the 27th of last month. We were all at a concert having a fantastic time; enjoying each other's company.'

'I checked, and the concert ended at 11 p.m. Why weren't you with Ravi up until the end if you were all at the gig together?'

'You know what these places are like. We were dancing, going back and forth to get food and drinks. Maybe I saw him later than I thought. Why are you asking me these questions?'

'Are you left or right-handed, Mr Greene?'

Norton looked at the DCI with a bemused face.

'Left. Why?'

'I notice you have a bandaged left hand. How did you hurt it?'

'I trapped it in my car door. Stupid mistake to happen. I was obviously distracted.'

'The post-mortem performed on Mr Patel showed a left-handed, clenched fist impression on his skin, with intensive internal bruising to his muscles. The person that inflicted this punch would have been left with an injured left hand.'

Norton realised that he hesitated too long after DCI Davidson had spoken.

'Yes, it was me. We argued, and I lashed out. It was a pent-up situation that got out of control.'

'What were the circumstances that led to the altercation?'

'I don't remember. We had all been drinking, and you know how it is. Someone says something slightly wrong and then everything becomes fragile.'

'Did you also kick Mr Patel?'

'No, but I know who did. His husband. They didn't know, but I was standing nearby and saw Rakesh do it.'

The detectives made notes and pondered on what they had been told. Something didn't feel quite right to the DCI. Norton was looking fidgety and this was ringing alarm bells.

'Before we leave you to get on with your day, can you tell us who you think would want to hurt Mr Patel?'

'No, not really. He had upset his cousin and his business partner, Parveena Johal, but they aren't likely to be killers. Wasn't it a random attack?'

'We're keeping an open mind. Did you notice anything strange about Mr Patel in the months and weeks leading up to his murder?'

Norton thought for a few moments.

'He did develop a nervous habit of rubbing his head and repeating himself. He said he'd been told it was stress-related. To be honest with you, his husband was unfaithful on many occasions and the rest of us thought this was the reason for his nervousness.'

'Thank you, Mr Greene. If we need to speak with you again, what is the best way to get hold of you?'

'If,' replied Norton, emphasising the word, 'we need to speak again, DCI Davidson, please address me as Dr Greene and not Mr.'

Norton wrote down his number for them and then showed them out.

'In death, you still haunt me, Ravi Patel,' he said as he watched the detectives from his office window get into their car.

As they drove back to the police station, the two men discussed Norton.

'Thoughts?' Jian asked.

'Slimy. There is more to that relationship that he was telling. I want a background check on that man. Also, I want us to go and see those other two names given to us by Mr Kumar, Agatha Hawksworth and Parveena Johal. We also need to pay the said husband another visit. He withheld from us that he attacked our victim.'

43

Updates

6th November 2019

08:30 a.m.

The crime board was now showing four faces. Norton's had been added with the ones of Ravi, Rakesh, and Dipen.

'I'm declaring these three as official suspects,' Isaac stated. 'Both the husband and a friend assaulted the victim on the evening of the murder, and Dr Greene mentioned Dipen Patel as a person who may have also inflicted harm. They are therefore staying on the board. I'm also keen to talk with Miss Hawksworth and Miss Johal. This already feels like a crime of intent and not a random attack. Ravi was not the victim of a robbery.'

The mutterings between the detectives were a good sign of thoughts and ideas being shared.

'Updates, please,' Isaac called out.

'Train CCTV has been requested,' shouted back Anne. 'Phone records not back yet.'

'I'm still looking through his laptop. There are emails to sort through. I was also going to go over to Mr Patel's veterinary practice today,' Lily said.

'I'll come with you, DC Tovey,' Isaac said. 'We can interview his work partner at the same time.'

'Still looking through data from his bank,' Faisal stated. 'However, I also scouted out Rakesh Kumar's banking details. They both banked with the same provider. I can see transactions being transferred between both of their accounts. But, here it gets interesting; Rakesh has a stand-alone account with a different bank. There has been £10,000 in it, but currently only showing £1500. The deposits are always large amounts. £300-£500, and lately by companies rather than individuals. There is no link to Ravi Patel throughout the statements. It is my thinking that only Mr Kumar knows about this account. I would therefore suggest that it is a secret bank account.'

There was an air of excitement building up as always did when more information was gathered.

'DC Potter?'

'Yes, sir,' Hamish responded. 'I found out that on 1st October he presented to a London A&E. He said he'd been mugged. They took X-rays and sent him home with painkillers. There was nothing else on his records. Zero on their system about a brain tumour. I'll contact the local hospitals, north and south of the river with a neurology-oncology department and ask if they were aware of him.' Hamish then sat down, but soon bolted up again. 'Oh, I also spoke with his GP, who was reluctant to speak with me at first. She was embarrassed that she had misdiagnosed him as having just stress-related headaches. In hindsight, she said she should have sent him for an MRI scan.'

'Great work, team. DC Potter, please carry on with hospital checks and keep up the digital footprint investigations. DC Michaels and Asher, I want you to go door to door and speak with Ravi's neighbours. Try to build up a picture of the Patel-Kumar household.'

With tasks allocated, the team went to the kitchen to grab themselves a hot drink, apart from Lily who was getting herself ready to leave with DCI Davidson. As she waited, Hamish came over.

'So, you're the favoured one this morning.'

'Meaning?' she snapped.

'I'm sick of this job. The Superintendent wants this section of the department to make cuts. If I go, cut made!'

Lily saw a real sadness in her colleague's face for probably the first time and her opinion of him changed instantly.

'Hey, come on. You're a brilliant detective. DCI Davidson won't let you go. He is doing all he can to prevent anyone from leaving. He is having meetings all the time. It isn't about just getting rid of someone. If we do that, they'll come back and say we have to make more cuts. This is about fighting and proving our worth. Sticking together and making a united stand.'

'Can I have a hug?' Hamish asked.

'Absolutely,' DC Tovey replied.

44

Parveena

6th November 2019

11:30 a.m.

Having a late breakfast, Parveena was re-watching the news from two days ago, asking for witnesses to come forward. Ravi's picture, which had been taken when he was on holiday in Greece last year, was in the top right corner. A number was scrolling across the bottom of the screen. She rewound and watched it again and again. She couldn't help the smile etched on her face.

The day had started with some sun but was now overcast and it would seem that rain was coming, maybe even a storm. Standing by her window peering out, Parveena watched as a black car approached her driveway. She knew exactly who they would be, as she had been waiting for them to come to see her. She took a deep breath and then headed for the front door.

Parveena, studying DC Tovey as she got out of the car, couldn't believe that the police allowed detectives to have pink streaks running through their hair. For this reason, and this reason alone, she already hated Lily. After introductions, they proceeded to the kitchen, which was larger than the lounge. Parveena offered to make some hot drinks, but they both declined.

'It looked like you were waiting for us, Miss Johal,' Isaac said.

'It's Parveena,' she replied. 'Well, I'd be stupid not to be expecting you, wouldn't I? There has been a murder.'

'We went to your practice first, but it's shut up.'

'Well, of course it is. Someone has killed my business partner. Do you really think I'd be working?'

The atmosphere had been noted by DCI Davidson. Parveena had barely looked them in the eye, choosing to either look straight through them or over their shoulders. She clearly did not want them there.

'We are very sorry for your loss,' Lily added. Parveena sneered back.

'What do you want?'

'When did you last see Mr Patel?'

'27th,' she responded to Isaac. 'I'm sure you already know that we were at a concert. It didn't end well, so we all left early and went our separate ways.'

'All?' questioned DC Tovey.

'Let's not play games,' Parveena hissed back. 'I've spoken with both Rakesh and Norton, so I'm fully aware of what they have told you. I even know that Norton informed you about the beatings Ravi got. I assume they didn't tell you about the pint of beer I poured onto Ravi's head? No? I didn't think so.' Parveena opened a cupboard and took out an unopened bottle of whisky.

'Why was Mr Patel treated like this by his so-called friends?' asked Isaac.

'If I'm being honest, he'd been a complete arsehole lately. Prim and proper, thinking that it's his way or no way. I've known him, knew him since we were kids playing in the streets. Over the past year he'd changed significantly and managed to fall out of favour with his friends, and I believe he'd alienated himself from us. But that doesn't mean any of us would hurt him. He was just different.'

'Anything in particular?'

'Repeating himself, forgetting things. It really disrupted our business. That's the main reason we're closed. I just couldn't trust him.'

'I'm sorry to hear that,' Isaac exclaimed. 'Can you think of anyone that would have wanted to hurt him? Maybe a disgruntled customer? Anything that you can think of would be really helpful.'

Parveena poured her second glass of drink. The detectives could tell she didn't want them there any longer than necessary.

'No,' she said. 'No one comes to mind.'

'Who else works at your practice?' DC Tovey asked.

Parveena hated this young woman.

'We had a practice nurse, but he left.'

'Why?'

'Why do you think? One of his bosses was murdered. The practice has shut down due to Ravi's conduct over the past year, resulting in financial losses. I couldn't afford to keep Kwasi on. Does that answer your question?'

Lily nodded but had a stern face.

'What is his full name?'

'Why is that important?'

'Please, just answer the question, Miss Johal.'

'Kwasi Moses,' Parveena said sharply.

The interview wasn't going well. The hostile reception they were getting was giving off "suspect" vibes and Isaac was already picturing Parveena's photo on the crime board.

'Can anyone vouch for your whereabouts once you left the concert?' he asked.

'Why are you asking me that? Do you think I had something to do with his death? Am I a suspect in his murder?'

'Routine question, Miss Johal, that's all,' Isaac smiled.

'I drove to the concert. Once we left, I came home by myself. So, no, I don't have anyone who can vouch for me.'

'Are you left or right-handed?' he asked.

'Right-handed. Why?'

'It's of no importance. Thank you for speaking with us. We will need to speak with you again.'

Once back in their car, Isaac could tell how angry his DC was. He gave her time to calm down and adjust herself.

'She is definitely going up on that crime board when I get back into the office and print off a picture. Even if it takes me hours to find one. Aaargh, what an annoying woman!' Lily vented.

'Oh, I've had much worse,' Isaac said.

'We didn't push her too hard, sir. Why not?'

'Because, DC Tovey, she isn't a suspect yet. We need to dig into their business. Look at her emails, digital footprint, computer and while you're at it, check out her bank account. We also need to track down Mr Moses and get his take on the day-to-day running of that practice. Also do an ANPR: Automatic number plate recognition, and let's see if she is telling us the truth.'

'She didn't look strong enough to carry out the murder, sir. What do you think?'

'Oh, she is. Did you not see her upper arms? She had defined muscles, which I guess comes from lugging big animals about. Especially dogs.'

Lily began rubbing her hands together with a sense of glee all over her face.

45

Isaac

7th November 2019

05:00 a.m.

Ever since Alan had moved out, Isaac struggled to sleep. He didn't know why this would be. Yet, with each passing morning, he found himself waking up earlier than the day before. Being lonely was an emotion Isaac wasn't expecting to feel. Now he was living on his own, it allowed him to reflect on the life they had been living, which had been isolating.

It had been quite closeted from the outside looking in. Following Alan's accident, they devoted most of their time to each other and initially seemed to keep others at bay. On reflection, this probably hadn't been the healthiest of decisions. Isaac was thrilled that his brother was now in a loving relationship and he wouldn't change it for the world. He just missed the life he had with him.

Outside, a dog could be heard barking. He knew by the sound of its bark that it was from a large breed. It belonged to a new family which had moved in a couple of months ago. It seemed that they put the dog into the garden when the husband departed early for work. The animal would then bark non-stop for at least an hour before being allowed back into the house. Isaac had thought about taking some sort of action but hadn't got around to it. Lately, he had no motivation to do much.

After his shower, he made himself two poached eggs; two and a half minutes in simmering water with vinegar produced the perfect breakfast. Mushrooms, grilled tomatoes and a slice of wholemeal toast had also been added to his plate. The plunger on the cafetière was pushed down, and he poured himself a strong black coffee. He then took his turn on his Scrabble app, for which he currently had two games on the go. One with his brother and the other with Jane; he was losing both.

When he had cleared away the breakfast things, he got himself dressed and headed off to work. Glenn would be waiting.

08:30 a.m.

The team slowly arrived. Jian and Faisal arrived together for the first time and looked happy with themselves. Anne flounced in with her usual coffee and pastry. Today's choice was a pain au chocolat. After their DCI, Hamish and Lily had been the next in the department and were already at their desks and logged on.

'How's Nathan?' enquired Lily.

Just hearing his name brought a smile to Anne's face.

'Well,' she said. 'He hasn't ghosted me yet.' She saw a hurt expression on Hamish's face and instantly regretted her choice of words. 'We had our first actual phone call last night. He suggested a WhatsApp video call, but I had my hair in a towel and a face pack splattered all over me.'

'What was it like?' probed Faisal.

'Dead Sea and Witch Hazel, you know, for purifying the skin.'

'I meant the call,' Faisal said as he laughed.

The team all smiled, even DC Potter.

'We are going out for dinner at the weekend. There is a nice French bistro near me, and I can't wait. It's the first date I've had for donkey's years.'

Everyone felt genuine delight for DC Michaels.

DCI Davidson left his small office and entered the main room. As he did, a text message came through to his phone. It was from Alan.

"Hey, I need to speak with you about Daisy. I'll call you later."

Isaac was now concerned that something was wrong with his brother's relationship, but he tried to put it out of his head.

'Morning everyone. I'm going to be very brief this morning. I want to speak with Agatha Hawksworth this morning. She is the final person mentioned by Rakesh Kumar. Jian, you will come with me, and everyone else please carry on with the given tasks.'

46

Agatha

7th November 2019

09:30 a.m.

Agatha had been up since 7 a.m. She had made herself a healthy breakfast and was now at her bedroom mirror straightening her hair. On her bedside cabinet was her booklet given to her yesterday when she had joined the slimming group. She had exchanged her usual vibrant colours for pastel hues, and her new glasses were of a regular size with transparent frames.

'Today is the start of the rest of your life,' she said to herself as she sorted out her hair. 'He is dead and gone, and no longer plays a role in your life.'

The doorbell rang.

When she opened the door Agatha saw two men standing in drenched raincoats. Their hair was dripping, and both looked incredibly uncomfortable.

'Miss Agatha Hawksworth?'

'Yes,' she replied to Isaac.

'I'm DCI Davidson and this is DS Wong. Can we please come in?'

Agatha stood back and gestured with her arm for them to enter. She then momentarily disappeared, coming back seconds later with a towel for each of them, which they gratefully accepted.

When they had dried themselves and Agatha had made them both a coffee, they finally sat and started the interview.

'Miss Hawksworth, do you know why we are here?'

'Ravi?' she replied to the DCI.

'Indeed. Can you tell us when you last saw him?'

'27th October, we had all been at a concert,' she said with a smile. 'Parveena has called me, so I know you are aware of how the evening ended. None of us overly liked him, except perhaps Dipen.'

'Then why was he with you at the concert if you didn't like him?' questioned Jian.

'Because when the tickets were bought, we were sort of getting on. Then we had a party for his birthday and he disgraced himself. Told terrible lies, broke confidences and upset all of us. It destroyed the relationships that we had.'

'What lies did he tell?' Jian asked.

'Not for me to say,' she said. 'Are we suspects?'

'Can you tell us what he said that particularly upset yourself?'

'He blurted out that I had had a termination. It wasn't his news to do that.'

'And what did he reveal about the others?'

'Ask them. It's not my place to say. Are we suspects?' she asked again after being ignored the first time.

'We are at this time just gathering information. Are you right or left-handed, Miss Hawksworth?'

'Right, why?'

'Just asking,' was all DS Wong would say.

Agatha continued to give quick and sharp answers. The detectives couldn't tell if she was being defensive or this was her personality. It was extremely off-putting.

'How long have you known the victim?' Jian asked.

'Don't be disrespectful! Call him by his name,' she snapped. 'Since we started at university. We were housed together along with Norton and Parveena. She is a stuck-up cow who never really liked me. I think she was jealous of my friendship with Ravi.'

'And what was your relationship like with the vic… Ravi?'

Agatha glared at DS Wong.

'People who once shared accommodation. We all stayed in touch and I suppose you'd class us as friends, but we are a strange group. We go out with each other, celebrate birthdays, Christmas, Diwali, and have in the past had holidays together. However, I don't believe we even like each other.'

The interview was drawing to a close. Agatha had remained calm and almost without emotion. She had answered the questions posed to her, but at the same time had revealed very little.

'Can you think of anyone that would want to hurt Mr Patel?' Isaac asked.

'Have you spoken with his husband? He has been cheating for years, and what he was told at the party is definitely a motive. I'd start there if I were you.' She now stood and took back the towels and showed them out.

As they walked back to the car, both pleased that the rain had stopped, Jian stopped and asked his DCI a question.

'Would you kill someone for saying you'd had a termination?'

'Yes,' said Isaac. 'I have known people kill for a lot less.'

'So, is Miss Hawksworth now a suspect?' Jian queried.

'I believe that she is. I am aware that our investigation is in its early stages and there is still a significant amount of evidence to collect, yet I am convinced that the perpetrator is among the five individuals we have already interviewed.'

'Not Dipen,' Jian volunteered.

'Let's just see what happens next,' said Isaac.

47

Alan

7th November 2019

7:00 p.m.

After finishing work for the day, Isaac headed to the supermarket. He had the notion of making a citrus chicken with garlic and honey, served with a salad. Mid-afternoon, he had texted his brother back and asked if he would like to come over for dinner and discuss his concern about Daisy. Alan declined, explaining that his girlfriend felt too fragile to be left alone. They agreed on a 9 p.m. call.

The shop was relatively quiet, so he wasn't long inside. In addition to food, he purchased an expensive bottle of white wine, fully aware that he would finish it and hoping to wake up with a clear head in the morning. Since Alan had moved out, his alcohol consumption had increased. He didn't drink every night, but whereas a bottle used to be shared, it now wasn't.

He spent the drive home pondering what his brother might want to discuss with him concerning Daisy. He went from thinking it was a relationship issue to wondering if he wanted to discuss a dinner party or a holiday abroad. Nothing prepared him for what he was soon to hear.

9:00 p.m.

Isaac cleared away his dinner things and replenished his glass with the wine. He then started a video call.

'Hey,' he said when he saw Alan's face. He felt himself instantly feeling happier. 'How are you?'

'Great, you?' was the reply.

Isaac knew his brother better than anyone else. The "great" didn't sound sincere. He was now worried but didn't want to push the issue so early into the call.

'So, I made a citrus chicken tonight. It was nice enough, but something was missing.'

'Chillies or spring onions?' Alan volunteered.

'Yeah, maybe.'

The brothers spent the next fifteen minutes catching up with each other. Alan was missing his brother as much as he was being missed.

'She,' meaning Daisy, 'calls me, Al. You know how much I hate my name being shortened. It doesn't matter how many times I ask her to call me by my full name, she doesn't. She even introduces me to people as Al. Drives me demented.'

Part of Isaac wanted to laugh, but he also knew at the same time that this would be causing his brother some distress.

Their conversation was flowing, and both were enjoying themselves. It had been some time since their last conversation, and Alan was fully aware that the silence was of his own doing.

'Sorry, Isaac. I'm being a crap younger brother. To be completely honest with you, things aren't great here. She takes a sleeping pill just after dinner and is asleep soon after. During the early part of the evening and at weekends, I'm on tenterhooks that she is going to flare up and start arguments. I know she has a complex family history and was seeing a psychologist, which is why I wanted to speak with you tonight.'

Isaac took onboard what his brother had said about the relationship, but Alan seemed ready to speak about something else.

'After the TV news report the other day about Ravi Patel, Daisy was convinced that she knew him. It's taken a couple of days, but she has worked out where she saw him. On the 1st of October she had a final session with her psychologist. She said he creeped her out and made her feel uncomfortable. She remembers the date because she spoke with the receptionist, Sorel, and said she wanted no more appointments. Daisy said that Ravi was there, and he was having an argument with the therapist. She couldn't hear what was being said, but could easily tell by their tones that it wasn't friendly. As she left, they both stormed off into his office. She saw or heard no more. However, the receptionist might have?'

'Wow,' Isaac exclaimed. 'I wasn't expecting this when you said you wanted to speak about Daisy. Was the psychologist, Norton Greene?'

'Yes,' Alan almost screamed. 'You know him?'

Isaac nodded.

The rest of the call went back to general chit-chat. A little more about the relationship, ending with Alan saying he wanted to see how things go.

'Come for dinner soon?' Isaac asked. 'Bring Daisy if you want.'

'I'll come soon, but let it just be us.'

The call ended and Isaac was delighted to have spoken with his brother, but concerned that he was generally unhappy. Dinner would need to be soon.

48

Crime Room

8th November 2019

1:00 p.m.

The detectives had spent the day scouring the internet and scrutinising the faces on the crime board, which now included Agatha and Parveena. Furthermore, following the television report, three individuals emerged as persons of interest for questioning: Daisy Christmas, Stuart Schumann and Jade-Marie Khan. Earlier, Daisy and Stuart had been interviewed by Isaac and Jian, and they were expecting Jade-Marie shortly.

Isaac called a halt to their current work and asked everyone to gather around the board. He relayed what Daisy had said to himself and Jian, which echoed what Alan had told him the previous night. He then spoke about Mr Schumann.

'Now, listen up! This is interesting. Stuart Schumann, like Daisy, was also having therapy with Norton Greene.' Isaac tapped the doctor's picture and grimaced. 'But it sounds like the psychologist abused his power, and although Stuart says he went through with the sex acts, it wasn't something that he wanted to do. The dreadful things that happened to him had a massive impact on his mental health, and sadly, he was going to throw himself off London Bridge. That is until a man came along and talked him down. Can anyone guess who that man was?'

'Ravi Patel!' exclaimed everyone gathered around the crime board.

'Wow,' said Hamish. 'What are the chances of that happening?'

The detectives continued chatting and theorising about what they had just heard. Faisal looked the most concerned.

'Sir,' he said with some hesitation. 'Was it repeated rape?'

'That is an excellent question. Stuart says that he consented by allowing the sexual acts to continue. He doesn't want to press charges. What he endured was appalling, particularly because it was inflicted by someone who was supposed to be a professional, governed by ethical codes of conduct and should have been caring for his mental well-being.' Isaac looked truly angered. 'What is nice is that we now get to hear a little more about our victim. Stuart says that Ravi was kind to him, and showed compassion after he stepped down from the bridge. He took Stuart for food and drinks to help him calm down. When he found out that Ravi and Norton were friends, he says he was so shocked and disgusted that he ran from Ravi. He regrets this now. However, since then, a few other young patients of Dr Greene have come forward all over social media; he is being named and shamed. I will leave you to research this. So,' he continued without stopping, 'I want motives found. Look at the five suspects on this board and get me motives. Anne, talk me through what we know so far.'

Anne stood and shook off the crumbs. Lily tried to stop a laugh from breaking free.

'Rakesh Kumar: Husband and serial cheater. Kicked Mr Patel at the concert. But why? We do at least know why he lied about how he hurt his leg. Has a secret bank account and Miss Hawksworth said he was told something at a party. What? Dipen Patel: Cousin. The only one who genuinely seemed upset when told the news of the murder. He lied about staying at the concert. Why? Parveena Johal: Business partner and angry with Ravi. Norton Greene: Friend who punched our victim at least once. Agatha Hawksworth: Friend who says that at a party, Ravi told lies about them all, or revealed things that he shouldn't have.' Anne scanned the room. 'Any motives spring to mind?'

The whole team shook their heads. Isaac stood again and looked mystified.

'Lily, what's outstanding?'

Lily jumped up and opened her notebook.

'Well, firstly, what happened at this party, and what was said? DC Michaels is awaiting the CCTV from the trains on the night of the murder. She is also waiting for the mobile phone records. DC Potter is chasing up neuro-oncology. Miss Johal and Dr Norton have both spoken about symptoms Ravi was showing in relation to the tumour but were obviously not aware of why he had them. I'm still going through the laptops, both work and personal. We are all still searching social media, and no news about the scarf used as the weapon.'

Everyone had taken in what both DCs had said.

'Anything else?' asked DCI Davidson.

'Anne and I started with the door-to-door interviews, but nothing has flagged yet,' said Faisal. 'We will go back out today.'

'Great, thanks everyone. Can someone please contact Ravi's husband and find out which solicitor is holding Mr Patel's will, if he has one? I want to see who stands to gain from it, and how much.'

'I'll do that,' Lily volunteered.

'Thanks,' Isaac replied. 'We are expecting Mrs Jade-Marie Khan in a few moments. Let's hope she isn't another crank and gives us some information that we can work with.'

49

Jade-Marie

8th November 2019

3:00 p.m.

Jade-Marie Khan was shown into interview room one. As she walked in she saw DCI Davidson and DS Wong sitting at a table and instantly became nervous. There was no reason for her to feel like this, but it all seemed so surreal that she was even here.

She was a black, slim woman with warming, walnut brown eyes. She had defined cheekbones and large hooped earrings secured in small earlobes. Mrs Khan was regarded by many as beautiful.

Isaac rose to his feet, extended his hand in greeting and expressed his gratitude for her visit as introductions were exchanged. Jian proposed fetching her a cup of tea or coffee, which she courteously refused opting instead to dive directly into the purpose of her visit.

'I had to come and see you when I saw the TV appeal. I met that lovely man on 26th October. He came for a massage that he thought he'd booked but hadn't. Oh, my goodness, he looked so vulnerable and I knew I had to help him. He was upset and seemed so lost. What I'm about to say to you will sound unbelievable, but I promise you it's the truth. What you need to know about me, is that I have a memory unlike anyone else I know. My brain absorbs information and I rarely forget. First, I'm married to a man from New Delhi who isn't always the best at speaking about his feelings. It's probably a cultural thing, but he feels there is a need to prove himself by being stoic in difficult circumstances. I'm sure his father's influence on his upbringing impacted him hugely. Actually, having said that out loud, I'm not sure that has any part of what I'm about to tell you. I think I'm trying to say that men struggle to talk about their feelings. Ravi was different which is why I took notice. He told me he was gay, but didn't speak of his parents, so, I don't know what part they played on him as an adult. However, within moments of our meeting, he told me so much and how those who should be close to him, were causing him such stress. DCI Davidson, he was distraught.'

The woman before him, who exuded not only confidence but a strength of character, captivated Isaac.

'We are genuinely interested in what you have to tell us. Please continue,' he said, smiling.

'He told me that his husband had numerous affairs. The two names he gave me were Edward and Ivan. No, Edvin. I'm not sure if you know this already, but Mr Patel told me that he recently told his husband and friends that he was a millionaire many times over. He was concerned that his husband would feel angry and betrayed.'

The two detectives turned and looked at each other with stunned expressions written all over their faces.

'Are you sure?' Jian said. 'Sorry, I didn't mean that to sound patronising.'

'DS Wong, your job is to ask questions and wheedle out the cranks. I get that.'

The revelation had caused a silence. DCI Davidson was wondering why DC Asher hadn't picked up on this information when he was searching through their finances.

'His cousin, I believe, is Dipen?' She saw the men nodding. 'Owes £200,000. Ravi said that Dipen wasn't aware that he had so much money when he asked him to help him out, just thought he had more from an inheritance than he was letting on. He turned the request down as he thought his foolish cousin should get himself out of trouble rather than letting someone else do it for him.'

Jian was writing everything down, despite the tape machine recording the interview. Isaac was picturing the crime board tomorrow morning with so much more detail. They both sat in intrigue, wondering what this storyteller was going to say next. Surely there wasn't anything else as revealing?

'There was a male psychologist, but I can't remember his name. Norman? Nigel? I'm not going to recall it, sorry. Ravi described him as "*a nasty man.*" He had been seducing his clients in the name of "therapy." One young man tried to take his own life, but Ravi said he stopped him. His business partner, Parmella, no Parveena, was a drinker and recently some animals had died under her care. However, the interesting part of these two, is that he reported them both to their governing bodies and both their practices had ceased operating due to pending investigations.'

The wave of unbelievable information that was flooding out of the woman in front of them was overwhelming. The detectives each were hoping that Jade-Marie didn't turn out to be an eccentric. They desperately wanted her information to be true. What she was saying was blowing their case wide open.

'Shall I continue? I have more to say.'

The men simultaneously nodded their heads. Jian even had his mouth slightly open.

'There was an ex-girlfriend, but I really can't remember her name, but she scared him. He actually used that word; scared. At some point, he had got her pregnant, and she insisted that he made her go for termination. Ravi said this wasn't true. She made him go with her for it, but he told her she didn't need to. Oh, I'm hoping I'm remembering all of this correctly. That man had such an emotional impact on me, and maybe that is why I remember so much of what he divulged. When I was having my dinner and watching TV, and the news report came on, I actually burst out crying. My husband didn't understand what was going on. I had massaged him. That poor, poor man. He was so delightful, but seemed scared, lonely, disorientated and miserable. Please find out who did this to him. I only knew him for the briefest of moments, but I felt such a connection with him.'

They all rose and went back into the main office. Jade-Marie had tear stains on her cheeks that were genuine.

'Mrs Khan,' DCI Davidson uttered. 'Thank you for all this information. It is evidently a lot for us to process, and verify, but we thank you for coming forward.'

'I just want poor Mr Patel to rest in peace, and for the culprit to get what's coming.'

Isaac walked Jade-Marie to the main entrance. There was definitely something about her that he resonated with. She gave off such a warm vibe that he already believed everything she had said.

'If we need to contact you again, what is the best way?'

'Mobile please, I rarely check my emails.'

'Before you go, is there anything else you can think of that might be of any use to us?'

Jade-Marie screwed up her face, and Isaac could tell that she was thinking through his question.

'Well,' she said. 'Of the ex-girlfriend, he said that she worried him the most.'

'That's interesting,' Isaac replied.

'Oh! I'm not sure if this is anything to go by, but the only one he said he loved, was Dipen.'

50

Further Information

13th November 2019

8:00 a.m.

It had been a few days since Jade-Marie had revealed so much about the five suspects on the crime board. DCI Davidson had given each of his team one of them to investigate; he had taken on Ravi. He wanted as much information as he could get before returning to interview each of them again.

Everyone was waiting for their DCI to join them. They could all see him in his office talking on the phone. The way he tugged at his hair and the scowl on his face suggested that Superintendent Chandra was making demands of him.

'He seems extremely irritated,' Hamish observed.

'If he doesn't tell us what that call was about, then after our briefing I am going to go and ask him,' Lily stated. 'By the way, DC Michaels, how was the date on Saturday with Nathan?'

Anne went a little red in the face.

'It got postponed, but only until this coming Saturday. No issue. His son was down unexpectedly from Ayr, and he rarely gets to see him so we just changed the date. We have been chatting each day, so all is good.'

Isaac came out of his office and was taking in deep breaths trying to calm himself down. As expected, he said nothing to his team, but they were all aware of what had been said. Further cuts were needed, and that likely meant one of them.

'OK, let's get started,' he said, with more of an irritated voice than he meant. 'I want us to speak about each person on this board, updating us all on where we are with them. Then I want to go back and question them. I'll start. Mr Ravi Patel was murdered we believe on 27th October 2019. Once strangled, his body was subsequently dumped into the river. Ah, that reminds me. I had a call with Alex Poole last night who said that the scarf report came back and there were no fingerprints on the fabric. There were small amounts of blood, but it only belonged to the victim. Probably from his fingers as he tried to pull the material from his neck. However, the label interested him, but he didn't say why and I forgot to ask. The water and river conditions had practically faded the writing, so he sent it off to a laboratory. He hopes that by using fancy techniques such as vacuum chambers, potions, and special lighting, we will get a name from it. Once the results are back he will notify me straight away.' He watched as they all nodded. 'What I can make out about our victim was that he appeared to be a nice guy. Of all the people we have spoken with so far, they have mostly said that he was genuine and were upset by his death, apart from four of the suspects who didn't seem that affected. Jade-Marie was more traumatised than Ravi's husband. Lily got me the name of his solicitor, so I can now tell you what was in his will. Certain animal charities benefit, as well as his friend Bilam, who is the executor, and following my telephone conversation with her yesterday, is deeply distraught about his murder and told me that he was a good person. Norton Greene and Agatha Hawksworth both get £300,000 and Dipen and his sister, Beena, both will get £500,000.' There were whistles around the room as they comprehended the amount of money in play.

'There are certain legal considerations concerning their veterinary practice; however, Parveena Johal is also set to receive £300,000. The rest, and we are talking millions, goes to his husband, Rakesh Patel-Kumar. The money was concealed in a bank account in India, which is why DC Asher couldn't locate it in his UK accounts. That amount of money gives each one a vastly transparent motive.'

The mood in the room was electric, and each detective was buzzing with excitement and keen to get their turn in speaking.

'Hamish,' Isaac said as he nodded in the Scotsman's direction.

'So, I took Rakesh. He is such a snake and not a nice person. He was employed at a shop but was let go recently because of the number of sick days he took in the last year. His workmates didn't overly like him. They said he was materialistic and was obsessed with money. He does possess a "secret" bank account, as Faisal has mentioned, but there's nothing out of the ordinary about it.' Hamish took a seat, signalling that he had finished.

The next to go was Anne.

'I had Norton, and what a creep he is! I managed to speak briefly with his secretary, Sorel Mawsby, who confirmed that there was an altercation between the psychologist and our victim on 1st October and Ravi left the office holding himself awkwardly and in obvious pain. That's the day he went to A&E, and we have now confirmed that Dr Greene has punched Ravi at least twice.' The room noises were in agreement with DC Michaels. 'Social media is full of hashtags warning people to stay away from him. As you told us following your interview with Jade-Marie, he was sexually inappropriate with his patients, and they have united to come forward with their allegations. That man is never going to work as a psychologist again. This now leads me on to his practice. I called his governing body yesterday who confirmed that he is under investigation and that it was Mr Ravi Patel-Kumar who reported him; motive number two for Dr Norton Greene, first being the reveal at the party.'

This was the part of a case that thrilled DCI Davidson. When finally evidence started coming in, and the momentum was driving his team forward to solve the murder. He couldn't help standing by the board and smiling at them all. His conversation with his Superintendent was momentarily forgotten.

'Parveena Johal,' Lily said as she got up from her seat. 'Like the others, I do not like this woman and that's just from meeting her once. I have been through the computer at their practice, and there were more animal deaths this year than any other. Not only that, but I am also trying to get hold of Kwasi Moses who was their nurse. I want to find out what he knows and which of the animals were potentially killed due to malpractice by the vet. Also, I did find on her personal email address just one email from Ravi, and it was about a presentation she did in Paris on 25th September. It didn't go well for her. The email is fairly abusive, considering we think he was a nice person. He uses the hashtag #Parisvetconference2019 throughout. I have searched this, and she basically made fools of them both and their practice.'

'Check how many of them, if any, were in Paris. I don't know why I want to know. I just do,' Isaac said.

Lily stood and waited to make sure her boss had finished before continuing.

'Like Anne, I also spoke with her governing body, and yep, Ravi also reported her as well, which has all but destroyed the business; also motive number two for Miss Johal'.

Those who had spoken now looked at both DC Asher and DS Wong. Jian nodded at Faisal to go next.

'I took Dipen Patel, cousin of our victim. Following the information from Mrs Khan, the first thing I did was check out his finances, and oh, my goodness! They are shocking. Just in credit cards, loans and store cards, he owes £66,000. How did these companies even allow him to get into this much trouble? If you were told correctly, and he does owe £200,000, then my guess is that he is now the property of a loan shark. Dipen was aware of Ravi's fortune and desperately needed that money.'

'Sir,' Anne interrupted. 'I got some phone records back for Mr Ravi Patel's mobile from his phone company. There was no text from Dipen stating that he was leaving the concert early; so where was he and why has he lied?'

Isaac was immensely impressed with his team and was eager to hear from his DS.

'Agatha Hawksworth,' Jian said. 'Friend of the deceased since uni days. Was at one time romantically involved with Mr Patel until he told her he was gay. We're not sure how she took this news. There are also mixed messages about a termination that she had and whether it was his decision or hers to have it done. DC Michaels also shared with me a text message that she recently sent him: *"I hate you. You, and you alone, have made my life a living nightmare. I should've kept our baby, but you made me get rid of it. Our so-called friendship is over. I never want to see you again."* She sounds angry.'

Jian observed that Faisal was making faces and seemed distracted. DC Asher then stood up and went over to the crime board and took down the photo of Agatha, and scrutinised it. The others looked at him, and some shrugged their shoulders at each other.

'I don't believe it,' Faisal finally said. 'I thought I recognised her. It has been playing on my mind since I first saw her picture on the crime board, and I remember exactly what she said. I was in a café with my mate, Maggie. In the corner were Ravi and Agatha, and she was screaming at him. She was talking about a party and she was angry, really angry. Sir, I remember she mentioned Paris. She then stormed out, but not before screaming: You've changed Ravi Patel. You've destroyed my life. She also threw her breakfast all over him.'

They all sat with their mouths open to different degrees. Anne's was the widest. Agatha's picture was placed back onto the board, and Faisal sat back down looking incredibly proud of himself.

'Money and such anger, I think we could call that two motives,' he said, crossing his arms and smiling.

DCI Davidson paced and was taking in all the information that had been gathered. The team were chatting amongst themselves as Lily went to the kitchen to get them all a hot drink. Anne went to her desk and fetched a packet of biscuits.

'Hang on, team,' Isaac called out. 'What's outstanding? Anne?'

'I'm going through the phone records and still waiting on the CCTV from the train. Faisal?' Anne said.

'Final bit of door-to-door with DC Michaels. We should get that completed today. Lily?' he said.

'I'm chasing up the ANPR on Parveena's car and still looking through laptops. Hamish?'

'Chasing up the brain tumour side of things,' he replied to DC Tovey. 'Jian?'

'Well,' DS Wong said with a grin. 'I don't think you've left me anything to do. Sir?'

'Jian, you'll be coming with me. It's time we re-interviewed them all. I think our killer is one of these five. Does anyone disagree?' Isaac scanned the room, but no one moved. 'Great! Jian, be ready to go in about an hour.'

Isaac returned to his office. Meanwhile, Lily prepared two cups of coffee and grabbed some of Anne's biscuits before following him.

51

DC Lily Tovey

13th November 2019

10:00 a.m.

DC Lily Tovey gently kicked the door to Isaac's office and then showed the DCI that she had two cups in her hand. Isaac opened it for her.

'I've also got biscuits,' she said, as she put the drinks down on the table and removed the Bourbons from her pocket.

'What can I assist you with?' he asked.

Lily, raised in Cardiff and cherished her Welsh heritage. She was always her father's girl until his untimely death from a heart attack. The move to London about eighteen months ago had been exciting, and since she had been part of Isaacs's team she had learnt so much. Outside of work, her passions were reading, films and dark chocolate. Lily had remained single since arriving in the capital, but it wasn't something that bothered her. Her constant talking probably put people off, but she liked nothing better than engaging in conversation.

Isaac was exceedingly pleased with his DC since she had arrived. She blended into the team seamlessly and was a popular member. She was hardworking, thorough, and compassionate. Being a detective was all that mattered to her, and relationships would always need to come second.

'What can I help you with, Lily?' DCI Davidson enquired.

'Does one of us need to go?' she asked directly.

'Yes,' was the honest response. 'However, I am fighting with everything I have. We're an important team, and I need you all.'

Lily digested what she had just been told. One thing she always admired about her boss was his directness. Whenever there was something that needed to be said, he communicated it so clearly that there was no room for doubt.

'Why should I keep you on?' he asked with kindness.

'Ever since I was a little girl I wanted to do something with my life that benefitted others. My parents thought I'd become a nurse, but I'm not interested in healing the sick. That is not where my talents lay. Logic fascinates me and I want to face problems and strategically find solutions. Oh, I know that is also the role of a nurse, and I think it is a magnificent profession, but it wasn't for me. I'm a team player and get excited by crime and justice. I love reading "whodunnits" despite rarely guessing correctly. The day I graduated as a police officer, my wonderful dad spent the day crying. He was so proud of me and knew the direction my life would take. The whole time that he was alive, I couldn't leave Wales. Although it broke my heart when he died, it also opened up a whole new world to me; London!'

The two detectives drank their drinks, and Isaac dunked his biscuits. His team outside in the main room were busy with their tasks. Isaac had listened intently to his young DC, and over the past year, he had been immensely pleased with her progress.

'Where do you see yourself in five years?' he asked.

'I want to be a detective sergeant. I'm not overly ambitious, but I do want some progression in my career.'

Isaac enjoyed finding things out about his team. As the boss, he rarely got an insight into his detective's lives.

Appraisals were all very good, but as far as he was concerned they were mostly a paper exercise. Talking in an ad hoc way was how he gathered the information that he wanted.

'Who do you think is our murderer?' he said. 'I am interested to know where your thoughts are. Being a detective uses lots of skills, both inherent and learnt on the job. Sometimes we just need to go with our gut reaction.'

DC Tovey pondered deeply. There was much questioning left to do since they were only at the beginning stages of the case.

'I want to say Parveena because I don't like her! But my gut is telling me that Agatha is our killer.'

'Tell me why?' Isaac asked.

'Mrs Khan told you that Agatha was the one that worried Ravi the most. There are mixed thoughts on the termination, and a large amount of money is in play. She is a large woman and would definitely have the strength to pull the scarf around Ravi's neck. There has to be something in a woman scorned.'

Lily left the office, and DCI Davidson was feeling guilty. He knew that despite what he was going to tell his team; one did have to go. Asking Lily to talk through her hunch was just a way that he could assess her skills as a detective.

52

Rakesh

13th November 2019

11:30 a.m.

The car journey was mostly routine. The detectives were lost in their own thoughts, only speaking sporadically. DCI Davidson was worrying about losing a member of his team; and soon. DS Wong's mind was wandering all over the place.

A sudden lightning flash and a booming thunderclap snapped the men back to the present. Abruptly, the skies opened, unleashing a torrential downpour that made driving a challenge. Fortunately, they were just two streets away from their destination.

As they pulled into the driveway, Jian could see Rakesh through the shutters and saw that he appeared to be dancing.

'He seems remarkably unperturbed by the fact that his husband was murdered two weeks ago, doesn't he?'

The DCI looked at what his DS was seeing and shrugged.

'Grief affects us all differently. Have you ever lost anyone of significance?'

'Only my grandparents have passed away, which was naturally sad but anticipated. I haven't experienced the loss of anyone else. And you?'

'My parents died in my late twenties. I was twenty-eight and Alan was just twenty. Dad drowned in a boating accident, and three months later, Mum had a brain haemorrhage. Two years after that, Alan was involved in a road traffic accident. The driver who had caused the crash walked out of her car without a scratch. Alan was left unable to walk.'

Jian wasn't sure what to say to his DCI but saw him smiling back so he knew he didn't need to respond.

The rain wasn't stopping, so the two men dashed to the porch and rang the bell. After a few moments, Rakesh opened the door and his face dropped when he saw who was standing there.

'Good morning, Mr Kumar. Can we come in?' asked Jian.

Rakesh stepped aside and allowed them to go through the lounge.

Joseph, the family liaison officer, was no longer at the house so Rakesh was alone. He was, however, making daily calls and helping Rakesh with anything he didn't understand.

'Leg feeling better? I saw you dancing.'

'Oh, yes thanks,' he replied to the DS.

'Remind me, how did you hurt it?'

'I don't remember,' Rakesh squirmed. 'In a fight with a guy I was seeing, that's right. Silly of me to forget.'

'Really?' said DS Wong. 'I have it on good authority that you hurt your leg by violently kicking your husband in the stomach whilst he was lying defensively on the floor, possibly breaking some of his ribs when you both attended the concert.'

Rakesh's eyes widened in surprise, and he slumped into a chair, burying his face in his hands.

'I'm so ashamed. Who saw me? I guess it doesn't matter as I assume it was one of the other four. In my defence, Ravi had just said that he wanted to divorce me. I loved him so much, and those words frightened me. I know I wasn't the best husband in the world, but I didn't want to lose him. You have to believe me.'

Another clap of thunder could be heard rumbling in the distance, and the rain was hitting the windows.

'Where did you go when you left the concert?' asked DCI Davidson.

'Home. We all went our separate ways.'

'Tell me about that, please,' Isaac said. 'You all live close to each other, and to the crime scene, and yet you all chose to leave the concert on your own. Why would that be? Doesn't it seem odd to you?'

Rakesh didn't answer straight away, giving himself time to process the question.

'I don't know. Dipen must have just buggered off as no one actually saw him apart from Ravi.' He choked when he mentioned his husband's name. 'Norton was in a foul temper following a fracas with Ravi, so I assume he stormed off in a mood. The women I have no idea about. Why do you need to know this?'

'We just need to gather all the information, Mr Kumar,' Isaac said with an exaggerated smile. 'When did you last see your husband?'

'At the concert,' was the snappy reply. 'I'm disgusted to say that after I kicked him, for which I'm so sorry for doing, I then left him on the floor. That is my final memory of him.' Rakesh erupted into tears.

After a few moments, the sobbing began to ebb. Rakesh tried to compose himself but found it difficult. He excused himself to go and get some water from the kitchen, offering to get the detectives some if they wanted; both declined but followed him.

'Did you notice any changes in your husband over the past year? Anything that worried you?'

'Yes,' Rakesh replied to the DCI. 'His personality changed. He got hung up on silly things and was becoming more pedantic. It was extremely annoying. We had a party for his birthday, and he basically attacked us all, verbally I mean.'

'Can you confirm what he said?' asked Isaac.

'Told us he was a millionaire, which shocked me to my core. He had never once mentioned having money. To be honest, we didn't live like he was rich. Money was never important to him.'

'Is it to you, Mr Kumar?' Jian said.

'Yes, it is. I want to live a life of luxury, and before you say it, no, I didn't kill my husband to get hold of the money. I only found out about it the night of the party.'

'Who do you think would want to hurt him?'

'Dipen,' he said back to DS Wong. 'Ravi told us all that his cousin was in deep debt and had asked Ravi to bail him out; Ravi refused. When Dipen heard about his millions, the look that spread over his face was pure evil.'

'What else was said at the party?' asked the DCI.

'Parveena had killed animals when she was drunk. Agatha had tried to kill herself multiple times and had terminated Ravi's child. Norton was abusing his patients, or at least that's what I think was said. Look, I'll be honest with you; I've never liked those four. They were friends of Ravi, not mine.'

Believing the interview had concluded, Rakesh began walking toward the front door. He then noticed that the detectives didn't leave the kitchen.

'Aren't we done?' he asked.

'Not quite, Mr Kumar,' Isaac said. 'What else did you notice about the changes in your husband?'

'He started tapping or rubbing his head. It was so irritating. His memory was getting worse, and he kept repeating himself. It was like he'd say something, and then less than a minute later he would say the same bloody thing again. So annoying.'

The detectives both turned to look at each other and then DCI Davidson spoke.

'Our forensic pathologist identified that he had an aggressive brain tumour, Mr Kumar. Your husband was a dreadfully sick man and only had a few months to live.'

'Wwwhat?' Rakesh stuttered. 'That can't be true. I would have known something like that. Not my Ravi.'

They could both see how distressing this news was for Rakesh. Tears that now seemed of genuine anguish streamed down his cheeks as he trembled visibly. Isaac passed him a glass of water, which was gratefully received.

'Mr Kumar,' said Isaac. 'Are you left or right-handed?'

'Left,' Rakesh replied, still shell-shocked.

'We will leave you now. Is there anybody you'd like us to call before we go?'

Rakesh thought for a few seconds and then replied to the DCI.

'No, but thanks for asking. I'm expecting a call from Joseph.'

53

Dipen

15th November 2019

06:30 a.m.

The terrified man sat on a rickety chair with his hands tied behind his back. There was no noise and he had no idea where he was because of the scratchy hood that was covering his head. He had taken a severe beating a few hours ago, and his face was hurting him; his nose must be broken. Wherever he was, it was freezing cold and he was naked, apart from his socks.

A heavy door creaked open that unnerved the man. He could now hear voices, but they were still distant. This led him to believe he must be somewhere vast, maybe a warehouse. The voices were getting stronger, as was his fear. He could make out two male voices. He recognised the South African accent and thought the other might be Eastern European.

The chair was suddenly kicked from beneath him and he fell to the floor, scraping his knees. He was terrified and shaking uncontrollably. This was partly because of the cold conditions, but more because of the panic he was experiencing.

'Please, don't hurt me,' he called out, disorientated because of the hood.

He felt a kick to his stomach and screamed out. The next thing he knew the hood was violently pulled from his head, causing pain in his neck. He had been correct, he was in a warehouse, but he didn't know whereabouts it was situated.

Looking up he saw three men staring down at him. One of them had two gold teeth in the front, was unshaven and wearing a blue suit. Behind him was a young man who looked as terrified as he was feeling. The other man was long-haired, clean-shaven and wore a checked shirt.

Using his hair, they pulled him up so that he was now in a kneeling position. The coarseness of the ground was cutting into his knees and was extremely painful. His nakedness was adding to the humiliation that he was feeling. He looked back at the younger man, who turned from his gaze.

'Please,' he said again. 'Don't do anything to me. Please don't kill me.'

'Why shouldn't we?' asked the unshaven man with the Eastern European accent.

'I know I've been stupid and owe a lot of money, but please, don't do this.'

The man from South Africa stepped forward and punched him in the face. The terrified man fell to the side and hit his head; hard. He was then pulled upright again by his hair. His face bore severe bruises, and blood trickled from his fractured nose. His hair was clumped with sweat, and his tongue felt parched.

'What do you want from me?' he begged.

'It has gone beyond that, Mr Davenport. Donna needs payment.'

The young man standing behind the henchmen grimaced at the loan shark's name and instantly took pity on the naked man on the ground. For the first time, he properly looked at him. Through tears and distress, the frightened man looked back at the young man, saw sympathy on his face and hoped there might be a connection between them.

'Please, help me!' he mouthed to him.

Crouching down so that their mouths were at the same level, the South African man spoke.

'Payment is required,' he said, as he spat into the man's face.

The other tyrant went behind and untied the petrified man's hands. He was then pulled up so he was standing. However, he had no strength in his legs; they gave way, and he fell to the ground.

'Get up!' screamed the man in the suit.

The naked man did his best to get back up. The young man went to help him but was pushed back.

Eventually, he managed to stand, but soon wished he hadn't. The man who had untied him was standing with bolt cutters in his hand.

'Noooooo!' he shrieked and felt his legs buckle.

His hand was forced out in front of him, and the cutters were handed to the young man.

'Take off his little finger on his right hand,' said the man in the blue suit.

'I can't,' he replied.

The naked man was screaming, crying, and trying to get away. However, his strength didn't come close to the large man holding him.

'Take off his little finger,' repeated the large man.

'Please, don't make me do this. This isn't me. I'm not meant to do things like this. Please, don't make me.'

'Dipen,' the man screamed. 'Cut off his finger, or I will tell Donna, and I'm sure she will find a punishment much worse for you.'

Dipen had no idea why his loan shark had chosen him to work for her, rather than being tortured like the pathetic man standing in front of him with his right arm held out and his fingers forcibly spread wide. At this very moment he didn't know which role he'd prefer.

'DO IT!' the man screeched.

Dipen snapped the bolt cutters shut as he heard the blood-curdling scream from the tortured man as he dropped to the floor.

'Your next payment is due in three days, or else you'll lose another finger,' Dipen hissed.

1:00 p.m.

Following a few hours of sleep, Dipen was now standing in the shower. When he first got in this morning, he had been exhausted and had collapsed onto his bed without removing his clothes. As he placed his face under the flowing water and then looked down at his feet, he was shocked to see streaks of red.

'Shit,' he said to himself. 'His blood.'

Dipen took a large amount of shower gel and was liberally applying it everywhere on his body. He washed with a sense of urgency and at times hurt himself. Feeling distraught, he dropped into a crouching position, and then onto his bottom, pulled his knees up to his chest and put his arms around them. He started to cry as he gently rocked himself.

'Ravi. Why?' he whispered to himself.

He had stayed under the water for a long time. Just sitting there, letting the water bounce off his body. Visions of his actions that morning were still vivid, and he was traumatised by the person he had become.

In his bedroom, he dried himself off as he looked out into the street. The day was dark and bleak, and this reflected his mood. He then took in a deep sigh when he saw a car approaching. He instinctively knew who was going to get out: DCI Davidson and DS Wong.

By the time the detectives had got out of their car, Dipen was already standing with the front door open and welcomed them in.

'Do you have any news for me? Is that why you're here?' he asked.

'Not quite, Mr Patel,' answered the DCI. 'We are still making enquiries, as I'm sure you'll understand.'

'I didn't kill my cousin. I loved him.'

'Many people are tragically killed by those who love them,' Isaac remarked. 'We must also consider other factors that come into play, such as revenge, jealousy, compassion, money and other things. Anything there that you can tell us about?'

'No,' Dipen said. 'Is that it? Can I get back to my day?'

'You appear especially agitated, Mr Patel. Why would that be?'

Dipen looked at DCI Davidson and shrugged his shoulders.

'Also, that graze on your nose still looks sore. It might be infected, so I'd get it checked if I were you.'

'I will, thanks. Is that it?'

'No, Mr Patel,' Isaac said with anger. 'There was a party and Ravi revealed certain things that you didn't mention the last time we met. Why?'

'What things?'

'You tell me,' Isaac said forcibly.

'Who told you?' Dipen asked.

'Told us what?' smiled the DCI.

'That I owe a lot of money and Ravi refused to bail me out.'

'There you go,' Isaac said. 'How did that make you feel? That you owed money and could have been helped. Bad enough when you first asked, thinking he had some inheritance, but how did it feel when you heard he had millions and still declined to help you? I'm sure it must have made you extremely angry.'

Dipen glared at the detectives with a slightly curled lip. His disdain for them both was growing.

'How do you think it made me feel? Ravi humiliated me in front of them all. He knew how bad my debts were. So, yes, I was deeply hurt. As a matter of fact, for that moment I wanted to punish him.'

'And did you?' Jian asked.

'I wouldn't hurt Ravi.'

'Mr Patel,' Isaac chipped in. 'Your cousin had a terminal brain tumour and had only a few months to live. Did you know this?'

Dipen thought for a few moments.

'The constant rubbing of his head, memory issues and repeating himself. Oh, dear! It makes so much sense now. He was told that he had stress-related headaches. Oh, poor Ravi. Did he know?'

'We aren't sure,' Isaac said. 'We are checking out with local hospitals, but his GP wasn't aware.'

Jian observed Dipen as his DCI asked the questions. There was an edginess about him today that hadn't previously been there. His legs were juddering, and he kept touching his nose like he had a nervous tick.

'Where did you go when you left the concert before everyone else?' asked Isaac.

'I already answered that the last time we spoke.'

'You also said that you texted Ravi to let him know you were leaving, but you didn't. Did you? We have his phone records.'

'It doesn't matter where I went. It hadn't anything to do with my cousin.'

'Mr Patel, everything matters in a murder case, so I will repeat my question. Where were you?'

'I don't remember. I may have taken myself off for a quiet dinner. My head is full of issues. The debt is crucifying me and messes with my thoughts.'

'Are you right or left-handed?'

Dipen looked at the DCI with a confused expression but answered the question.

'I'm right-handed.'

'Do you know of anyone who would want to kill your cousin?'

'Good question! We were a dysfunctional group. I've no idea why we kept meeting up. No one seemed to like anyone. Parveena was bitter with him about their practice and once, when I went to see Ravi, I heard her and their nurse shouting at each other. The nurse was asking for extra payments. Could that be something?'

After being informed that they would need to speak with him again soon, Dipen escorted the men out and was reminded to make himself available for future discussion. Once back in their car, Isaac spoke.

'Something isn't ringing true about that man. I want you to check with phone masts in the local areas and see if anything "pinged" concerning Dipen Patel. Sadly, we don't know where Ravi Patel entered the water, but something may show in phone records.'

'He was definitely on edge today, that's for sure,' said DS Wong.

DCI Davison put the car in first gear and slowly drove off.

Standing at his bedroom window, Dipen stood and watched them go. A smile crept over his face.

'Your turn, Parveena.'

54

DC Anne Michaels

16th November 2019

7:00 p.m.

The reservation for the table was set for 7:30 p.m. Anne, feeling anxious had arrived ahead of time. This was the first date she had been on in more years than she cared to remember. She had never regretted caring for her father, especially in his declining years, but it heavily impacted her seeking intimate relationships. They had always been a tight unit since her mum died when she was only seven years old. She had hanged herself and Anne was the one who found her.

Although she hadn't been prepared for her father's passing, once the funeral was over and she had taken enough time off work to grieve, Anne was ready to move forward with her life. Mr Michaels would've been delighted that she was on this date tonight. He only ever wanted the best for his daughter, and hated being a burden to her.

The server had shown her to the booked table and asked if she wanted a drink. Anne had chosen a red wine, and at the same time apologised for being so early. The restaurant was beautifully French, from the tablecloths to the decorations. The candle on the table had already been lit, and an accordion was being played.

Anne sipped her wine, then grabbed her phone and opened the camera app. She studied herself and pulled a face.

'Oh, you look awful. Why didn't you make an effort?'

In truth, DC Michaels had spent the entire afternoon treating herself to a long, hot bath with bath bombs. The rest of the time had been spent putting hair removal cream on herself, followed by a revitalising vitamin-infused face mask. She realised too late that she should have used the cream before her bath. The next part was the most difficult, the make-up. Anne wasn't used to spending so much time on herself, so applying foundation, blusher, eye-shadow and lipstick was alien to her.

'You look hideous,' she said as she looked into her phone's camera. She suddenly felt very depressed.

'Hello,' a voice said. 'Anne? I'm Nathan.'

Anne became flustered, and as she stood to shake his hand, she knocked over the breadsticks on the table.

'Yes, that's me. Hello,' she said as she put out her hand, ready to shake.

Nathan sat down, and Anne was instantly hooked. He was fifty-two but looked younger. His thinning brown hair seemed just the right amount for someone his age. He had hazel eyes and a chiselled jaw. The clothes he was wearing looked expensive, and his aftershave was gorgeous. Anne was immediately impressed.

'I don't normally start like this, but may I say, you look lovely,' he said.

'You may say,' Anne blushed. 'That does make it sound like you have been in this situation a few times.'

More drinks were ordered, and the menus were perused. Anne regretted posing such an uncomfortable question, and Nathan's silence filled her with concern. However, her worry was unnecessary.

'Dating is difficult, as I am sure you can imagine,' he finally said. 'I won't lie. I have met a fair few from the apps. Sadly, some look nothing like their profile pictures or the photos were taken years ago and don't represent who they are today. I met a few women who as soon as I sat down, I knew they weren't for me. However, I have met some lovely ladies along the way, but they just haven't worked out for either me or them.'

After studying the menu, orders were placed along with a bottle of red wine.

'Tell me about you,' asked Nathan.

'Well, you know that I'm a detective and working on a murder case. I haven't dated in so many years, hence I'm frightfully nervous. The youngsters at work warned me about dating apps, so I'm delighted to see you match your profile pic.'

'Likewise,' Nathan said.

Following enough time for them to start feeling relaxed with each other, the food arrived and they chatted like they had known each other for years. Anne blushed when compliments were made, and Nathan intervened if a rare silence cropped up. The entire experience was thrilling DC Michaels; her dad would be so proud of her. They were talking the night away and finding lots out about each other. Desserts were served, and the conversation continued.

'Do you mind if I say something to you, Anne?' Nathan said.

'Go on,' she apprehensively replied.

'You have a massive blob of custard that you have dropped onto your right boob.'

Anne looked down and felt awful.

'Oh, damn! What must you think of me?'

She reached for a napkin to wipe it off herself, and as she pulled it towards her, she knocked over her glass of red wine.

Anne felt embarrassed as she used other napkins to soak up what she had spilt. She didn't want to look Nathan in the eye, as she felt mortally ashamed. His voice then boomed.

'I have loved this evening,' and a huge smile spread across his face as he righted her glass and poured in some more wine. 'When can we do this again?'

Anne did everything she could from screaming out her delight.

55

Bad News

19th November 2019

9:00 a.m.

The entire team had been at their desks going through their outstanding tasks. Lots of the unresolved information came in at the weekend and the rest of it, yesterday. Isaac had been called into a meeting with his Superintendent, and it had turned into a whole day affair. This was time DCI Davidson could ill afford, and the result of the day was bad news; Isaac was dreading telling his team.

'Bloody hell, Anne,' Lily called from her desk. 'I'm so sorry! How did Saturday go with Nathan?'

The team all stood and crowded around DC Michaels' desk. They were all eager to hear how her date had gone.

'Well,' Anne began to say. 'If I'm being honest, it was fantastic!'

Their faces all lit up, and they could see the joy in their colleague's smile.

'I'm so pleased,' Hamish said.

'Tell us what happened,' Faisal said, sounding excited.

Anne then told the team of her lovely evening, and let them know that date two wasn't that far away.

'Gather round, please,' DCI Davidson said in a raised voice.

The team went over to the crime board and immediately noticed the worried expression etched across his face.

'Sir,' Jian said with a concerned tone. 'What's up?'

Isaac let out a deep sigh.

'It's happened, guys,' he said in a depressed tone. 'I've been fighting this for a long time, but I've been instructed that roles within the department need to be reduced, which unfortunately means parting with one of my DCs. I'm so sorry.'

The silence that descended upon the room was a clear testament to their collective emotions. Anne reached over and grabbed Lily's hand and squeezed it.

'I'll go,' a quiet voice said.

Everyone turned around and looked at DC Potter.

'It doesn't work like that,' Isaac replied. 'DS Wong, your post isn't at risk, but the rest of you will need to reapply for your job. There are four of you and three vacancies.'

'I'm going out for coffee and pastries,' chimed Anne. 'Hamish, you come with me and to hell with Superintendent Chandra. At least for today.'

56

More Information

19th November 2019

11:30 a.m.

DCI Davidson had been on the phone with his Human Resources department for the last hour. Things were moving quickly, faster than even he imagined. The plan was that whoever wasn't successful in the job application process would be gone by January. They had little more than six weeks left. Isaac put down the phone and looked out of his office and into the main room. The entire team were either on calls themselves or at their computers. The loss of one team member would be difficult, not only for Isaac but also for the remaining team members.

Isaac summoned everyone to provide updates and share their current thoughts, but not before updating them himself.

'I spoke with Alex, and details on the scarf aren't back yet. Also, we now know that Rakesh and Norton are left-handed, and Parveena, Agatha and Dipen are Right-handed. The five of them were in Paris as confirmed by checking their passport details for leaving the UK and entering France. Why is that important? I still don't know. Parveena, Norton, Rakesh and Ravi ordered Euros through their bank. Parveena ordered a lot more than the others.'

He then asked DC Michaels to present first.

'The train CCTV finally came through on Sunday. I came to work to go through it and finished it last night. Sadly, it isn't overly helpful. I can plainly see Ravi, and I'm not going to lie to you all, he looked so sad. It actually broke my heart watching him. It looked like he was in a lot of pain, as he was not only sitting awkwardly but also the way he was holding himself and rubbing his side. His facial expressions were also a clue to how much pain he was experiencing. So sad. However, he stays in the same seat for the duration of the journey and gets off at his station. There is a little more footage from the CCTV on the station, but once he steps outside, we lose him.' Anne then brings up an image on her computer. 'This is a person of interest,' she says. 'As you can see they are wearing a padded jacket and a hood. Unfortunately, I can't tell what they look like as their face or any features aren't revealed. If this is our killer, they knew what they were doing to avoid being seen. However, they may also be no one of importance.'

The team scrutinised the picture. As with most CCTV footage the image was fuzzy and blurred.

'Thoughts?' Isaac asked.

'Female?' volunteered Faisal.

'Small or medium male?' suggested Jian.

'Well, it can't be Parveena Johal,' said Lily. 'The ANPR picked her car up along the straightest route home for her, so she was driving. She was last seen at 10 p.m., but as we aren't sure of the time of death, she could have parked up at home and then gone to the station and waited for our victim to get off the train. She knew that she left the concert before him.'

Isaac welcomed their views and enjoyed hearing what they had uncovered. Hamish was next.

'So, Mr Patel did have an awfully aggressive brain tumour. I heard back yesterday, early evening from the neuro-oncology department. He had what is called a Glioblastoma Muliforme, GBM for short. The symptoms include headaches, nausea and vomiting, personality changes, and memory loss, to name a few. The hospital did not have him on their records and kindly contacted other NHS Trusts that deal with this type of brain tumour and got zero results back. It would appear that no one was treating his tumour. I then spoke again with the GP who had told him they were just stress-related headaches. She is convinced that Mr Patel didn't know he had it. However, the hospital is surprised by this as his symptoms would certainly have been severe. With treatment the mean survival rate for GBM is thirteen to eighteen months, but far less without. Sadly, with no treatment, Ravi Patel only had weeks to only a few months left to live.'

Hamish's revelation had an impact on the team. An unplanned silence followed as they thought through what they had just heard.

'OK,' Isaac said. 'As sad as that may be. We need to move on. Who is next?'

'Phone records,' said Anne. 'There aren't huge amounts of texts to get through. I assume as a group of so-called friends, they tend to use WhatsApp, which is encrypted. So apart from the one sent by Agatha, there isn't much to go on.'

'Same with social media and laptops,' Lily said.

'Were there no messages between the Patel-Kumars?' asked Hamish. 'Rakesh said he hoped his husband was going to come home, but was then told that Ravi intended to divorce him. Surely there would be text messages going back and forth?'

'No, nothing,' said Anne.

This wasn't what their DCI wanted to hear. Social media usually dragged up some evidence.

'Sir,' Jian said as he raised his hand into the air. 'DC Potter has made an extremely good point. I'm going to ask Mr Kumar to give me access to his phone, and if he refuses, I'll get a warrant.'

'DC Michaels and I have finished the door-to-door interviewing,' declared Faisal. 'Again, not much of interest. Those who were aware of them spoke highly of Ravi but said Rakesh was the grumpy one. However, the house opposite did have some CCTV footage that may be useful. We can't hear what is being said, but the two of them look to be having a heated argument outside their front door. I have asked my mate Maggie, who is deaf and can lip-read brilliantly to look at it. That way it won't cost the department anything. In the beginning of the video we can mainly see Rakesh talking. Ravi has his back to us most of the time, but finally Ravi moves and we can see his lips talking just before Rakesh slaps him hard around the face and Ravi hits his head on the door frame as he falls to the ground.'

'Mr Kumar failed to tell us about this,' uttered Hamish.

Just as Isaac was congratulating his team. A uniformed officer came into the department, and he handed DC Potter a note. Hamish read through it and his eyes widened.

'Sir,' he said. 'This is a note from Amanda on the front desk. Parveena Johal was brought in last night and put in one of the cells overnight. She was picked up for being drunk and disorderly. She has only just woken up.'

Isaac pondered on the information. He had planned to visit Miss Johal again today, so now he just needed to head to the ground floor.

'Lily, with me, please.'

'Coming, sir,' she replied.

57

Parveena

19th November 2019

12:30 p.m.

The cells were pretty grim. The walls were a dirty-looking white, and the heavy doors were a standard dark grey. There was a bed but very little else. The blankets provided were scratchy to the skin, just like school jumpers were in the 1980s. Parveena sat on the edge of her bed with her head in her hands and a vomit bowl placed at her feet. The throbbing in her head was worse than she had ever known and when she saw the detectives approaching, she groaned.

'Go away,' she said out loud.

'Good afternoon, Miss Johal,' Lily replied with an exaggerated loudness, relishing in the discomfort it caused. 'How are we feeling?'

Lily and Isaac stood in the doorway of the cell, and could only imagine how this woman was feeling. Parveena's hair looked like it needed a good wash. At some point during the night, she had clearly vomited in it. Her eyes were dark and pained, her lips chapped and parched. Isaac's first thought was that this was someone who hadn't been looking after themselves. She had a broken heel on her silver designer shoes, and her white suit was stained with blood and other bodily fluids.

'Go away,' she repeated.

'We need to ask you a few questions, Miss Johal,' Lily said, without lowering her tone.

'What?' was the only response she got.

At that moment someone arrived with a sandwich and some water. Parveena drained half the bottle as quickly as she could. She pushed the food under the bed so she didn't have to see it.

'Can you remind us of the reason your business has closed?'

'Ravi,' was the only word that came back.

'Are you a good vet, Miss Johal?' asked DC Tovey.

'Go away.'

'Because rather than Mr Patel destroying your practice, we now believe that the unexplained deaths of three animals under your care might be the reason.'

'Kwasi,' Parveena uttered under her breath.

'No,' Lily responded. 'Not Mr Moses. We have heard that you killed three pets and Ravi Patel reported you to your governing body resulting in your practice closing, pending an investigation. Do you care to expand?'

'No comment!'

'Furthermore, the last time we spoke, you informed us that it was due to Mr Patel's health concerns that you were struggling financially. You also said you had to let your practice nurse go because you could no longer afford to pay him. Is that correct?'

'I told you so. Yes, that is correct.'

'Then why, Miss Johal, has £300 a month been leaving your personal account and going into his since August? This is in addition to his usual wage paid from your business one?'

No immediate came back.

Parveena took more water from the bottle and looked at DC Tovey with pure hatred. 'You'll need to speak with Mr Moses.'

'Yes, we are trying to locate him. Do you know where he is?'

'No comment!'

Lily was enjoying watching the suspect squirm. She didn't know if her DCI would agree with her methods, but at this moment, she didn't care.

'How was Paris?' Lily asked.

Parveena slowly pushed back her hair and glared at the DC.

'Why?'

'We found many hashtags throughout social media that, well, let me be honest, don't paint you in a very good light. Does it? Then we found an email from your partner, Mr Ravi Patel, who was disgusted by your performance at the conference. He doesn't mince his words and I'm sure this would have made you especially angry.'

Parveena's head was pounding and her thoughts about DC Tovey weren't changing. She looked over at DCI Davidson and wondered why he had even bothered coming along. Her tongue felt dry and hard, despite the water she had been given, and there was a smell coming from her armpits that she never wanted to experience again. However, what angered her the most, was a snotty DC standing in front of her with pink streaks running through her hair and odd socks on.

'Are we done?' Parveena croaked at Lily.

'Not quite,' was the reply. 'When we last met, you told us you poured a drink over Mr Patel's head. Why would you do this? It feels like a childish action, or was there more to it?'

'If you bothered to take notes,' hissed Parveena, 'I told you I did it because he was an arsehole.'

'Or because he reported you to your governing body for malpractice whilst under the influence of alcohol?' replied Lily.

'No comment.'

Isaac could tell that his DC was getting frustrated and wanted to keep her calm. He signalled to her that he would ask the next question.

'Miss Johal, did you kill Mr Patel?'

'I don't suppose either of you has a hip flask? Pinky, do you?' Lily ignored her.

'Please answer the question,' Isaac said in a gruff tone.

'I didn't! But I'm glad someone did.'

'And who do you think could have wanted him dead?' Isaac asked.

'Miss Hawksworth? I never liked her. Or Norton Greene? That man is so slimy. I have hated them since the day we met back at university. I have only ever tolerated them because Ravi liked them. At the party, I assume you know about the party?' The detectives nodded. 'He humiliated Agatha. I'd start there if I were you, but to be honest, Ravi was asking to be killed.'

'What do you mean by that?' jumped in Lily.

'He pissed people off. He pissed us all off. Maybe we all did it!'

'Did you know that Mr Patel had an aggressive brain tumour and he had probably less than a couple of months to live?'

Parveena looked at Isaac.

'No,' she said. 'I didn't.'

Both detectives were perturbed by her lack of emotion at this piece of information.

DCI Davidson and DC Tovey left Parveena to sober up some more. She had practically stopped talking by the time they left.

'What do you think, Lily?' asked Isaac.

'Oh, she is very clever. Did you notice that she never really answers the questions? I don't trust her at all. Did you hear her remark, "maybe we all did it!" The woman is hiding something, and we need to find Kwasi Moses.'

58

Susie

21st November 2019

10:00 a.m.

The main room bustled with activity. Isaac vigilantly monitored his team as they conducted the required searches. Hamish appeared to be in another bothersome mood if his facial expressions were anything to go by. Anne was pulling faces at Lily as they witnessed their colleague breaking a mug as he slammed it into the sink. DC Tovey went over to him.

'Hey, what's up?'

'Nothing,' he said.

'Come on, DC Potter. I'm not stupid.'

Hamish sighed as his bottom lip protruded and his cheeks flushed a pinkish red.

'Usual story. I was chatting with a woman I met at a pub last week. We seemed to get on well and arranged a date for last night. I waited for over an hour at the wine bar, but she didn't turn up. This morning I got a text, "*Sorry, not interested*" and it has just left me feeling crap about myself. What is it about me that scares them off?'

'Ah, mate. That's rubbish. I'm sorry she did that to you. There is nothing wrong with you. You're a kind man and anyone would be lucky to be in a relationship with you.' Lily hoped her words were making him feel better.

'Look at those two,' Hamish said as he pointed to Faisal and Jian. 'I'm jealous of what they have. They are so great together, and I want that.'

Hoping not to be patronising, Lily rubbed DC Potter's back and offered to clear up the broken pieces of mug and then take him out for a coffee. Hamish accepted.

A knock at the door jolted Isaac from his thoughts, which weren't of the case but of what he would be cooking tonight. He fancied fish.

'Yes, Anne?'

'Sir,' DC Michaels said. 'Downstairs have just called. There is a Susie Hudson in reception who would like to speak with the detective leading up the Ravi Patel investigation.'

'Do we know her?' he asked his DC.

'No, we don't.'

Isaac knocked back the remaining coffee dregs in his cup and winced at the coldness of it. He then headed out to speak with the woman who had come forward. Upon reaching the lifts, a pang of guilt struck him and he opted for the stairs instead. It was just four floors down, and he would remind himself to take them back up on his return.

DCI Davidson arrived at the reception and saw a woman with striking ginger hair. He assumed this was who he was meeting.

'Susie Hudson?' he enquired.

'Yes.'

Isaac asked the desk sergeant if there was anywhere available that they could talk and they were shown to a windowless, stuffy room which had a smell of residual body odour. He apologised, and Susie just smiled.

'I hope you don't mind me coming to see you, and maybe I shouldn't even be here. She's my friend you see. Oh, I shouldn't have come, it's wrong of me.'

Susie got up to leave but was persuaded to stay.

'I saw that news report about Ravi Patel. You see, I knew him. Well, not actually to speak to, but knew of him. I have a friend, Agatha Hawksworth, and she was obsessed with him. She is an ex-girlfriend from many years ago. However, she never got over him. Under her bed is a box full of memorabilia of their time together, which was only a few months as a dating couple. It even has a pair of his used pants in it. I find that a little creepy. You obviously know that they have stayed in touch ever since.'

Isaac sat and listened. The woman in front of him was talking so fast that there wasn't a space for him to ask questions. He therefore let her continue and would ask things once she had finished.

'Agatha, and God forgive me for saying this, was obsessed with the man. She never got over the end of their relationship. She followed him and found him with another man. It broke her heart, and if I'm honest, it changed her. I didn't know her back then, but from the things she told me about herself and what I know now, she is an incredibly damaged woman.'

Once Susie had stopped, Isaac took a moment to consider the information he had received and to think of a question or two.

'Interesting,' he finally said. 'How has she been since the murder?'

'Amazing,' Susie quickly said. 'Her usual appearance has completely changed. Her previously frizzy and sometimes untidy hair is now meticulously straightened every day. She has joined a slimming club and has already lost one and a half stone since joining. She has toned her clothes down and seems, well, happy.'

'And this is all since Mr Patel's death?'

'Yes, that's what I'm telling you. It's like she has started a new life. Moved on at last, but why? I am so worried about her mental health. This isn't the Agatha I know.'

Susie leaned back into her chair and breathed for what felt like the first time since she arrived in the building. She studied the DCI and wondered what he was going to say next. A fly buzzed by her ear and caused her to jump.

'Do you know of a termination?' Isaac said.

This was the last thing Susie was expecting him to say.

'The abortion. Yes, I am aware of this. Has Agatha told you that Ravi insisted that she went through with it?'

'She told us that she had one, but the finer details of the event came from someone else.'

'It isn't true. One drunken night a couple of years ago, Agatha told me that Ravi said to keep the baby, but she insisted on an abortion. I honestly believe that Ravi did all that he could and because of her irrational obsession, she has altered the truth in her head. Agatha is unhinged and a danger to herself.'

'Susie, do you think she killed Ravi?'

'I honestly don't know. She has the ability to strangle someone, probably because she was part of a rugby team at university and has a lot of upper body strength. But, what I think makes me believe that she could have, was when we last met. It was eight days before the murder, and she kept going on that Ravi had destroyed her life. She was furious and said, *"For my life to have any chance of happiness, then Ravi Patel has to die!"* The intention behind those words was clear.'

Isaac thanked Susie for coming in to speak with him.

'You've been very helpful,' he said.

'I hope she didn't do it, DCI Davidson.'

'But?'

Susie took her time before answering the detective.

'But I think she did.'

59

Agatha

21st November 2019

1:00 p.m.

Agatha had got herself into a structured routine. She'd have a bowl of fat-free Greek yoghurt every morning before her shower. She would alternate what she had with it. Today she had blueberries, strawberries and blackberries. Tomorrow would probably be mangoes and bananas.

After her shower, she would spend time on her hair and then admire her weight loss in the mirror. Even though there wasn't much of a difference yet; she knew it was happening. Although not quite ready to apply, Agatha had also started to look for jobs to get a sense of what was out there. So far, nothing had grabbed her attention.

When her front doorbell sounded, she smiled as she instinctively knew who it would be.

'Hey,' she cried out enthusiastically to DCI Davidson and DS Wong. 'It's so wonderful to see you both again; and much drier this time.' Agatha giggled. 'Do you remember when you first came here? You were both soaking wet and I had to get you towels. Oh, how we laughed.'

The men looked at each other with puzzlement unsure about the exceedingly jolly persona they were being presented with.

'How have you been, Miss Hawksworth?' asked the DCI.

'Call me Ags,' she replied 'Actually, don't do that as I hate my name being shortened. I don't know why I even suggested it; sorry. Not that it isn't so lovely to see you both again, but it has been two weeks. I thought that you'd forgotten me. What can I help you with today? Can I get you a coffee?'

'No thanks,' they said in unison.

'Tea?'

'No, thanks.'

'Hot chocolate?'

'Miss Hawksworth, please settle,' Isaac said, a little frustrated. 'You don't need to make us anything. We have a few things that we'd like to discuss with you concerning Mr Ravi Patel.'

Her expression changed at the mention of his name, and the temples on the side of her head started to throb.

'What about him?' she grunted.

'Can you tell us more about your relationship with him?'

'No,' she snapped. 'Let's not talk about him.'

Isaac was concerned about the change in her behaviour. She was frenzied and not giving either of them any eye contact.

'I appreciate it might be a hard thing to talk about, but we do need answers.'

'There was no relationship. We were friends, that's all; not even that towards the end of his life.'

'We know that you had a brief romantic relationship,' Isaac continued, ignoring what she had said. 'And at some point it was sexual, hence the termination he spoke about at the party. Do you remember telling us about it the last time we were here? Please, can you expand on this?'

'No, I won't,' she said, getting louder. Her arms were beginning to flap about. 'He is dead, and therefore it doesn't matter what he said. My mother agrees with me. Can I make you both a sandwich? Cheese? Tuna? Ham?'

Both men were becoming exasperated with Agatha. She was deliberately avoiding questions.

'Miss Hawksworth,' Isaac said sternly. 'If you refuse to answer the questions, we will have to make it more formal and take you into the station.'

'ASK! Go on! Ask your questions,' she screamed, startling both men. Her calm face was now full of aggression.

'Your relationship?'

'It was about six months only. We weren't compatible. That's all there is to say.' Agatha dropped into a chair, tightly folded her arms and huffed.

'Go on?' Isaac encouraged.

'Nothing more to tell you.'

'Was the baby his?'

'Do you think I'm a slut? Is that what you are saying?' Agatha was gripping tightly onto the arms of the chair. Her knuckles were turning white.

'Of course, that isn't what I'm saying, and I believe you know that. Answer the question, please.'

'Yes it was his,' Agatha sneered at the DCI. 'He made me terminate it.'

'Did that make you angry?'

'What do you think?' she started shrieking again.

DCI Davidson allowed a few moments to pass, so Agatha could calm down, although it appeared to have the opposite effect. She stood and began pacing the room.

'Mr Patel was homosexual, wasn't he? Is that why the relationship broke up?'

'Well, I wonder if that was the reason?' she replied sarcastically, putting a finger to her mouth and pulling strange faces. 'I caught him with another man. If only he'd been honest with me. I would have adjusted.' She seemed to be slightly calmer as she said this.

'Agatha,' Isaac gently said. 'Did you want Ravi to die?'

She looked at him and her top lip began to curl.

'Why are you asking me that?' she croaked. 'He got what he deserved. Mum said so.'

'Ravi Patel was brutally murdered. Why would you say that?' DS Wong said, unable to help himself.

She ignored the question.

'We understand that you have a box filled with memories about your time with Mr Patel. Why do you hold on to something that would have the potential to cause you distress?' Isaac said, a little wary of the reaction he might get. He was right to be concerned. Agatha stormed over to her bed, grabbed a box from underneath and screamed as she threw it at DS Wong, scattering its contents all over the place.

'There,' she shouted. 'HAPPY! We had sex twice, and then he found a man. Is that what you wanted to hear? That I wasn't good enough for him. My body repulsed him and he left me! He destroyed my life!'

DCI Davidson could see that she was beginning to spiral out of control, but he wanted to get some answers, so he chose to continue.

'We were informed by a witness that you said Ravi had to die so that you could get on with your life. Did you kill Ravi, Miss Hawksworth?'

Agatha glared at DCI Davidson and then seized a vase from a shelf and hurled it across the room, shattering it onto the floor.

'Susie Hudson! She told you. Just wait until I speak with her next. I'll wring her bloody neck. She had absolutely no right to speak with you. I'm telling you this, and you'd better take note; she can't be trusted.'

Seeing the distressed state she had got herself into, and sensing that they weren't going to get anything more from her, they decided to leave. Just before they went, Jian pulled out the CCTV picture of the person on the train wearing a jacket.

'Do you recognise this person or jacket?' he asked.

Agatha snatched the photo, took seconds to look at it and then thrust it back to DS Wong.

'No,' was all she said.

Outside in the bright winter sun, the detectives glanced at each other and got into their car.

'Well,' Jian said. 'That was interesting. What do you make of that?'

Isaac took time to carefully think about how he wanted to answer this important question. He was already feeling upset with himself.

'I believe Miss Hawksworth has some concerning mental health issues, and therefore we need to be mindful of that. Today probably wasn't our best work. Actually, I know it wasn't. We screwed up! When we come back, and we need to, we will have to take advice first. However, she is an extremely volatile woman who has held on to a lot of anger and resentment for many years. That can build up inside you, and when it explodes out, anything could happen. Also, we have proof that she is right-handed, as that is the arm she used to throw the vase. She is also very strong and therefore we can't rule her out of killing our victim.'

DS Wong drove out of the street with both of them feeling guilty about what had just occurred. Isaac was particularly uncomfortable about the interview.

'We messed that right up!' he sighed. 'Jian, we also forgot to ask her about the text she sent to Ravi, and the fight in the café that Faisal witnessed. Damn!'

'We'll do better next time, sir.'

DCI Davidson barely said anything for the rest of the journey, but he spoke just as DS Wong parked up.

'Jian, check with Miss Hawksworth's GP and see if she has a psychiatric history. Also, ask them to give her a welfare call.'

60

Updates

25th November 2019

09:00 a.m.

Isaac sat in his office getting ready for the morning briefing. He had spent the first hour of the day ignoring emails from his Superintendent asking what was happening about cutting a DC from his team. Isaac had informed the four of them about the reduction required in the team, the process and timescales that Human Resources were following, and had encouraged them all to reapply for their jobs. If he was being honest with himself, he didn't want to lose any of them. Not because he was worried about less manpower, but because he genuinely liked them and thought that they did a great job, especially Faisal.

Isaac gathered them around the crime board, which was looking full. He informed them of the botched interview with Agatha Hawksworth and looked at his DS. Jian jumped up.

'I spoke with the GP, who agreed to make a welfare call. She was, however, reluctant to speak with me because of patient confidentiality and wanted to run it by information governance first. I remembered Agatha talking about her mother, so I rang her. Faith Hawksworth was helpful to a point. She told me that her daughter has manic episodes but hasn't had one for quite some time. Apparently, stress can bring them on. I described what happened to us, and she said it sounded mild, but would check in and ensure she was doing OK. Agatha is unfortunately non-compliant with her medications and therefore these outbursts can happen at any time.' Jian looked at his boss with a worried expression on his face.

'What else?' Isaac said, picking up on the facial concern.

'Mrs Hawksworth said that Agatha gets like this because of our victim. That ever since he dumped her daughter many years ago, there have been many attempts at ending her own life. The consequence being that she has often ended up with a Section Two being put in place and hospitalisation. Agatha's mother said she was glad Ravi was dead, as she blames him for everything her daughter has been put through. She also gave me some hospital discharge letters, and those I read all stated a broken relationship from years ago as her daughter's reason for trying to commit suicide. Mr Kumar did tell us about what was said at the party concerning Miss Hawksworth, but there have been historic difficulties with Agatha managing her mental health.'

Isaac thanked his DS as he processed the information.

'Does that make Faith Hawksworth a suspect?' asked DC Tovey.

'I don't know. Maybe.' Isaac replied. 'Faisal, did you get your friend to help with the lip-reading re the fight on the street between Ravi and his husband?'

'I did, sir.' Faisal opened his notebook. 'On the CCTV from the neighbour's property, we can see both men run out of the house. Ravi has his back to us, but Rakesh says, *"I hate you. You only want to live a quiet life. I want expensive holidays and everything the husband of a millionaire should have. I'm being held back by you. You were so lucky to have parents who loved and accepted you for who you are. My parents were different.*

They despised me for being gay. We could be living a life of luxury." At this point, Ravi turns and says, *"It isn't your money. It's mine. Do you think I'd give you anything now? If you do, then you are very much mistaken. You may hate me, but I loathe you. You're a slut."* Rakesh then slaps him hard and goes back into the house.'

What DC Asher had read out didn't seem to shock anyone.

'I think we know they weren't getting on,' DC Michaels said. 'However, Rakesh Kumar was the victim's husband. He was going to do well following divorce proceedings, so why risk killing Ravi?'

'He'd get more from the will,' Hamish replied.

'Yes, but why risk losing it all if you're caught for murder?'

DCI Davidson summarised the morning conversation and items were moved around the crime board.

'Anything else?' he asked.

'Yes,' Lily shouted, louder than she meant to. 'I have located Mr Kwasi Moses, Ravi and Parveena's nurse at the veterinary practice. He is expecting you and me today, sir.'

'Good work, Lily,' Isaac smiled at his newest DC. 'Is that it?'

'Rakesh's phone, sir,' Jian said. 'I called in to see him, and to be fair he willingly let me look through his phone. Anne was right, very few text messages between him and his husband. However, there is a WhatsApp group with the six of them. Ravi sent a message on 16th September, *"Not completely sure what I said last night because my memory of events is vague. Sorry if I revealed too much."* This follows the party. No one responded to it. There were some messages between Rakesh and Ravi, but nothing of great importance, and certainly nothing following their break-up and Ravi moving out. Rakesh said he was hoping his husband was going to move back in soon. Doesn't it seem strange that there are no messages about a reconciliation? Just like Hamish said.'

'Deleted?' voiced Lily.

'Maybe,' said Jian. 'Should we get his phone looked at properly, sir? However, what was on it were hundreds of messages between him and other men. The photos on it would shock most people.'

'Let's talk with him again and decide about the phone. And, just before we go, Alex told me the processing of the scarf label had been delayed due to these ongoing strikes, but is finally being looked at and he hopes to get an answer to us as soon as possible.'

61

Kwasi

25th November 2019

11:30 a.m.

Just as DCI Davidson and DC Tovey were getting ready to leave, a call came in from downstairs. Mr Moses had arrived to see them. Isaac asked Lily to fetch him and then escort him to meeting room one.

When Lily brought the man to meet the DCI, Isaac was slightly shocked at the sight that greeted him. Although he had never met the man, he didn't give off the impression that he was a qualified professional. He was unshaven, his chin was hanging like he'd lost a lot of weight too quickly, and his body odour was overwhelmingly offensive.

Kwasi was shown to a chair, and then DC Tovey went to the other side of the table and joined her boss.

'Dear Lord!' he said. 'Please forgive me.'

The smell coming from the veterinary nurse caught the back of Isaac's throat and made him wish he'd brought some water with him.

'Mr Moses, we have been keen to speak with you regarding Mr Ravi Patel. I understand you worked for him?'

'I'm so sorry for what I did. You must both believe and forgive me.'

'For what?' asked Lily.

Kwasi appeared increasingly anxious as he sat there, his head swinging from side to side while he clenched his fists tightly. His recent meeting with Agatha was running through Isaac's head, and he hoped this interview wasn't heading in the same direction.

'I knew what that woman was doing, and I should have stopped her. I need money for my daughter, but I should have said something. He was such a lovely, kind man and didn't deserve to die. I should have said something,' he repeated. 'My child has special needs and money is always needed to provide for her. Dear Lord, what have I done?'

The detectives could see how distressed Kwasi was, and Isaac intervened.

'Mr Moses, we can take a break if you like and speak again when you are calmer.'

'No, dear boy. We must speak now. I have done wrong, and I want to tell you. Please, you need to know that this isn't what I am normally like. Please believe me.' The detectives nodded. 'She is an evil person.'

'Who are you talking about, Mr Moses?'

'Dear boy, call me Kwasi, that would please me greatly. I'm talking about Parveena Johal. She killed three pets, and I watched and did nothing. I was scared that I would lose my job and the money. Each time she was drunk. Not paralytic, but enough to make her judgement poor. Oh, why didn't I say something to Mr Patel? Such a wonderful person. He used to look at me with such concern. I think he didn't like me, but I liked him. At first, we all got on well and I loved working for them both. Then it all changed. I started noticing that Miss Johal smelt of alcohol and she sometimes slurred her words. It scared me, but I just put my head down and tried to ignore what was happening. I broke my working code of conduct, and for that I have asked our Lord for forgiveness.'

Isaac felt relieved that Kwasi seemed to have calmed down and was starting to make sense. However, he couldn't help but feel a sense of compassion for the dishevelled man sitting before him.

'Please, Kwasi. Go on, you're doing extremely well.'

'Thank you, dear boy,' he replied. 'I have had trouble sleeping and eating. I have lost weight and haven't been caring for myself as I am sure you can see.' Kwasi lowered his head. 'The relationship between the two of them started to deteriorate during the past year. Miss Johal started to say bad things about Mr Patel. There was so much resentment coming from her. However, she was the one making mistakes, not him. I used to hear them shouting at each other, and this got worse over time. They went to a conference in Paris, and this did not go well for her. Mr Patel was very angry about this, and they yelled constantly at each other. Working with them had become increasingly difficult. I came today because I couldn't wait for you to come to me. My guilt was eating at me. I need you to know that he was a good man, but she is the devil.'

The detectives thanked Kwasi for coming in to see them and acknowledged what he had told them. As he stood, Isaac could see that there was a reluctance in him to leave.

'Kwasi? Do you have something else to tell us?'

'DCI Davidson, I have been a bad man. I took extra payments from Miss Johal for my silence.'

'£300 per month, yes we know,' said Isaac.

'I am so ashamed of myself, but my thoughts were of my daughter. If you think I need to, I can try to find a way of paying it back, although this would be difficult for me.' Kwasi was embarrassed. 'I am sure you know, Mr Patel reported her and the practice has been shut down. I am now jobless and have no hope of a reference. That woman has reduced me to tears on many occasions and I wish I'd never met her. Poor Mr Patel.'

Kwasi stood and thanked the detectives for their time. Lily also rose from her seat and walked the man back downstairs.

62

Norton

27th November 2019

08:30 a.m.

Isaac was studying the crime board and pulled a frustrated expression. He calculated dates in his head.

'Why has Norton Greene not been spoken with for three weeks?' he called out to the room.

There were then a lot of computers being accessed and notebooks shuffled through.

'I've been going through his social media,' called back DC Tovey.

'After Stuart Schumann came to see us, I have also been following up on his statement,' replied DC Asher.

'And I spoke with his professional institution about Ravi's report,' said DC Michaels.

'We need to speak with him again, and I mean today,' DCI Davidson expressed. 'We have left him alone for far too long, and there is something fishy about that man.'

The rest of the morning was spent combing through forensic reports and statements from suspects and witnesses.

'DC Michaels,' bellowed Isaac. 'I'd like you to come with me to interview Dr Greene. Then tomorrow, DC Potter and I will go back and speak with Mr Kumar. We will find the person who murdered Ravi Patel!'

1:00 p.m.

With his practice no longer operational, Norton hadn't been to the office for a couple of weeks, nor had he heard anything from his receptionist. He had preferred to keep himself to himself and almost shut out the world. Every morning, he would go to the local shop and buy just enough food for that day. Doing things this way would give him the excuse he needed to go out again the following morning. However, lately, he had been returning home to find dreadful things on his doormat.

Each morning, he feared the post being delivered. He had re-directed the mail from his office, so there were usually a few things he had to open. Lately, along with unpaid bills and returned invoices, there was a surge of hate mail. Some with postcodes he didn't recognise, but more alarmingly, some were being hand-delivered. It concerned Norton how they knew where he lived. Twice he had come home to envelopes with dog muck inside. One of them he had trodden on before he realised and it had exploded onto his shoes and carpet.

Depression was taking over the doctor. He had seen it so often in his patients but had never suffered himself. These last couple of weeks were giving him a real insight into this terrible illness. He ventured into the kitchen to make himself a coffee and a light lunch. His appetite had reduced significantly and his clothes were beginning to hang off him. He sipped his drink.

'Yuk! Such a dull drink,' he whispered.

The doorbell sounded just as he sat down with half a ham sandwich. Since the hate mail, he was reluctant to open the door.

'Dr Greene,' came a voice. 'This is DCI Davidson and DC Michaels.'

Norton continued to sit for a few moments, then reluctantly got up and opened the door.

'Can I help you?' he asked, as he allowed them in.

'We certainly hope so,' said Isaac. 'We need some clarification of some details. Just how many times did you actually hit Mr Patel?'

'Once,' said Norton.

'Let me try to ask that again,' Isaac said with an air of sarcasm. 'How often did you inflict pain on your friend?'

'Once,' repeated the doctor.

'DC Michaels, please hand me the A&E reports and our witness statement.'

Anne handed over the required documents and was looking forward to watching the doctor squirm.

'We know you hurt him at least twice.' Isaac read out the information in front of him. 'Your receptionist saw and heard what happened on 1st October. So why have you been lying to us?'

Norton glared at the detectives with disdain.

'People argue, DCI Davidson.'

'Yes, but they don't tend to beat up a friend though, do they?' Isaac raised his voice. 'Why were you fighting?'

'I don't see what bearing this has on his murder.'

'Answer the DCI's question, please,' said Anne.

'I don't remember,' he said.

'Not a problem,' Anne replied. 'Let me see if this jogs that memory of yours. Do the names Daisy Christmas and Stuart Schumann mean anything to you?'

Norton's expression froze as he reached behind to feel for the arm of the chair to steady himself.

'I see that they do,' Anne said cheerfully. 'Can you now explain why you felt the need to punch your friend?'

The atmosphere in the room was tense. In his head, Norton was cursing Sorel and at the same time wished he'd never laid eyes on those two patients. However, his anger was still directed at Ravi.

'That man has a lot to answer for!' he snarled through gritted teeth.

'Who?' Anne questioned.

'Ravi, bloody, Patel!' he snapped back.

'He reported you to your governing body, and now you're under investigation. We are also aware of the social media campaign against you. Now, we know that based on what these young people are saying about you may always have happened without you even being reported by Mr Patel, but it gives you a clear motive for murder, Dr Greene.'

Norton jumped up, stormed over to his table by his front door and picked up a handful of letters.

'These,' he screamed, 'are because of that interfering man. Are you going to start investigating these? Hate mail! I don't deserve what that fucking man put me through. Oh, he got what he deserved. He has ruined me!'

DCI Davidson took the letters and briefly looked through them.

'If you care to make a report to the police station, I'm sure they will be only too happy to help you, but this isn't a job for me and my team.'

Norton snatched them back.

'How did you get home from the concert?' Anne chipped in.

'Train.'

'Would that be the same train as Mr Patel would have got?'

'It would have been the same line, but not necessarily the same train. If your boss here remembers what I said last time he visited, I watched Rakesh kick Ravi, and then I left the concert. I have no idea what time they left.'

'Can you please look at this CCTV image and let me know if you recognise the person or the jacket they are wearing?' Anne said, handing him the picture.

Norton grabbed the photo, and his eyes widened.

'No, I don't.'

'Did you kill Mr Ravi Patel?' Anne asked.

'No!' was all Norton would say.

On their way back to the station, the detectives discussed what they had both heard. Isaac was keen to hear his DC's thoughts.

'You were right when earlier you said there was something fishy about him. Social media has him out to be the next creepy pervert that is hiding in plain sight. Also, sir, did you see how he hesitated when I showed him the photo? He knows more than he is telling us.'

'I picked up on that too, Anne. I don't like that man,' Isaac said. 'Now, changing the subject. Have you re-applied for your job?'

'Yes, sir.'

'DC Michaels, I am delighted to hear that.'

As Anne drove them back to the station, Isaac got a text message come through to his phone.

"Things not great with Daisy. I think I have made a big mistake. I'll tell you everything when I come home tonight. Hope that's OK. Alan xx"

"Absolutely! I'll be back at 8 p.m. Isaac x"

63

Isaac

27th November 2019

8:00 p.m.

In true keeping for a late November evening, the rain was lashing from the heavens and making driving conditions difficult. The streetlights were being reflected in the ever-growing number of puddles on the ground. Impatient drivers were honking their horns and driving too close to the car in front. As Isaac slowly drove home, he felt a deep sense of disappointment in the way people were behaving. However, he did smile when he saw the house at the beginning of his road already had their usual Christmas decorations sparkling away in the front garden, and the tree in their lounge window.

As he approached his bungalow, he could make out his brother sitting in their partially covered porch, getting wet.

'What are you doing?' Isaac called out as he got out of the car.

'I know! So stupid. I just wanted to get here, and the Uber turned up early. Don't worry, I've only been here a few minutes.'

Once inside and with a towel around his shoulders, Alan felt warmer. Isaac made them both a cup of tea.

'Working late?'

'No,' Isaac replied. 'I met Jane for a drink and a catch-up.'

'How is she getting on?'

'Great! She has started dating, and it's going well. I'm chuffed for her.'

The brothers took their hot drinks into the lounge and Alan was pleased that he was back. He had missed living here. On the mantelpiece, there were two Christmas cards.

'Let me guess,' Alan said. 'One from the local church and the other from Auntie Fiona, who isn't our auntie, but always signs her card that way?'

'Spot on,' Isaac chuckled. 'Now, what's going on with you?'

Alan took a swig of his tea, and the warmth felt good.

'We just argue all the time. It's still a fairly new relationship, so surely we should be in the honeymoon period. Don't get me wrong, Daisy is a great person, but I don't think we are as compatible as we first thought. On paper, we are perfect, but in reality it isn't working.'

Isaac listened intently and didn't miss a single word. He had missed having his brother at home so much and was enjoying being able to have an evening like this. The only downside was what his brother was telling him.

'Well,' Isaac said. 'From what I know about her involvement in my case, she has a lot going on.'

'I know,' Alan said. 'That is probably why I feel like a complete dick!'

'Tell me.'

'I understand what she is going through, because of this man, Dr Greene. He sounds horrendous. Daisy is on a huge campaign to take this man down, and I agree that she should, but there is nothing left for us. She has got together with Stuart Schumann and others. I didn't tell you this, but they are sending him hate mail and putting dog turds through his letterbox.'

Isaac couldn't help himself from smiling.

'Daisy is hell-bent on destroying this man,' Alan continued. 'But at what cost? I believe the price is us.'

'Ah, man. I'm sorry,' Isaac said. 'Maybe things will settle down for her once this case is over. After all, Dr Norton Greene may be our killer and could spend most of his remaining life in prison.'

'Do you think it's him?' Alan asked.

'I don't know. He is certainly a hateful person, but that doesn't make him a murderer.'

'I think Daisy and I are done.'

'You sure?' Isaac asked with genuine interest.

'Yes! I'm OK with it ending, so surely that is a sign that it shouldn't continue? Isaac?'

'Alan?'

'Can I come back?'

Isaac went over and put his arms around his brother and kissed his head.

'Alan, this is your home, and it always will be. Stay tonight, then tomorrow go and get your belongings. Please talk things through with Daisy first, though. She has a right to know how you're feeling.'

'I will. Now tell me about you and the case.'

'That needs wine, and a log fire!'

There were now flames roaring and red wine being enjoyed. Both brothers were happier than either of them had been for a long time. All thoughts of Daisy Christmas had temporarily left Alan's mind.

'Go on, tell me what's happening.'

'I'm annoyed with myself,' Isaac replied. 'I let a suspect; the aforementioned Dr Greene go three weeks in between interviews. It's sort of OK because we were gathering evidence, but I'm not happy.'

'Why did that happen?' enquired Alan.

'Muzzy feeling in my head. I have to let one of my DCs go. Those above haven't given me a choice.'

'So, DCI Davidson. What are your thoughts?'

Isaac lifted his glass and enjoyed the taste of the Malbec. It was a bottle given as a present a few months ago from DC Michaels.

'So, I do not want any of them to go, but one is.'

'Do you know if pushed, who you would choose?'

'They need to be interviewed, so it will depend on that,' Isaac said.

'Really?' Alan said. 'Now tell me the truth. Who would be your choice to go?'

This was a question that the DCI had been dreading. He was therefore pleased his brother had asked him; to get it out of the way.

'DC Anne Michaels,' Isaac said as he frowned. 'I am very fond of Anne, and I know she did great in the Sally Raines case, but before that I was getting ready to put her on a performance review. She has improved since her father died, but is it a bit too late? On the other hand, DC Potter doesn't give me the impression that he wants to stay. He has already volunteered to leave. That doesn't give me the feeling that his heart is still on the job, but he is a great detective.'

Alan topped up both their glasses and could see the confusion written on his brother's face.

'DC Lily Tovey,' continued Isaac, 'is great. She is coming along nicely and brings a great balance to the team. I seriously don't know who to choose. Therefore, I am glad that the decision is not entirely mine; it will depend on how they score during their interviews.'

'DC Faisal Asher?' asked Alan.

'That's a no-brainer; Faisal stays.'

The rest of the evening was spent reminiscing and laughing. When the second bottle of wine was opened, Isaac knew that his head would not thank him in the morning. However, he didn't care; he was happy.

64

DS Jian Wong

27th November 2019

11:00 p.m.

Multicoloured strobing lights were flashing around the room. The smell of cheap cologne and hair products permeated the air. The music was loud and lots of people were dancing. Jian and Lily were sitting at a table watching Faisal and his friend Maggie strutting their stuff.

'I can't believe we are out on a school night,' Lily joked.

'Faisal does like to dance,' Jian replied. 'Do you want another drink?'

'Go on then, but this is the last one. We've got work in the morning. Are you getting those two a drink?' Lily said, pointing to the dance floor.

'They don't need one,' laughed Jian.

At the bar, a gin and tonic and sparkling water were ordered. Jian then took them over to Lily. They sat for a few moments as they watched the dancing. There were so many moves happening, and that's what they both loved about disco. All those who were on the dance floor were loving the music. Maggie, who was deaf, enjoyed the thumping she could feel through the floor.

'They dance well,' Lily said.

'He's great, isn't he?'

'Yes,' Lily laughed. 'However, I meant they both were.'

Jian looked slightly embarrassed but laughed along with his colleague. They had become great friends since she had joined the team, and the thought that either Faisal or Lily might lose their jobs had been a concern playing on his mind. Jian liked the other two DCs, but there was no contest for him.

'Can we go outside?' he asked Lily.

Despite the time of night, a lot of activity was still happening on the streets. Sirens were going off all over the place, so the emergency services were being kept busy. The cool air initially felt good against their bodies, but it wasn't long before they realised they had come outside without their coats.

'Be quick,' teased Lily.

'I love him,' Jian said.

'I can't believe the two of you thought you'd been so discreet at work. That made me howl when the boss told you everyone knew.'

'I was so shocked. To be fair, I thought we'd done a great job hiding it.'

'Is he OK with it?'

'Yeah, as long as it doesn't interfere with work. Isaac Davidson is a good man.'

More people were heading into the venue than coming out, but this wasn't surprising as it was still early for clubbing in the grand scheme of things.

'Go on,' Lily said. 'You didn't bring me out here to freeze my tits off to tell me that you love him. I already guessed that. The way the two of you look at each other. I see the touching that goes on. I agree that you are very subtle with it, but I see the occasional hand touches and the locked eyes. Ooh, you two are delicious.'

'Lily,' Jian said. 'I'm going to ask Faisal to marry me. What do you think?'

The screams coming from the young woman outside the discotheque were drawing attention. People walking by were stopping to ask if she was OK.

'Oh, Jian Wong, that is the best news I have heard. I am thrilled for you.'

Lily embraced her friend and continued to scream.

'I love him. Maybe I should delay for a year or two, but why wait? I know he could say no, but I need to ask him. Every morning when I see him lying next to me, my heart beats faster. The noises he makes in his sleep are precious, and the way he cuddles into me as we fall asleep is something I have waited my whole life for. Do you think it is crazy? Should I wait?'

'Don't you bloody well dare!' Lily said.

As the two of them stood there in the cold November evening, they heard voices behind them.

'What are you two doing out here?' Faisal asked. 'Here are your coats. We'd better get going as we have work in the morning and we don't want the boss to be mad at us.'

65

Rakesh

28th November 2019

10:00 a.m.

Following the morning briefing, DCI Davidson and DC Potter headed out to talk with Rakesh Kumar again. This allowed Isaac time to speak with Hamish. He had been doing a lot of thinking following his chat with Alan the previous evening. Letting one of them go was going to be difficult.

'Have you submitted your application?'

Hamish nodded but didn't answer verbally.

'Care to expand?' asked Isaac.

'Form completed, but I'm still not sure about things. I have been looking for other jobs outside policing. If I go, you don't have to choose.'

'We've already spoken about this. The final decision will be based on the application form and the interview. If you do well, then you're the right person for the job. Please don't leave just to stop me from having to choose. That is for me and Human Resources to worry about and not you. Do you understand?'

'I do,' Hamish replied. Isaac wasn't convinced.

When they drove into the road leading to Rakesh's place, they noticed a car on the driveway that wasn't there before, and the shutters were closed. The rest of the street had their bins out but nothing outside the house they had just arrived at. Hamish noticed the serene quietness of the pleasant road. It was lined with detached houses with only a couple of semi-detached. Most front gardens were well-presented and the properties were beautifully maintained.

'I could live here,' he said.

'With Rakesh Patel-Kumar as your neighbour?' Isaac said, laughing.

'Oh, hadn't thought of that. That'll be a no then.'

DC Potter rang the doorbell and waited. Across the road, a curtain twitched. Then a man appeared on his doorstep and called over.

'Such a shame the wrong one was killed.'

The detectives walked over to speak with him.

'That sounded harsh, sir. Would you like to tell me why you said that?' Hamish asked.

'The other one, he was a lovely fella. He always gave you the time of day. That one,' he said, pointing over to the house, 'doesn't even say hello. Never has. And since his husband was murdered, he has had men coming and going. I'm no prude, but it hasn't been that long, has it? Only a month, so it doesn't seem right.' He turned and went back inside his house and the detectives went back to Rakesh's.

DC Potter banged on the door this time, seeing that there was no answer using the bell. However, it took two more loud knocks before an unknown man wearing just a pair of boxers opened the door.

'Can I help you?' he asked with little enthusiasm.

'We'd like to speak with Mr Kumar, please.'

'Raks,' he called out.

Rakesh came excitedly running to the door, almost as if he was dancing. When he saw who was waiting for him, his demeanour drastically changed.

'Oh, come on, you have got to be joking. I have told you everything I know.'

'Can we come in?' Isaac politely asked, at the same time as stepping forward.

In the lounge the four men stood looking at each other. Rakesh almost made it his mission to make the detectives feel uncomfortable with the two of them just in their underwear.

'I suggest you leave us,' Isaac said to the friend. 'Mr Kumar, please get dressed.'

The two men huffed off towards the stairs, leaving Isaac and Hamish to look around.

'The pictures of Ravi have all gone?' Hamish noticed. 'Didn't take long for that to happen.'

'We can't judge DC Potter, but we can note it.'

Five minutes later Rakesh appeared, now wearing joggers and a T-shirt.

'Better,' he said, as he spun himself around.

'Mr Kumar,' DCI Davidson said, ignoring Rakesh's floor show. 'If you don't mind me saying, you seem pretty chipper. It has only been a month since your husband's death.'

'Nothing is going to bring him back, so I need to start living again. And when the inheritance comes through, I can tell you right now that I'll be moving away from here.'

'Can it really be that straightforward?' Isaac asked. 'You learned that your murdered husband had an aggressive brain tumour with a very short time to live, and we find you doing a hot-shoe shuffle.'

Rakesh glared at the DCI.

'Firstly, DCI Davidson,' he snapped. 'You have no right to judge me. I can react however I like. Ravi and I were finished, over! Do you comprehend? The relationship was dead. Excuse the pun. The person I no longer wanted to be with was a millionaire. So, by death or divorce, I am now an extremely rich man. My scum parents can look down from heaven, or wherever they ended up and see I will now become the person I wanted to be and live the life I was born to have. Yes, it's sad that Ravi is dead, but so what? He was going to die anyway.'

Hamish recoiled at the callousness of what he had just heard. The man across the street had been right about Rakesh.

'Are you left or right-handed?'

'Left,' he replied to DC Potter.

The friend who was asked to leave came back into the room and draped his arms over Rakesh's shoulders and gently kissed his neck, hoping to get a reaction from the detectives; he didn't get one.

'Last time we were here, you told us that you hoped that you and your husband could work things out and get back together. When did that change?'

'Oops! I lied. Incredibly bad of me. The moment I kicked him was the end of any possible reunion. I am free of that miserable, penny-pinching excuse of a man, and soon I'll have millions, so bite me!'

'One final thing,' Hamish said. 'Please look at this CCTV picture of a person of interest. Is there anything you can tell us about it?'

Rakesh glanced at the photo.

'Nice jacket.'

When they were back in the car, DCI Davidson could sense the rage his DC was experiencing. He liked that he was showing so much emotion as it showed he cared.

'What a vile, toxic human being,' Hamish belted out.

'Agreed. Why did you ask him about which hand he uses? We already knew that.'

'I was testing the idiot.'

'OK, good call,' Isaac replied. 'But stay focused, DC Potter. Being toxic doesn't make him a killer.'

'I know, he just got under my skin.'

Isaac drove them back to the police station, and Rakesh and his friend giggled and waved them off from inside the house and then headed back upstairs.

66

Dipen

2nd December 2019

08:30 a.m.

Everyone was sitting around the crime board and DCI Davidson was going over things that they already knew, but he wanted to make sure that they weren't missing anything.

'Rakesh, a horrible man with a motive; millions of motives. He was cheating on his husband and had a secret bank account where he kept the money he earned from sleeping with men. Ravi's death seems to have been a good thing for Mr Kumar. Parveena Johal, a drunk who was reported by Ravi and has all but lost her career. Norton Greene, a predator of young adults, was also reported by Ravi and is now ruined thanks to the power of social media. Agatha Hawksworth, a bitter former girlfriend who never got over their relationship breaking up. That leaves Dipen Patel.' Isaac looked frustrated. 'I feel he is the one we know least about. I got the feeling that he sincerely loved his cousin, but the amount of debt he is in could trigger anyone to commit murder. The last time we met him, he was decidedly edgy.'

There was a consensus among the group and some breakout conversations. Isaac called out to get back their attention.

'Sir,' Faisal said. 'DS Wong asked me to look further into Dipen Patel. It seems he has a reputation as a "lad about town," but he is well-liked. We have already discussed the amount of money that he owes but here is where it gets interesting. We have traced his phone on the day of the murder, and a mast "pinged" in a desolate part of London. Doing a postcode search, he was only about a twenty-five-minute drive from where the body was found. The phone notification was 9:07 p.m. His location was by a lot of abandoned warehouses. I have made some calls and this area is known to be unsafe, and managed by a woman known only as Donna. She's apparently the head of an organised crime group and loan shark. I am only assuming, but what if Dipen Patel was seeing this woman? She is piling on the pressure about the money he owes her, and he kills Ravi to get money from the inheritance. He would know what trains Ravi would be getting home on, even if he didn't know the exact time. He could wait.'

'Good work DC Asher,' said Isaac. 'DS Wong, we need to go back and speak with Mr Patel.'

1:00 p.m.

Dipen looked at his face in the bathroom mirror. The graze on his nose was finally beginning to heal. The antibiotics were doing their job. There would be a scar, but there was nothing he could do about that. His hands, however, were in a bad way, more so his knuckles. He had beaten up a terrified man in his sixties only a couple of hours ago in a disused warehouse, and he was feeling sick. The sight of the poor man's face with each punch taking out more teeth. Dipen hated what he'd become, but carrying out these tortures on other people kept him alive. He took out his phone and texted Rakesh.

"When will the inheritance money be released? I'm desperate!"

Not able to face food, he cracked open a can of lager and drained the entire thing in one. He then opened another one, but took his time. The loud knock at his front door frightened him.

'Mr Patel,' Isaac said. 'Can we come in?'

Dipen stood aside but didn't say anything. His phone vibrated in his pocket.

"No idea. I think they have to solve the crime first. I'm contacting a solicitor next week."

'Damn!'

'Did you say something?' asked the DCI.

'No. So what can I help you with?'

'If I said the name, Donna, what would it make you think of?'

Jian immediately saw the fear in Dipen's eyes, and when he brought his hands up to his face, the cuts and bruises were obvious.

'Are you working for her?' Isaac asked.

'No comment.'

'Ah, we are going to be playing that game, are we? Mr Patel, we can place you on 27th October at 9:07 p.m. at the part of London where this Donna operates. Why were you there?'

'No comment.'

'Is she your loan shark?'

'No comment.'

'How did you get those marks on your knuckles?'

'No comment.'

Although frustrated with Dipen's behaviour, the detectives could see how terrified he was at the mere mention of the woman. His legs were quivering, as were his hands.

'We can help if you let us.'

'No one can help me,' he replied to DS Wong. 'Only money can do that. I can't believe what I've done. I am a nervous wreck whenever my phone makes a noise, or someone is at my door. Sleep is out of the question; if I have to leave the house, I spend the whole time looking over my shoulder. Ravi could have stopped this from happening, but he didn't. He chose to let me live this life. I think I now know how Agatha feels before she attempts to take her life. I would be better off dead.'

Dipen fell to his knees and began sobbing hard. His tears were stinging the cuts on his hands, but he couldn't stop himself. Isaac crouched down and gave his shoulder a sympathetic rub.

'You need to go into the police station and report what is happening to you. It is the only way to make it stop.'

'Not wishing to be rude,' the frightened man said, 'but you don't know what you're talking about. I have been told that only by paying everything I owe will stop what is happening. They have warned me that if I go to the police, or stop working for them, then they will hurt me. I have seen what they do DCI Davidson. I'd rather kill myself, but if I do that, Donna has said she'll come after my sister, Beena. Ravi's money from his will is what I need. Nothing else will save me.'

Jian brought Dipen a glass of water and then helped him to his feet. When things had calmed down, he was shown the CCTV image.

'I don't recognise anything,' he said. 'Sorry.'

The detectives left, and as they went, they heard the sound of bolts locking and chains being put back in place. They also heard Dipen crying.

'I think he did recognise something in that picture. I can't be sure, but his eyes enlarged, just a smidge, but there was something there,' said Jian.

67

Parveena

3rd December 2019

2:30 p.m.

DC Tovey was eager to get back to interviewing Parveena Johal. She had got under her skin and Lily wanted the woman to feel uncomfortable. The last time they saw her she had been covered in her own vomit and reeked of alcohol.

Isaac drove and Lily looked through her notes. She didn't want to miss a thing, and wanted to get the names right.

'DC Tovey,' Isaac said.

'Yes, my application has been submitted, sir.'

'Good show.'

They pulled up to the veterinary practice and saw a car parked outside. The number plate matched the one Lily had traced via ANPR. Parveena was in the building. They had taken a chance on her being here rather than at home, and it looked like it had paid off.

'Look at the graffiti,' Lily said. 'It doesn't take people long to find out when a building is barely used.'

'It amazes me, and at the same time it saddens me. I'll never understand why idiots have to behave like this. It is actually a lovely looking building, but now has that all over it.'

DC Tovey agreed with her boss.

When they tried the main door it was locked. They circled the practice but couldn't see another way in. However, through a window they could see Miss Johal. Lily bashed hard on the window and they were eventually let in.

Parveena was looking so much better than when they last met. Her hair was glossy and even though she was just wearing jeans and a T-shirt she looked fantastic. There was an energy about her that was exuding confidence. She greeted them warmly and made tea.

'Miss Johal, we need to catch up on a few things. I hope that is OK,' said Lily.

'Of course, my dear,' was the reply. Any sarcasm hidden.

'What's happening with this practice?'

'As I am sure you are already aware, if you're doing your job properly, I am still under investigation. There is still an outstanding enquiry, but I'm sure there is nothing for me to worry about.'

'Mr Patel must have made you incredibly angry when he reported you.'

Parveena smirked at the DC.

'He did what he felt he needed to do, I guess. Totally unnecessary, as I kept pointing out to him. Kwasi, our nurse, was with me on the three occasions that Ravi questioned and told him that I was in complete control and the animals died as they would have done if Mr Patel had been operating. I really don't understand why the matter keeps rearing its ugly head.'

Parveena went through to the kitchen and brought out the teapot to top up their drinks. She had a majestic air about her that the detectives hadn't seen before. Lily was suspicious though.

'How did you get on with Mr Moses?' she asked.

'Kwasi? He was a delightful man. I am sorry all this nasty business has meant we have had to part company.'

'He recently told us about constant arguments between yourself and Mr Patel. They had been building up for a long time, but a conference in Paris made things so much worse. He told us that you loathed Ravi.'

'If you will forgive me for saying, Kwasi did not know the ins and outs of this practice. People that work together argue, especially when finances are involved. Ravi and I were trying to run a successful business, and therefore, at times, things got heated.'

Lily smiled, but was getting ready to play her trump card.

Parveena had acted like the perfect host. She was polite and courteous, and didn't seem at all bothered that they were there. However, Lily had a couple more questions first.

'We have looked at the Paris conference times and your train schedule. It would appear that you would have had very little free time. Can I ask why you took the huge amount of euros with you? We checked the amount with your bank. Was there anything in particular you wanted to buy?'

'Really? That's your question! Dearie, it was Paris. I made myself have time to shop. Honestly, I can't believe that you asked me such a stupid question. I'm assuming you're new to the job?'

Lily ignored the question.

DCI Davidson was enjoying watching the two women trying to outdo each other. So far, DC Tovey was winning.

'Please look at this CCTV picture and tell me your thoughts.'

Parveena took the photo and gave it her best attention.

'Well, it's a man wearing a jacket. Why is that important?'

'What makes you think it's a man? Do you recognise him?' Lily said.

'No. It could be anybody.'

DC Tovey put the picture away, but she was far from finished with her suspect.

'Where did you go when you left the concert on 27th October?'

'I drove home.'

'The six of you all live relatively close to each other. Why didn't you give anybody a lift?'

Parveena scowled at the detective.

'The guys had train tickets and Agatha was in a strange mood. I told you the last time we met that I don't care for them.'

'Did you strangle Ravi Patel?' Lily asked, staring Parveena directly in the eyes.

'No,' was the reply. 'Anything else?'

'Yes,' Lily said, finally playing her trump card. 'Just three names for you: Rudge, Peanut, and Twix.'

Both detectives saw a sudden change in Parveena's body language.

The mood in the room had now dramatically changed. DC Tovey was loving the anger spreading across the vet's face.

'Get out!,' Parveena screamed.

'I think not,' Lily responded. 'These are the names of the pets that Ravi Patel accused you of killing whilst under the influence of alcohol. This is backed up by Kwasi Moses, and the reason Ravi reported you. This gives you a very clear motive for murder.'

'They got it wrong! I did not kill those animals. Get OUT!'

'Why pay Mr Moses £300 per month, extra to his wage if you had nothing to hide?' Lily continued, ignoring Parveena.

'Because Ravi was coming for me. I did what I thought I should do. Kwasi was angry, and I thought he was going to run to Ravi and give him more ammunition to sack me as a partner. I was sure that this is what Ravi ultimately wanted.'

'So,' Lily said. 'With Kwasi's help, I have contacted the owners of the dead pets and two of them had asked for their pets to be given back to them so they could bury them in their gardens.' DC Tovey was enjoying the panic on Parveena's face. 'Rudge and Twix are at this precise moment being exhumed and will go through a thorough post-mortem to give a precise cause of death.'

Parveena looked exhausted, and DC Tovey, triumphant.

'You bitch,' the vet hissed. 'OK, you win! I killed those animals. I never meant to, but I was drinking heavily and made mistakes. Kwasi was getting hysterical, so I had to pay for his silence. Ravi reporting me has ended my career.'

'Did you kill Ravi?' asked Lily.

'I believe that's for you to find out.'

The detectives drove back to the station, and DCI Davidson could feel that his DC was proud of herself.

'Great work, Lily,' Isaac said.

'Did you see her squirm?'

'I had no clue that you had arranged for exhumations.'

'Oh, that was a lie,' she said. 'But it worked. Parveena Johal has one huge motive for wanting Ravi dead, and I just proved it.'

68

Norton

4th December 2019

1:30 p.m.

Norton sat in his chair and listened to some music by Schubert. Of all the composers, he was his favourite. The glass of brandy by his side was empty, as was the bottle on the floor. Lost in thoughts of Austrian lakes and mountains, he pretended to conduct the music. At one moment, he even thought he could smell the alpine flowers, hear goats, and see the chalets on the hills.

Coming from outside was a chanting noise that he tried hard not to focus on. He wanted the classical sounds to wash over him and keep reality far away. His flat was on the first floor of a four-storey building. It had cost a small fortune to buy, but it was his sanctuary. He reached for his glass and was disappointed to see nothing inside. As he stood, he kicked the bottle on the floor under the chair opposite. He then staggered into the kitchen and got out another full bottle and swigged a large mouthful. He wiped the back of his hand across his lips and then opened the fridge.

'Chocolate is needed.'

Outside, the chants were getting louder.

After a further twenty minutes, Norton eventually got sick of the noise and was going to scream at them to go away. When he got to the window, his heart felt like it had stopped. Outside his building was a crowd of young people. Some he recognised, and some were complete strangers. Daisy Christmas and Stuart Schumann were leading at the front. There were placards and banners, all calling Norton Greene a pervert, child molester, predator and much worse. The chanting that he had shut out, were these young people demanding answers and also letting anyone know who could hear them, that Dr Greene had violated them and caused an enormous amount of psychological damage.

Cars were honking horns in solidarity, and things were now being thrown at the windows. They obviously knew he was one floor up from the ground because their aim was spot on. In moments, he had eggs being thrown at his windows, as well as dog muck and rotting vegetables. One man was even spray-painting the walls. Norton opened the window to yell at them to leave him alone but was hit in the face by something that smelled disgusting.

The baying mob were getting louder and others not even part of the original group had joined in and were creating madness among everyone without even knowing what the cause was. Upon seeing Daisy, Norton decided to confront her and dashed out of his building.

'Leave me alone!' he screamed at her.

She hadn't even realised he was standing in front of her. She seemed to be arguing with someone on her phone.

'I hate you,' he heard her say. 'You're better off with your brother. There's something odd about the two of you. Don't ever contact me again.' Daisy ended the call and then turned to see Norton standing in front of her.

'PERVERT!' she screamed as she pointed towards the Psychologist.

'LEAVE ME ALONE,' Norton continued to shriek. Nobody was listening.

The masses were rocking cars in the street, and shops had windows broken. People were taking videos on their phones and photos were being taken from all angles and then uploaded to social media. Norton seized Daisy's wheelchair, began shaking it, and attempted to tip her onto the ground. Stuart noticed Norton's intentions and swiftly kicked him behind the knees, causing him to collapse onto the road.

'Leave her alone,' Stuart yelled. 'PERVERT,' he screamed as he pointed to Norton.

Some of the group had started to hit the psychologist with their placards.

From the ground looking up, Norton saw angry faces looking down at him. He knew they were kicking him, but it didn't seem to matter. Now the spitting started and then a kick landed in his genitals. He turned and vomited into the gutter. More cameras were clicking away and people were holding up their smartphones and recording every second. Social media was yet again going to be full of Dr Norton Greene.

As he lay there, allowing the attacks to happen, Norton caught sight of Stuart and grabbed his ankle. The young man fell and landed next to the psychologist.

'Please make them stop,' he begged Stuart. 'I didn't know that I was doing wrong.'

'Yes, you did,' he snapped back. 'You raped me! Time and time again.'

Norton felt the anger surge through his body. Then, with an unknown strength, he flipped himself over and seized Stuart's head and started to pound it onto the road. He wasn't sure how hard he was doing it.

5:00 p.m.

From inside his cell, Norton was petrified. Having never been in one before, he had no idea what was about to happen. He could hear voices outside but didn't recognise who was speaking. He closed his eyes as he lay on the uncomfortable bed, but shot up again as he saw Stuart's head and the blood seeping from it. Tears began streaming down his cheeks as he curled up on the bed.

Just as he settled himself, the large, heavy door opened and he saw DCI Davidson standing there. From his position, the detective looked nine feet tall and filled the space in the door. Behind him was DC Michaels. He wasn't sure how to explain it to himself, but he took comfort in seeing them both.

'How is he?' Norton asked, knowing they would have been informed.

'He has a severe concussion, needs many stitches, an MRI scan and undoubtedly years of therapy with a reputable psychologist. We can only hope that he'll be fine.'

'Thank you, DCI Davidson.'

The detectives had only seen Dr Greene less than a week ago, and yet he looked like a tramp off the streets of London. He hadn't shaved in weeks, and his hair was all over the place. His large teeth were even more prominent because of the gauntness of his cheeks. His hands were bruised and his shirt was half-open due to being ripped in the fight earlier.

'I'm so ashamed of myself,' he uttered. 'Hurting them was never part of my plan. I truly never thought I was doing wrong. They knew what I was doing and enjoyed it. I'm not to blame. I relished seeing their skin and nipples as the sun shone on their thin tops and I honestly believed they enjoyed me looking. Young people are so delicious in so many tantalising ways. Stuart begged me to take his virginity, I'm sure he did, and Daisy wanted her brother to do things to her. I wanted to help, and make them see different ways of seeing things. I shouldn't be punished for allowing their enviable youth to be enjoyed; and savoured. They need me as much as I need them. They are my necessary drugs! My daily medication that keeps me alive. If I had diabetes or high blood pressure, you would know that I need to take my tablets and not deny me. I want to feel them surging through my veins, engorging my very being. Don't you see? They need to fill me with desire. The older need to feed from the young, and even though I am only in my late thirties, I was only just getting started. The plans I had for Stuart Schumann would have been sensational, and he would have known such greatness. Ravi stopped me! He reported me and ended my practice. Just think of those young people who will never get a chance to come and see me; and be touched by me. For me to help them and release their innocent and fresh essence. Ravi has destroyed my creativity. That monster told us at that awful party that he was going to report me. How could he not see the beauty of what I was doing? The young are my fuel and my drive, and I would have educated so many through my work. They need me, and I will be there for them; to feed them.'

Isaac and DC Michaels were feeling astounded by what they had just heard. How this man had been able to work as a psychologist for so long and never be caught in his wrong-doings was unbelievable. They weren't sure if they had just witnessed a confession or a psychotic episode. Not knowing what else to do, the DC asked the only question on her mind.

'Did you kill Ravi Patel?'

'Does it really matter?' was the only reply offered.

Once back in his office, DCI Davidson called for a rapid psychiatric assessment to be carried out, and Anne called the hospital to check up on Stuart Schumann.

69

DC Hamish Potter

5th December 2019

10:30 a.m.

The morning briefing had been brief. DCI Davidson had updated everyone on Norton Greene. He was being detained pending a full psychiatric review, and would then most likely be charged for grievous bodily harm against Mr Schumann. A sexual assault charge could also follow if the young man felt able to press charges.

Stuart was still in hospital, but his MRI showed no concerns, and his wounds were not as bad as first thought once they had been cleaned and dressed.

The entire team was typing up their notes and reviewing the case. At times, they would shout out questions or thoughts to each other. Every moment was dedicated to constructing the case and determining who was responsible for the murder of Ravi Patel.

Hamish sat at his desk but wasn't doing what his colleagues were doing. DC Potter was checking his emails for job application results. Over the past two weeks he had sent five. They had all been to various sports centres looking to train those interested in becoming personal trainers. This was Hamish's perfect job; he wasn't meant to be a detective.

DC Potter could see his boss was rarely off the phone, and maybe only appreciated how busy his DCI was when he needed to speak with him. Hamish thought he could hear some keywords coming through the office door: "Imminently," "cost-cutting," and "decisions."

When DCI Davidson finally put the phone back on the receiver, Hamish knocked on the door.

'Come in,' called the DCI.

When he saw it was DC Potter, he relaxed a little and welcomed his DC into his office.

'Everything OK?' Isaac asked.

'From a case point of view we are all pulling everything together. Currently we all have different ideas about who did the murder. Not exactly helpful, is it?'

'Who do you think it is, DC Potter?' questioned the DCI.

'Rakesh Patel-Kumar, sir. Without a doubt!'

'Tell me why you think that.'

'Not yet. Give me a couple of days to think things through.'

'Do you know who the others think it is?'

'DC Michaels thinks it's Norton Greene,' answered Hamish. 'DC Tovey believes maybe Miss Johal but most probably Miss Hawksworth. Jian and Faisal are playing their cards close to their chests. Who do you think did it, sir?'

'At the moment, I think it is between two of them, but I won't say who.'

'Do you enjoy your job, sir?'

'Some days are better than others, but yes, I love it.'

'Am I a good detective?' Hamish asked.

'I believe so,' Isaac replied. 'If I'm being perfectly honest with you, you've lost direction a little in the past few months. I get the feeling you don't enjoy the job as you once did. Would I be right?'

Hamish nodded.

Even though it seemed that all questions had been addressed, Hamish didn't move.

'DC Potter?' Isaac said. 'Is there something else you want to speak to me about?'

'I adore visiting the gym. However, of late, I haven't managed to do so. I feel as though I've lost my way in life. Sir, my aspiration isn't to be a detective; my true calling is to be a personal trainer. It's my life's ambition and what I'm destined to do.'

DCI Davidson contemplated what he had just been told, and felt a sudden sadness.

'Did I fail you?' he asked.

'Oh, sir, not at all! I have loved working in this team. This is about me! I have experienced what happens on the streets. The lack of respect towards us, and our government doesn't give a toss about us. They make constant lies about fixing things, but at the end of the day they only care about themselves. I'm done!'

Isaac looked at his DC and felt nothing but compassion. He knew exactly what he was saying. This current government, and previous had let them down so badly, and therefore, destroying any enthusiasm left.

'I'm still trying to fight.'

Hamish smiled and thanked his DCI.

'Where does it all end? Are we left constantly fighting for our jobs? When will they ask you to make further cuts?'

Isaac could understand exactly what Hamish was saying.

'What are you telling me, DC Potter?'

'I'm going. I will stop you from having to worry about the others. Why should one of them lose a job that they care so much about?'

Isaac fell back in his chair. He looked at the detective in front of him and sighed.

'Hamish, I don't want to lose you.'

'I'm already gone, sir.'

'Are you sure?'

'Absolutely!' he replied. 'I will finish this case and then move on. Faisal is so much better than me.'

'I won't process this until the case is finalised,' DCI Davidson said.

DC Potter thanked his boss and went back to join the others. Isaac felt a pang of sadness but was also relieved that he didn't have to put the team through interviews to make the decision. Hamish's selfless act had probably just saved DC Michaels from losing her job.

70

Agatha

6th December 2019

06:30 a.m.

Mrs Faith Hawksworth sat on the bed with her daughter's head in her lap. She was gently stroking her hair.

'Do you remember me doing this for you when you were a little girl?'

'I do, Mum.'

'I used to love picking you up from school and seeing your excited face when you saw me waiting in the playground for you. You'd usually be carrying something you'd made using inners from toilet rolls, empty cereal boxes and bits of tissue paper.'

Faith continued stroking Agatha's hair.

'I'll never forget your school's production of The Wizard of Oz. You wanted to play the part of Dorothy, but they gave it to that horrid girl. What was her name? Oh, yes, Amy Flood. You were so good as the Cowardly Lion. You made the whole audience laugh so much. I was so proud of you.'

'Thanks, Mum.'

Mrs Hawksworth looked down at her daughter and felt an enormous surge of love.

'You loved being in the girl guides and looked adorable in your uniform. You couldn't wait for a Friday evening to come along so you could meet with your friends and do arts and crafts. Agatha, you were such an outgoing person until you met him. Why did it have to change? I remember how you loved making cakes with me. Chocolate was your favourite, and like all children, you enjoyed licking the bowl clean. I believe you preferred that more than the actual cake. Grandma would always make you a special birthday one, and after she died, I tried my best, but I was never as good as her. Where does the time go?'

Outside, the barking of a dog could be heard.

'You've never liked dogs, have you?'

'No, Mum.'

'There was that snappy little thing that Mr Andrews used to have. It always tried to nip at your ankles. I was glad when he moved away and that lovely family moved in. That's where your interest in rugby started because their daughter was part of the after-school team. I wonder what happened to them? We lost touch when we moved to our current address. Oh, well. You can't stay friends with everybody, can you?'

Faith leaned over to the bedside table and picked up a brush. She ran it through her own hair a few times before brushing Agatha's.

'Then the time came for you to move on with your life and go to university. You were so excited to be heading off to study economics. I always thought that was a strange thing to get a degree in. Maybe a sports degree would have been better for you. Your father and I had hoped your time there was going to be filled with happiness. That you'd meet people that enriched your life. Instead, you met them; him! I'll never understand why you became friends with them all. Such awful people. Agatha, I wish you'd never met that man. Ravi Patel turned you from a beautiful, fun-loving person to an emotional wreck within six months of meeting him. He treated you so badly. My gorgeous daughter, you were never the same. Something inside of you died, and we never got you fully back again. Your weight ballooned and the suicide attempts started. All because of that man! Did you kill him? Don't answer that, I don't want to know. Then, after his death, I began to see a change in you. You were styling your hair differently, losing weight and wearing new colours. I thought you were finally getting over him. You even began smiling again. That face of yours lights up when you smile.'

A sudden knock at the door caused Agatha's mother to jump.

'They are here for you, my darling. They will look after you now. You be a good girl and go with them.' She bent down and kissed her daughter on the head. 'I love you so much, my darling girl.'

'I love you too, Mum.'

Faith rose gently and opened the door, where she was met by two members of the ambulance crew wearing their green uniforms.

'She's on the bed. Sadly, she died during the night. She took an overdose late last night and then texted me to tell me what she had done. I only read it this morning when I woke up to use the toilet. She's done this sort of thing before, but I still rushed over. However, she was already dead. I know it's silly, but I thought I could hear her voice speaking back to me. There are empty blister packs scattered all over the floor. There are so many of them. She finally did what she had tried so many times to do. She was my beautiful daughter and maybe now she is finally at peace. I hope Ravi Patel is burning in hell for what he put her through!'

Mrs Hawksworth collapsed onto the floor and sobbed.

71

DC Faisal Asher

7th December 2019

8:30 p.m.

Jian had called beforehand and requested a private table. They had been given the one in the window and it was perfect. A red and white checked tablecloth was in place and a container full of breadsticks was on it. There was Italian-style music playing in the background at just the right volume. The restaurant was busy, but it was a Saturday night and the two of them had just the correct amount of privacy they wanted, but were still able to enjoy the ambience.

They had both ordered a red wine, Jian a Merlot and Faisal a Shiraz. There was a candle on the table to help make the evening as romantic as possible. Faisal couldn't stop looking at Jian.

'Are you ready to order?' asked the waiter.

'I'll have the sea bass, please,' said Jian.

'I will have the seafood linguine. Thank you.' Faisal passed back the menu to the waiter.

They sat in silence for a few moments and were both thinking how lucky they were to have found each other. Jian was just about to speak when the waiter came over with a basket of bread.

'You look gorgeous,' Jian said.

Faisal was wearing his favourite pair of jeans and a red, plain T-shirt. Dressing up was not his thing, and he felt more comfortable being casual. Jian had gone for a black polo neck top.

'You're biased.'

They reached across the table and held hands.

'I'm so happy you're in my life,' Jian said. 'I love work, and sharing it with you is wonderful, but I can't wait for us to get home in the evening and just be us.'

'I feel exactly the same,' Faisal said. 'It feels so right.'

As they waited for their food to arrive, they discussed the case in hushed voices. Although not for long, as they tried not to talk about work when they were out.

'Do you think we are close to finding our killer?'

'I think so,' replied Jian. 'We have asked them all the questions we need to, so we just need to re-examine what we have found out. Agatha not leaving a suicide note wasn't helpful. Did she kill herself out of guilt for murdering Ravi?'

'I don't think it was her,' said Faisal. 'She came across as an extremely unwell person who had been deeply impacted by the aftermath of their break-up. Her mental health issues must have been difficult to live with, especially having Ravi constantly in her life. Why didn't she just move away or stop having anything to do with him? Why put yourself through all that pain?'

'Some people thrive on those feelings. Maybe the thought of not seeing him was worse than what she put herself through.'

'So killing Ravi was never going to be the answer for her?'

'That's true,' said Jian.

Faisal took a breadstick, broke it in two and passed one half over to Jian.

'So thoughtful of you.'

'I like this place,' said Faisal. 'Why have we never been here before?'

'Because it took some finding,' was Jian's response. 'I wanted to find the perfect restaurant for a special night.'

'Special? Have I forgotten a significant day?'

Jian laughed and reached out his hand again to grasp Faisal's.

The waiter came over with their main courses and they both ordered a second glass of wine. Faisal picked up his phone and took a photo of his food.

'That's Instagram-worthy,' he said with a smile. 'I'll send it to Maggie as well. She loves seeing food pics.'

Their wine arrived and they enjoyed the food, the music, and the atmosphere, but not as much as they loved being together.

Once they had eaten, plates cleared away and desserts were ordered, Faisal remembered what Jian had said earlier.

'Special? Why is this evening special?'

Jian put his hand into his pocket and took out a small box.

'Because, my darling, I have something that I want to ask you.'

Jian stood up briefly and then went down on one knee. The entire restaurant stopped talking and looked over in their direction. Faisal's mouth was wide open, as were his eyes. He couldn't believe what was about to happen.

'Faisal Asher. Will you marry me?'

There wasn't a sound coming from the restaurant. Even the music had been switched off.

'Yes!' shouted Faisal. 'A hundred times, YES!'

As Jian stood and embraced his partner, the other customers cheered and clapped.

Faisal, feeling slightly overwhelmed, just sat back down and couldn't help smiling. This was the best thing to have ever happened to him.

'Is it too soon? It's too soon, isn't it? Is it too soon?' he said with a glorious smile etched across his face and his eyes were soaking in the man in front of him. He knew it wasn't too soon.

'I can't wait for you to become Mrs Wong,' Jian said with a slight giggle.

'How about Wong-Asher?' was Faisal's excited answer.

'Asher-Wong sounds better.'

'Perfect,' Faisal replied as they embraced again.

'By saying yes, I can't begin to tell you how happy you've made me,' said Jian. 'Every moment that we're not together is a moment I don't want to have. I love you so much, Faisal.'

'I love you more, Mr Wong.'

Their desserts arrived with a complimentary glass of champagne.

72

The Scarf

9th December 2019

08:30 a.m.

The team were sitting by the crime board watching their DCI talking on the phone in his office. He was looking very thrilled about something and gave them all a thumbs-up.

'Hamish, did you hear back from any of those jobs you applied for?' asked DC Tovey.

'I did. I have an interview next week.'

'Good for you, DC Potter,' said Anne.

'We also have some news,' exclaimed Jian. 'DC Asher and I got engaged at the weekend.'

'That is fantastic news,' DCI Davidson said as he approached his team.

Everyone hugged the two men, and congratulations were given.

They could all tell that their boss had just heard interesting news as he was pacing and thinking things through.

'Right! That was Alex from forensics on the phone. The results on the scarf have finally come back. Whatever clever tests were used on the label; they have been able to tell that it was bought in a shop called La Fabien. Alex says he has googled and there isn't a shop by this name in the United Kingdom, but there is one in Paris. It is a small boutique off of the Champs-Élysées. Faisal, I need you to go home and get your passport. I have booked you onto a flight at 11:30 a.m. Take the scarf and see if the owner can tell you anything about it, and more importantly, who bought it. We're close team. I can smell victory.'

Most of them went back to their desks, but Faisal remained where he was, looking petrified.

'What's up?' Jian asked.

'I'm scared of flying. Why did he pick me to go?'

'I didn't know that about you.'

'Well, it hasn't come up. We've only used the Eurostar so far. Jian, what if the plane crashes? What if I die?'

'Faisal, calm down. Flying is the safest form of travel. We have only just got engaged, so nothing is going to happen to you. You will be fine.'

DC Asher wasn't sure.

3:00 p.m. French time.

The weather in France seemed much colder than back in England. DC Asher was wearing a thick coat, gloves and a hat and was still feeling cold. Because he was trying to use Google Maps, he had to keep taking his gloves off. He currently had the Arc de Triomphe behind him and was walking in the direction of the Louvre Museum, although this was quite a distance away.

The bustling street was alive with people engaged in Christmas shopping. Enormous decorations dangled from wires above, and trees sparkled with white fairy lights. Faisal consulted the map on his phone. He turned left onto Rue de Berri and then right onto Rue d'Artois. This was the street he needed, and there in the distance, he saw the shop.

It was definitely a boutique establishment, as it was tiny. Faisal stepped inside and the warmth hit him straight away. It was filled with fashionable clothes and accessories. There was a section in the corner with a lot of scarves. Behind the counter, a tall woman in her fifties, with glasses on a chain was serving a customer. Faisal took the opportunity to go over and see if there was a scarf the same as the one he had in the bag he was carrying.

When the customer finally left, he approached the woman.

'Bonjour. Parlez-vous anglais?'

'Oui, Monsieur,' she said in a gentle tone. 'I lived in London for a few years. How can I help you?'

DC Asher took the scarf out of the bag and handed it over to her.

'I'm a detective from England investigating a murder.' He showed her his identification. 'Can you tell me anything about this?'

'Murder? Oh, my goodness.'

The woman took the scarf from Faisal and scrutinised it. She took her time and looked at both sides.

'Oui, this is one of mine. It would only have been available to buy from this shop. As you can see, no scarf is the same as another. The designs are exclusive and this is one of the more expensive ones. Was it used in the murder?'

'I'm afraid so. It is the murder weapon, but has completed its forensic tests.'

The woman dropped it onto the counter.

'Oh, how awful! To think that something so beautiful, bought from my little shop would be used to do something so terrible.'

There was a ringing from behind and another customer entered the shop. Faisal grabbed the scarf and stood to the side. He could tell that the woman was now rattled and he felt bad for making her feel like this. Luckily, the customer knew exactly what he wanted and was gone quickly. The woman followed him out and then turned the sign on the door to fermé.

'That should stop us from being disturbed. Now, please tell me how I can help.'

'Do you maintain purchase records? And if so, could you determine the purchase date of this scarf?'

'Yes, we itemise our stock. I will go and look for you.'

She was gone for about five minutes and returned carrying a book.

'It was bought on 24th September.'

'Yes, they were all here on that date,' DC Asher mumbled to himself.

'As I was looking for this information, I remembered something about the person.'

Faisal's eyes widened, his heart began to race and a lump formed in his throat.

'Please, tell me.'

'They were willing to purchase the most expensive scarf, opting to pay with Euros instead of a credit card. I remember them saying something along the lines of, "Only the best will do for," although I can't recall the name they mentioned.'

'Ravi,' Faisal said.

'Is that the name of the poor person who was killed?'

Faisal nodded.

The woman picked up the scarf again and closed her eyes at the same time. It looked like she was trying to remember something.

'They inquired about the durability of the scarf's material. "Can it be pulled tight?" I presumed they were referring to wrapping it snugly around their neck for warmth during winter. I assured them it was crafted from top-quality textiles, which pleased them greatly.'

'You refer to the person as "they" but were they male or female?'

'If I remember rightly, I don't believe I knew. They wore a garment with a hood pulled over their head and dark sunglasses. Their head was constantly looking down when I was serving them.'

'Their voice?'

'Again, I couldn't say. They spoke gently, so either they were disguising it or that's how they speak. I'm not being much help, am I?'

'You're being a great help. Can you think of anything else?'

The woman thought long and hard.

'Yes,' she blurted out. 'As I handed them the bag with their purchase, their sleeve moved up slightly. I would say judging by the skin tone, that they may have been of Indian descent. Does that help?'

Faisal was delighted and it showed all over his face.

'You have helped us eliminate two suspects from our enquiry. Can you think of anything else?'

'No, I'm sorry.'

DC Asher thanked the woman and prepared to leave. However, once he got to the door, she called out.

'Monsieur, wait.'

She ran out the back again and then called Faisal through.

'Please forgive me. I have been so silly. Here, look. I have what you call CCTV. I never look at it to be honest, because I have no reason to. I delete it only every six months. Maybe they will show up on here.'

Faisal's excitement grew with each passing minute. The woman was highly organised and they located the necessary month with relative ease. She left Faisal to scroll through and went to make him a café au lait.

Two hours later, DC Asher screamed out. He froze the tape and took a picture using his phone. The killer made the mistake of looking up at the CCTV camera just as they were leaving the shop.

'Caught!' laughed Faisal.

10:00 p.m. French Time.

DC Asher had contemplated calling DCI Davidson and telling him what he had found out but was keen to get to the airport to get the last plane back to Heathrow. He also wanted to run things through his head and try to piece together what possibly happened the night Ravi was killed.

Unfortunately, the only seat available was at the back and a middle seat. This was the worst combination he could imagine. The weather was atrocious and heavy rain was falling, which had delayed the flight already by fifty minutes. Faisal had a horrible feeling.

'Ladies and gentlemen,' the pilot's voice suddenly boomed out. 'As you can see the conditions outside aren't the best, but we will be taking off in the next fifteen minutes. I can already tell that there will be a lot of turbulence back to London. However, I can assure you that the plane is perfectly safe and you have nothing to worry about.'

73

A Murderer Revealed!

10th December 2019

08:00 a.m.

Despite it being early, there was already a commotion in the police station. The front desk was trying to deal with incoming calls and drunks from the night before who were being sent on their way. Hamish had called in to speak with his ex-girlfriend to update her on his plans. Regardless of breaking up after only a couple of months, they had managed to forge a new friendship, and the DC was pleased about this. He didn't have a wide circle of friends, so Amanda was still important to him.

'When do you leave?' she asked.

'As soon as the case we are working on is finished. The boss has completed all the necessary paperwork, so I'm free to go.'

'Are you going to miss being a detective?'

'Some aspects of it, but personal training is what I need to be doing. I know you told me I was boring, but it's what I love.'

'Stop reminding me that I called you that.' They both laughed.

Just before he was getting ready to leave, a familiar face arrived at the front desk. Hamish moved slightly out of sight and watched the rat-like man approach Amanda.

'I'm Rakesh Kumar. I was told I had to come in and collect my dead husband's belongings. Why it had to be so bloody early, I don't know.'

Amanda just gave him a quirky smile and went out the back. After a few moments, she returned with a bag. Rakesh signed for the items and left, still huffing about the time.

'That man gives me the creeps,' Hamish said.

'I can see why,' was the reply.

09:00 a.m.

Everybody was enjoying the coffees and Danish pastries that DCI Davidson had brought in with him. Alan had moved back into the bungalow nearly two weeks ago, so he'd already had a scrumptious breakfast. However, he still wanted to treat his team. Anne was especially delighted.

'Anyone heard from Faisal?' he called out. 'Jian?'

'Yes, he called late last night. The weather deteriorated rapidly after he boarded, leading to his flight being cancelled. Consequently, he had to spend the night in a hotel. He's scheduled for a morning flight and mentioned he has news, but he didn't elaborate further.'

'Anne,' said Lily. 'How's Nathan?'

'Great,' she replied with a mouthful of food.

With their refreshments in their hands, DCI Davidson started the morning briefing around the crime board. DC Potter seemed eager and had his notebook ready for action.

'What are your thoughts about Agatha Hawksworth?' asked Isaac.

'Killed herself out of guilt?' volunteered DC Tovey.

'Stayed as strong as she could for so long?' was Anne's suggestion.

'Faisal and I have discussed this, sir,' said Jian. 'We can't rule her out. Not having a suicide note wasn't great, but I don't think she did it. Why keep Ravi in her life for so long, just to end up killing him?'

'Norton Greene?' was Isaac's next name.

'Creepy man with an unhealthy, depraved obsession with young adults,' said Anne. 'The motive is clear. His world has crumbled because our victim reported him. I think he did it. We know he beat him up on at least two occasions, so he has a violent temper.'

DC Potter sat in silence. He knew his turn would be coming, and he had a lot he wanted to say.

'Parveena Johal,' said Lily. 'Like Dr Greene, Ravi destroyed her. Could they have worked together and both killed Ravi?'

'It's a consideration, Lily,' the DCI responded. 'Yet, there's no evidence to suggest that multiple individuals committed this act. How about Dipen Patel?'

'Absolute tortured soul,' said Jian. 'The amount of money that he owes could drive some people to do anything. I was concerned by his appearance the last time we saw him. His loan shark, Donna, must be making him do terrible things. Do you remember how scared he looked?'

'I do,' said Isaac.

'He also said, *"I can't believe what I have done"* so Dipen has to stay as a very possible suspect. Although my gut feeling is that he didn't kill his cousin.'

There were murmurs between the team, and the suspect's names were being repeated. Hamish continued to watch and smile.

'You're quiet, DC Potter,' commented Anne. 'Why are you looking so smug?'

'I think I know "*Whodunnit.*" Rakesh Patel-Kumar, to give him his full title.'

The rest of the team was interested to see where this was going.

'Please continue?' encouraged Isaac.

'That man has always concerned me. He doesn't come across as nice or caring. Other than a few theatrical tears at the beginning, he seems fine that his husband is dead. He didn't even seem that bothered by the means of how it happened. And, before anyone says anything, I know that doesn't make him a murderer. However, I have been looking back at my notes and there are a couple of points that don't make sense to me. Rakesh said, *"I know we've been fighting, but couples do that. Don't they? We all left the concert separately, and Ravi was going back to his hotel. It won't be my Ravi."* Why did he assume that was when Ravi was killed? We didn't even know at that point! Also, when we were in the car and taking Rakesh to view the body, he asked if he should text the others to let them know Ravi was dead. He hadn't viewed the victim yet. It sounds like he already knew that his husband was dead because he was the one who did it!'

It was evident that DC Potter's remarks stimulated the interest of others, resulting in numerous responses.

'Good detecting,' said Isaac. 'Hamish?'

DC Potter had gone silent, and he couldn't hear what was happening around him. He was too busy looking at the crime board, and more importantly, the CCTV photo.

'Remind me what hand Mr Kumar uses?' he said with a sense of urgency. 'Quickly, left or right?'

'Left,' replied DC Tovey.

'Yes! He told me left. Twice,' said DC Potter.

'What are you thinking, Hamish?' asked DCI Davidson.

'Downstairs, about an hour ago. Rakesh came in to collect Ravi's belongings, which he had to sign for. He signed with his right hand! He told us he was left-handed to confuse us. That despicable man is right-handed. And this coat.' Hamish grabbed the CCTV photo and looked at it intensely. 'The stupid man came to the police station wearing this jacket, knowing we had been sharing this photo.'

'Unbelievable,' said Lily.

The doors to the department burst open and made them all jump. Faisal came running in and had a picture open on his phone.

'It's DIPEN! It's Dipen Patel,' he shouted.

Hamish slumped into his chair; his face etched with a wave of disappointment.

'I'm joking,' Faisal said. 'I only said it because Jian kept saying he was sure it wasn't Dipen. Sorry, everyone. Look,' he said, showing them the CCTV picture he'd taken in Paris. 'It's Rakesh. Rakesh killed Ravi.'

Everybody was congratulating DC Potter.

'I told you that you're a skilled detective,' said Isaac. 'Still want to go?'

'Absolutely, sir.'

'We need to proceed with the arrest of Mr Patel-Kumar. I suggest I go with DS Wong and DC Potter.'

All but one person were in agreement.

'Take DC Asher,' said Hamish. 'I'm done. He went to Paris and got the evidence. I'll start clearing out my desk. Honestly, Faisal, you go.'

With everybody going back to their desks to finalise their paperwork, Jian hugged his fiancé.

'I see you didn't die in a plane crash, then?'

'Nah,' said Faisal. 'You can't get rid of me that quickly.'

74

A Murderer Caught!

10th December 2019

1:00 p.m.

The weather was overcast and it kept drizzling. Christmas trees adorned the gardens along the tranquil street. Some residents had even set up snowmen and reindeer embellished with twinkling lights. One house stood out, blanketed in a display of illuminations suggestive of a scene from an American Christmas movie. For everyone that lived here, it was a day like any other. But then the shouting started.

'Rakesh,' shouted Dipen as he banged on the door. 'Open up. I need to speak with you.'

There was no movement from inside the house. The curtains were still closed, but Dipen could hear music playing.

'Rakesh!' he shouted through the letter box.

Dipen started to bang on the door with his fists and didn't stop until the man he wanted opened the door. He looked as if he had just woken up because he was only wearing his underwear and was yawning.

'What do you want?'

'Let me in,' demanded Dipen.

'Can't, bro. I've got what you'd call, company.'

Rakesh stretched but did not move to allow Ravi's cousin inside.

Up and down the street, people started peering out of their windows, drawn by the commotion.

'I need my inheritance from Ravi's will. He told me at the party that I was in it. Please, I'm desperate.'

'I can't help you. No money has been sorted yet. The solicitor keeps cancelling my appointments. It'll happen, so just chill.'

'You don't understand what they are making me do! She wants me to hurt the child of someone who owes her a massive amount of money. I don't want to be this person. If I don't do what she says, she is going to arrange for me to have an accident. I NEED the money.'

Before Rakesh had time to answer, sirens could be heard, getting louder. Both men looked panicked and Rakesh slammed the front door shut, leaving Dipen on the doorstep.

Two police cars and a black vehicle sped into the street. Sirens were blasting and their blue flashing lights were illuminated against the darkness of the sky. They pulled up outside Rakesh's house. In the street, anybody who was home looked out of their window or came outside for a closer look. Dipen stood aside.

The uniformed police stayed by their cars, but DCI Davidson, DS Wong and DC Asher went towards the house. Inside, Rakesh was crouched by the front door, shaking. The person who he had been with had already left by the back door.

'Rakesh Patel-Kumar,' shouted Isaac. 'Please open the door. We need to speak with you in connection with the murder of Ravi Patel.'

Rakesh had seen enough police dramas to know they only turn up like this when they know who killed the victim.

'Shit! Shit! Shit!' he cried out.

The knock at the door startled him, prompting him to dash into the kitchen and hastily pull an item from a drawer.

Rakesh paced back and forth, trying to think of something that the police would believe. He could come up with nothing.

'Rakesh, open the door.'

'No!' he screamed.

'The house is surrounded. Please, come out with your hands in the air,' Isaac said in a calm tone.

The front door cracked open a little and an eye could be seen.

'Get back,' Rakesh shouted.

'He's got a gun! I can see it in his hand,' roared Faisal.

Everybody stepped back away from the door and watched as it opened wide. In front of them was a man trembling with a gun shaking in his hand. He was pointing it at everyone in turn.

'Rakesh,' said Isaac. 'Why don't you let us come inside? You can put some clothes on, and we can have a chat.'

'Don't use that patronising voice on me, DCI Davidson.'

'Did you kill Ravi?' Dipen asked as he realised the seriousness of the situation.

'YES!' screamed Rakesh. 'I hated him. He held me back. Something snapped inside of me when I heard he was a millionaire at his party. I had already fallen out of love with him. The inheritance would be huge, and I could finally live the life I wanted; the life I was born to have!'

The detectives were listening to what was being said and at the same time, trying to position themselves where they would be safe. Isaac had yelled at the neighbours to get back inside their homes. Most of them didn't listen.

Rakesh was still randomly pointing the gun at different people in a concerning haphazard way.

'Did you never think about killing him for all that you're going through?' Rakesh asked Dipen. 'Knowing he could have ended it for you, just like that.'

'No,' Dipen croaked, trying to hold back the tears. 'He was my cousin, and I loved him. I would never have hurt Ravi. What I'm going through is my fault, and was never his.'

'I wish I'd had your strength of character!' Rakesh said, almost sobbing. 'The evening of the concert, Ravi told me he was going to give you the £200,000 to pay off your debt.'

'And you killed him that night? He was going to save me from what I have done! I can't believe what I have put people through.'

The street was now full of people. A lot of them had come from surrounding roads. The uniformed police who had arrived with Isaac were doing their best to push them back and out of harm's way. However, the unfolding incident was too good to miss.

'There was a moment at the concert when I looked at him after Norton had punched him. I started to feel sorry for him. He was on the floor and looked pathetic. But then the stupid fool said he wanted a divorce.' Rakesh had started to sweat, despite the coldness against his naked skin and was trembling. 'He told me he'd give the money away to charities before I could get my hands on it. Don't you see, Dipen? I NEED money. I crave it and want as much as I can get. My life growing up with embarrassing parents has driven me to become like this. Ravi was going to take away any chance I had to live how I wanted. He had to die. After the party, I lay awake all night with such raging anger soaring through my veins. The next morning, I was standing in the kitchen and he came downstairs, stood behind me and put his hands around my waist. I wanted to vomit! It was at that precise moment that I knew I was going to kill him, and how I was going to do it. I had bought him a cashmere scarf for his birthday a few years ago. It was sky blue with white and grey highlights. Such a beautiful piece of material and he never wore it. It did occur to me to use that scarf, but I thought it may be traced back to me, somehow. So, I bought the scarf I used to snuff out his life when we were all in Paris. The morning after the party I started to follow him, or stalk might be a better word. Then the concert, the night I killed him. Norton had already weakened him with the punch to his stomach. That was a gift I didn't see coming. I then kicked him as hard as I could. He was damaged already as he made his way home. I followed him and even got the same train home. Then we walked along the river and I made sure that he was frightened. He tripped, which was another gift, and I then put the scarf around his neck and I pulled it as tight as I could. It took a while, and bless him, he did try to put up a fight, but with all his other injuries, he didn't stand a chance. And then when the final breath was leaving his body, I whispered into his ear, *"It's Rakesh."* He died knowing it was me that killed him. Then, once he was dead, I pushed him into the river. It's amazing where strength comes from when you really need it.'

'You're a monster,' Dipen cried out and rushed at Rakesh.

'NO!' screamed Faisal, who then rushed forward.

Rakesh turned quickly and fired the gun. Jian grabbed Faisal and went to push him to the ground. The bullet hit the detective in the middle of his forehead and he was instantly killed.

'Rakesh,' shrieked Dipen. 'You've killed a police officer.'

For Rakesh, everything appeared to slow right down. He could see what was happening in front of him, but it didn't seem real.

'The money will come to you now, Dipen. You and Beena. Use it wisely and get yourself out of trouble. I'm not sorry that I killed Ravi. I hated him, but I'm sorry for your loss.' Rakesh then put the gun into his mouth and pulled the trigger.

Screams erupted from the crowd of spectators; while some fled back to their homes, others remained to capture the event on their phones, poised to upload it to YouTube or other social media platforms.

DCI Davidson was in disbelief at what had just happened. The thought of Rakesh possessing a firearm had never crossed his mind, and it should have. He knew he had let his detectives down and already anticipated a stern reprimand and investigation. Turning towards the source of the hysteria that he could hear, he saw DS Wong holding DC Asher, gently rocking him in his arms as tears streamed down his cheeks.

75

Three Months Later

The Memorial

7th March 2020

1:00 p.m.

As people entered the hall, they saw a large photo of DC Faisal Asher perched on an easel. It was a picture taken on the night Jian had proposed and he looked striking wearing his favourite red T-shirt. His smile enabled those who had come to see what a kind and gentle soul he had been.

Jian stood with DC Tovey, and they welcomed people as they arrived. Faisal's parents and sisters had been first, and Maggie, his best friend was next. Within the next twenty minutes, the hall became crowded and conversations about Faisal were everywhere. This filled Jian with happiness and emotion.

DCI Davidson had arrived with his brother and they had chosen to sit at the back. DC Michaels had come with her fiancé, Nathan. Hamish had come down from Edinburgh and was sitting with Maggie.

When everyone was gathered, Jian stood at the front, next to another photo of Faisal and started.

'Today belongs to the loveliest of men. Faisal Asher was kind, thoughtful, compassionate and a fantastic detective. He touched our lives and we are better for this. It was only in November last year that DCI Davidson asked me if I had ever lost anyone significant, and I said I hadn't. I couldn't have predicted that a few weeks later I'd experience such a significant loss. I've thought to myself these past few months, how am I going to be able to carry on? Then I realised; if my beautiful Faisal can no longer see each gorgeous new day, then I will see it for him.'

Jian spoke for a further fifteen minutes and most people had cried at some point. The reception then moved on to the local pub, The Lemon Tree.

'Our DCI isn't looking too good,' said Hamish. 'Is everything OK with him?'

'It's been really tough,' said Lily. 'He blames himself for Faisal's death.'

'If anyone is to blame, it's me,' replied Hamish.

'How?' asked Jian.

'I told him to go and arrest Rakesh Kumar. If I'd have gone, Faisal would still be here. I have cursed myself every day since it happened.'

'Hamish,' Jian said with conviction. 'You are not to blame for what happened and neither is DCI Davidson. Something terrible happened, and learning needs to take place, but Rakesh killed Faisal; no one else.'

The group agreed to move on and keep away from the day in question.

'So, what are your thoughts on this COVID-19?' asked Hamish.

'I'm frightened,' replied Lily.

'Not sure,' Jian said. 'I think we need to take it seriously.'

'Nah,' croaked Hamish. 'At most, it's a bad flu. There's nothing to worry about. I guarantee it.'

Alan had joined Maggie, and they were signing to each other. Because he was working in a school, Alan had taken British Sign Language classes. He was still learning but was making himself understood.

Anne had been talking with Nathan and Faisal's parents when she saw Isaac was alone. She went over to speak with him.

'We should see this as a good day,' she said. 'The funeral was for crying; today is for remembering.'

'You're right, Anne,' Isaac replied.

'Do you mind if I say you're not looking your best, sir?'

'I'd agree with you. The internal investigation into what happened is taking its toll on me.'

'Is there anything I can do to help?'

'Yes,' Isaac said. 'Go and cheer up Jian.'

Anne left and walked over to the rest of the team, but then felt something was wrong, so went back to her boss.

'Are you OK, Sir? You look a little flushed.'

'I believe so, DC Michaels,' he slowly responded. 'But you're right, I am feeling slightly warm, and I've picked up an irritating cough and have a strange taste in my mouth. It's probably nothing serious, just a common cold. Please, go back to the others. I'll be fine.'

About the Author

I am 55 and this is my third whodunnit book. For as long as I can remember I have loved murder mysteries. As an 11-year-old I read my Grandad's (we called him Barr) copy of Agatha Christie's "At Bertram's Hotel" and my passion for whodunnits started. I never believed I could write my own. It took years of self-doubt and then determination to finally come up with a story that ended up being my first book: "The Murder of Philip Oakes". The love of writing then produced "The Murder of Sally Raines". Never stop believing in yourself. If there is a story brewing inside of you, get it out and let others enjoy your wonderful imagination!

I am a cancer nurse for young people. I live in West Sussex and enjoy going for long walks in the countryside, cooking, reading, board games and I have a love for elephants!

Printed in Great Britain
by Amazon

51778341R00209